RISE TO
THE FLY

Can Welsh detectives catch a cunning killer?

CHERYL REES-PRICE

THE
BOOK
FOLKS

Published by The Book Folks

London, 2022

ISBN 978-1-913516-61-1

www.thebookfolks.com

Rise To The Fly is the sixth standalone title in a series of murder mysteries set in the heart of Wales.

Chapter One

The smell of burning wood filled the night air and clung to the clothes of those seated around the bonfire in the courtyard of Bryn Glas Farm, which sat at the foot of the Black Mountain in Wales. Faces glowed, glasses were refilled, and laughter carried to where Madog Jones stood in the shadows. He could see sparks floating on the breeze before falling as ash on the ground. Now he was away from the fire he felt a chill creeping over his body.

With shoulders hunched he dug his hands into his pockets. He just wanted to go home. Get away from the younger ones who seemed so far removed from the sadness he felt. Away from the talk of times gone by, and away from the woman standing in front of him. He had done his best to avoid being alone with Pippa Eccleston. He'd even taken to locking his cottage, something he hadn't done the whole time he had lived on the farm, and that had been his whole life. She had caught him off guard, followed him, and now he felt trapped, standing in the semi-darkness away from the family.

'Well?' Pippa asked. She had drawn herself up to her full height and folded her arms across her chest.

'I'm sorry, I can't,' Madog said.

'I wasn't asking you. I'm telling you,' Pippa hissed. 'Do you think I'm going to let you destroy my family?'

Madog shook his head. 'You've done that all by yourself.'

Pippa's nostrils flared. Madog could see the anger burning in her eyes. At this moment he thought she resembled the bonfire that lit up the sky behind her. A ball of rage with sparks flying in the air. She looked like she was about to charge at him. Given his age and her solid build he had no doubt she could knock him down. He wasn't afraid of her, at least not in a physical sense. It was confrontation that Madog feared. He was a gentle soul and stayed away from arguments. Maybe he could just pacify her for now; it would be over in a few days, he thought.

'You must know that I don't want to do it,' Madog said. 'I don't want to hurt anyone. I never asked to be part of it. It's not just your family that will suffer.'

Madog saw a little smirk on Pippa's face. He guessed she thought he had given her ammunition.

'No, and you don't want to do that to them,' Pippa said.

He was sure that she would like nothing more than to see his family humiliated. It was no good, he couldn't let her think that he would back down. It wasn't fair. Even if he didn't like the woman. It wasn't in his nature to be cruel.

'I need to do what's right. It's what he would've wanted,' Madog said.

'I won't let you.' Pippa stepped closer.

Over the top of Pippa's head Madog saw a figure heading towards them. Even in the darkness he knew it was his niece, Kitty.

'Are you listening to me?' Pippa asked. She turned her head to see what had caught Madog's attention. 'Great, I knew she wouldn't be far away.' She took a step back.

'Are you OK, Uncle Madog?' Kitty asked as she came to stand next to him.

'We were just having a little chat,' Pippa said. 'I better go home and check on Mother.' She pulled a torch from her pocket and flicked the switch. 'I'll see you tomorrow.' She gave Madog a pointed look before striding away.

'What was that about?' Kitty asked.

Madog shrugged. 'You know your sister-in-law, always complaining about something.'

'She sounded pissed off.'

Madog smiled. 'Doesn't she always.' He felt a sense of relief now Pippa had left. He would've liked to have told Kitty what Pippa wanted but he didn't want to burden her – not yet. She had a couple more days' peace left. He wanted her to have that time.

A howl of laughter came from the direction of the bonfire and they both turned to look.

'Escaping, are you?' Madog asked.

'Yeah, it's been a long day.'

'And a hard one for you.'

'It was a nice send-off for Mum. She's out of pain now, and with Dad. I just have to keep reminding myself of that.'

'Yes,' Madog agreed. 'I'm the last one standing.'

It had been hard for him to watch as his sister-in-law's coffin had been lowered into his brother's grave. The idea of him being next in the plot sent a shiver over his body. It also reminded him that he needed to get his own affairs in order, and that meant letting Kitty know where to look. How to do it was the difficult thing.

'Well, I hope you plan on staying around a lot longer,' Kitty said as she threaded her arm through his.

'I'm getting old, Kitty,' Madog said. Tonight he felt every one of his seventy-four years.

'Don't say that,' Kitty said. 'You have years left and what would I do without you? Come on, I'll walk you home.'

They took the path that led past one of the cottages that was rented out during the summer. Kitty switched on her torch and illuminated the gravel track that led down to a wide stream. Water could be heard tumbling over rocks, the sound mixing with the distant voices of those still enjoying the bonfire. When the stream was low they could cross at this point, but it was dark, and the rocks could be treacherous, so they headed for the bridge. They talked about Kitty's mother and Madog felt a weight in his heart. He had loved Connie almost as much as his brother had. He would miss her and that connection to his late brother.

When they reached the bridge Madog stepped back to let Kitty cross first. It was narrow with iron railings each side and they always had the habit of stopping halfway across and looking down into the water. Kitty leaned against the rails and shone her torch downwards.

'I don't want you to worry about what will happen on Monday,' Madog said.

'You mean the codicil?'

'Yes.'

'I'm not worried. Well, not really. We knew the time was coming. It will be a relief in some way. I always wondered what Dad wrote in his letter, and why we had to wait all this time to find out. As you have it I guess you already know.'

Madog knew he had to be careful what he said now. 'Yes, and I'm so grateful you've never asked me to tell you.'

'It wouldn't be fair. It was Dad's final wish. Whatever it is I will just have to accept it.'

'You know you'll always have a home here,' Madog said. 'No matter what happens. I don't want you to worry about that.'

'But what will surround my home? Will all this be gone?'

Madog looked out into the darkness. He didn't need the light to see the acres of land. The patchwork fields of yellow, green, and brown ever changing in the seasons. The trees with their russet autumn leaves and the dancing hornwort in the lakes. He knew it by heart. Kitty was right to be concerned about the land. Once he was gone who would be left to fight for it? He didn't trust the others, especially Kitty's husband, Quintin. He just hoped she would be strong enough when the time came.

'Come on, I'm getting cold,' he said.

They crossed the bridge and the lights from Madog's cottage came into view. They stopped at the gate. Usually Madog would invite her in and they would have a chat over tea. Not tonight – he still had things to do.

'I'm going to say goodnight,' Madog said. 'I'm tired and you should get some rest.'

'Are you coming for breakfast in the morning?'

'I think I'll give it a miss,' Madog said. 'Too many people and they'll be hungover.'

'I'll bring you something to eat later then.'

'That'll be nice. We can talk more then.' He looked over the garden that was lit with solar lights. 'Do you remember the games we played here when you were a girl?'

Kitty smiled. 'Yeah, we had so much fun.'

'Just remember the white moth.'

Kitty gave him a quizzical look. 'Are you sure you're alright?'

'I'm fine. Just thinking of old times.' Madog leaned down and kissed Kitty on the cheek. 'I'll see you tomorrow.'

'Love you,' Kitty said before turning away.

Madog watched until she faded into the darkness then went inside his cottage. He took a glass from the shelf above the sink and poured himself a large whisky. He took a sip and felt the liquid warm his throat and spread through his chest. Another couple of gulps and he felt warmer. He put the glass down. He didn't want to drink too much. He just needed enough to take the edge off his nerves. Once he put things in motion he wouldn't be able to back out.

In the sitting room he retrieved his brother's letter that he had hidden behind the clock. The paper felt brittle in his hands. It had yellowed over the years and mildew spots obscured some of the words. As he read he could hear his brother's voice and he was taken back to the day he'd first set eyes on the letter. It had been in this room and his brother, Llew, had been standing by the fireplace with tears tracking down his face.

'I don't understand,' Madog said. 'Why are you telling me this now?'

'I'm dying,' Llew said. 'I never wanted to put this on you, but I have no choice now.'

'What?' Madog felt like a shard of ice had pierced his heart. What Llew had done didn't seem to matter now. 'You can't be dying, what about the treatment?'

'I've stopped it. It's gone too far, so what's the point? I want to enjoy what time I have left, here, on the farm. You're the only one I trust with this, and I know you will do the right thing when the time comes.'

It had been very little time in the end. Madog wiped a tear from the corner of his eye and folded the letter. He hadn't known then that Llew's secret would cost a life. He had failed his brother and now he had to put things right. He was so tired, but he needed to return the letter to its hiding place. He couldn't risk someone finding it. Then there was one person he needed to speak to before he slept. Once he did that there was no turning back.

Chapter Two

DI Winter Meadows cradled a cup of mint tea as he looked out of the office window. He could see the occasional car crossing the bridge and the River Amman below. It was a clear autumn day. The type of sunny Sunday morning that made Meadows long to be outside. Either working in his garden or taking a hike up the mountain, preferably with his girlfriend, Daisy. The one consolation was that she was also working today so he wasn't missing out on spending time with her.

He turned away from the window and saw DS Edris resting his head on the desk. The cup of coffee that Meadows had placed in front of him lay untouched.

'If you're going to sleep you may as well go home,' Meadows said.

Edris lifted his head and groaned. 'Yeah, if I do that I'll never hear the last of it from Blackwell. If he hadn't been such a miserable git and swapped rest days with me then I wouldn't have had to come in.'

'Judging by the way Blackwell was throwing shapes on the dance floor I doubt he's in any fit state himself. Maybe you should've waited until next week to celebrate, you've got the whole weekend off.'

'It wasn't me. Mum couldn't wait to tell everyone that her son is now a detective sergeant, and the family don't need an excuse for a party.'

'Well, you don't look the part today,' Meadows said. 'You haven't even shaved.'

Edris usually took great care over his appearance. Meadows had to admit that he looked rough. His sandy hair was in all directions, and he looked like he'd been half-asleep when he picked his clothes. 'Go on, off you go. I won't tell anyone.'

Edris picked up his coffee and took a sip. 'Nah, I'll stay and keep you company.'

Meadows laughed. 'Is that what you call it? If it's any consolation I think you're not the only one that's suffering this morning. Valentine was knocking them back and you two looked very cosy when I left.'

A flush travelled up from Edris' neck to his face. He stood up abruptly. 'I think I'll take a walk and clear my head.'

Meadows watched Edris leave and chuckled to himself. He got the impression that Valentine, the pretty, bubbly young DC, and Edris got a little too close last night. She would be back in the office Monday morning, and he hoped there wouldn't be any awkwardness between her and Edris. He sat down at his desk. A faint smell of paint and new furniture still hung in the air. He was now the head of the major crime investigation team which covered the large, mainly rural area of Dyfed Powys and beyond the borders if called for. He had initially been apprehensive about taking the position, but with his old team making the move with him he felt comfortable in his new role, although he was still under pressure to take up promotion to DCI.

As Meadows typed away at the computer Edris walked back into the office.

'I've just heard something that may be of interest,' Edris said. 'Hanes is up at Brynarian, that small village just before you get to the Usk Reservoir. A couple staying in a holiday cottage there have gone missing.'

Meadows looked up from his screen. 'I'm not sure that counts as major crime.'

'I just spoke to Hanes. He said they were supposed to check out this morning, but there's no sign of them. He says it's odd.'

'They've probably forgotten the day and have gone out somewhere. I'm sure they'll turn up. Besides I've still got some loose ends to tie up on the Beavan case. My brother is coming for a visit soon and I want everything wrapped up so I can spend some time with him when he turns up.'

'Are you meeting him at the airport?'

'No, Rain doesn't do schedules. He'll probably wander around London for a day or two then phone me to say he's outside my house.'

'He's been in India, hasn't he?' Edris asked.

'Cambodia for the last two years. The longest he's stayed in one place.'

Edris sat down, put his head in his hands and groaned. 'You never know, it could be a kidnapping,' Edris said.

'What?'

'The missing couple.'

'Oh.' Meadows laughed. 'There's more chance of an alien abduction given the location.'

'We could take a spin, get out of the office. There's nothing much happening, and Hanes sounded like he could do with a hand.'

Meadows didn't need much persuading. Getting out of the office would make the day pass quicker. 'OK, but I'm driving. I don't think you're in any fit state.'

Edris smiled. 'Fine by me.'

Meadows took the Black Mountain Pass keeping a watchful eye on the sheep that grazed on the rough yellow grass. They always made him nervous as you never knew when one of them would step onto the road. Edris was unusually quiet as he sat in the passenger seat gazing out of the window. The road climbed and twisted with the scraggly mountain stretching up on the right. At the top Meadows saw the usual ice cream van in the car park. People were dotted around enjoying the view from the top of the limestone quarry that overlooked the rolling valleys below. The road snaked downwards, across the river at the bottom and flattened. Meadows picked up speed and by the time he turned off onto a single-track road Edris had his head out of the window and was gulping in air.

'Don't throw up in the car,' Meadows said. 'I can stop if you want.'

'I'm OK,' Edris said. 'Just drive a little slower.'

They arrived in Brynarian which had a post office, chapel, and a few farms and cottages. Talgarreg holiday cottage was positioned at the foot of a track leading up to a farm.

Meadows pulled up behind a police car and Edris jumped out of the car before he had a chance to unclip his seatbelt. Meadows joined PC Matt Hanes who was standing outside the cottage talking to a woman whom he introduced as Alma Perkins, owner of the cottage. Alma was watching Edris who was walking up the road.

'Mrs Perkins, I understand a couple who are renting your cottage are missing,' Meadows said.

'Call me Alma.' She smiled at Meadows. She was a stout woman who Meadows judged to be in her late fifties. She wore a pair of jeans and T-shirt with a navy gilet. 'I wouldn't have bothered calling the police, but I have new guests due this afternoon.'

'David and Anna Wilson were due to check out by ten this morning,' Hanes said. 'All their stuff is inside and that's their car parked in the driveway. When Alma went inside the cottage she found the oven on with last night's dinner cooking.'

'It was all shrivelled up,' Alma said. 'Looks like it was supposed to be a casserole. Lucky it was on low, or it could've caused a fire. As it is the whole cottage smells of overdone food.'

'Was the cottage locked?'

'Yes.'

'When was the last time you had contact with the Wilsons?' Meadows asked.

'I saw them when they arrived last Sunday. I made sure they had everything they needed and gave them my phone number in case they had any problems. Once I let people in I leave them to it. Most don't want to be disturbed on their holiday. I'm sure if there'd been a problem they would've called. They've stayed here before.'

'Are they a young couple?' Meadows asked.

'No, both retired so in their mid-sixties. Maybe older. Difficult to tell.'

Edris came to stand beside them, and Meadows was pleased to see he looked a little better.

'Do you have a home address for the Wilsons?'

'Yes. Well, at home I do. It'll be on the booking form. If I remember correctly, they come from Bristol.'

'If you could get the details for us whilst we look around that would be very helpful,' Meadows said.

'Right.' Alma appeared a little hesitant to leave but when Meadows didn't comment further she turned and made her way up the track.

'I called the local hospitals in case there had been an emergency. No one by the name of Wilson was admitted last night or this morning and no ambulance pickups from this address or emergency calls. Bit odd isn't it,' Hanes said.

Meadows nodded. 'OK, let's look around.'

The door opened into a kitchen and Meadows could feel the warmth from the oven having been left on. A meaty smell permeated the air. He stepped up to the hob and took the lid off the casserole dish. The contents, which appeared to be chicken casserole, were congealed on the bottom.

'Ew,' Edris said, looking over Meadows' shoulders.

'Feeling a bit delicate, are you?' Hanes asked.

'How are you looking so bright?' Edris asked.

'Lemonade, mate. I was on early this morning.'

'How long would you usually cook a casserole for?' Meadows asked.

Both Edris and Hanes shrugged.

Meadows smiled. 'Not cooks then? I would say a couple of hours, given it was on low heat. Table is set. Looks like they didn't intend to be out for long. It gets dark at seven-thirty so if they went out about five-thirty for an evening stroll, they've been missing for over eighteen hours. Let's check upstairs.'

As they passed through the sitting room Meadows noticed the car keys on the coffee table. There was only one bedroom upstairs. The bed had been made and two cases were open on top, both filled with clothes. Next to one of the cases was a lady's handbag. Meadows unzipped the bag and peered inside.

'No mobile phone,' he said as he moved the contents, 'but her purse is here.' He snapped open the clasp and looked in the card compartment. 'Anna Wilson.' He handed it to Hanes. 'Address in Bristol. Give the local police a call to see if they can track down the next of kin.'

He took another card out and read the information. 'Looks like Anna Wilson is a diabetic. Edris, search around and see if you can find any insulin. We need to know if she took it with her.'

While Edris searched the bathroom Meadows went downstairs and checked the kitchen cupboards; they were empty apart from condiments and a packet of tea bags. He opened the fridge and found an insulin pen with spare cartridges.

'Found it,' Meadows called to Edris. 'We need to get search and rescue out and uniform to help with the search.'

'How long can you go without insulin?' Edris asked.

'I think it varies but given the time she's been missing she could be in trouble.'

Meadows stepped outside the cottage and scanned the area. 'If you were going to go for an evening stroll which way would you go?'

'Dunno,' Edris said. 'The Usk Reservoir, I suppose. It's close, but so is Llyn y Fan.'

'I can't see them hiking up there in the evening. Besides, it's open and not easy to get lost.'

'Glasfynydd Forest surrounds the Usk, easy enough to get lost in there,' Edris said.

'If they've gone in there it could take a while to find them and I doubt Anna Wilson has much time left.'

Chapter Three

The whir of helicopter blades sent sheep and wild horses scattering as it circled the mountain and woodlands. Meadows and Edris approached the last property on the road leading to the Usk Reservoir. They were awaiting the arrival of the Wilsons' daughter who had insisted on driving from Bristol the minute she had heard her parents were missing.

Meadows knocked on the door and it was immediately opened as if the occupant was expecting them. Meadows introduced himself and Edris to the elderly man and asked if he had seen the Wilsons.

'Seen them most days,' the man said. 'They usually pass here about five, taking an evening stroll. Nice couple. English. They always stop for a chat if I'm pottering around in the garden.'

'Did you see them yesterday evening?' Meadows asked.

'No, sorry.'

'On the occasions you talked to them did they mention where they go in the evenings?'

'Erm... no, he did ask me about badgers. Yeah, that's right, he asked if there was a badger set in the woods.'

'OK, that's very helpful. Thank you for your time,' Meadows said.

Edris looked up at the helicopter as they made their way back to the holiday cottage. 'You'd think they would've found them by now. They've been searching for hours. Maybe we should leave Hanes to it and go back to the station. I'm bloody starving.'

'Didn't you eat breakfast?'

'No, I couldn't face it.'

'Well, you're the one who wanted to get out of the office. We'll stay and see this through. Something isn't right. If one of them had fallen and injured themselves the other could've gone for help or phoned. I didn't see a mobile phone in the cottage so I'm guessing they're carrying them.'

'Signal is crap here,' Edris said. 'I've only got one bar and if they're in the forest the phones are probably useless.'

Meadows nodded. 'Still, it sounds like they know the area as they've been here before. If they went into the forest I shouldn't think they would've gone far in. Say they got lost, and it got dark, by first light they'd have been moving around. At least Mr Wilson if he was looking for help. The helicopter has thermal imaging, surely they would've picked up something by now.'

'Only if they're still warm,' Edris said.

'That's what worries me. What could've happened to incapacitate both of them? The cameras have picked up a few images. Hikers and anglers. All checked out and no one has seen the Wilsons. A few of those hikers were on the woodland trails, and search and rescue are on the ground. You'd think someone would've come across them by now.'

As they approached the holiday cottage a car pulled up and a woman got out. She was slim with dark straight hair that hung down her back.

'Lucy Wilson?' Meadows asked.

'Yes, have you found them?'

'No, not yet. We have a search team out and the helicopter. We're doing everything we can to find them.'

'I saw an ambulance parked in the village and I thought…' Lucy's voice trembled.

'We have the ambulance on standby, just as a precaution. Let's go inside,' Meadows said.

Once inside Meadows made the introductions and persuaded Lucy to sit down.

'When was the last time you spoke to your parents?'

'Yesterday. They called me at lunch time.'

'Did they give you any indication of their plans for the evening?'

'I don't think so, I don't know. I was out shopping with the kids when they called. I was distracted. I should've listened more carefully.' Lucy ran her hand across her forehead. 'I'm sorry. I can't remember what we talked about.' She stood up. 'I need to go and look for them.'

'Please sit down, Lucy. I understand this is difficult but anything you remember could help.' Meadows was sure that Lucy's lack of recall was because she was worried and stressed. The trick was to ask the right questions to prompt her memory.

Lucy sighed and perched on the edge of the chair. 'They said they'd had a good time and I told them I would have lunch ready for when they got home.'

'Do you know where they were when they called you?' Meadows asked.

'Erm… Brecon, I think. Yes, they said they'd been to the cathedral and were having lunch.'

'Did they talk about what they had been doing for the week?'

'They sent some photos.' Lucy swiped the screen on her phone and handed it to Meadows.

Meadows looked at the couple smiling into the lens. It was a close-up and looked as if David Wilson was holding the phone at arm's length. There were more of the couple individually posed near a body of water.

'It looks like the Usk Reservoir,' Meadows said as he handed the phone to Edris. 'Do you mind if Edris sends a copy to his phone? It will help to have a photo of your parents to circulate.'

'Of course. There're plenty of them. They sent photos every day.'

'So the one by the water would've been taken yesterday?' Meadows asked.

'Yes, they said they'd walked all around the reservoir. They like that sort of thing. Dad said something about going on a boat.'

'That they had been on a boat or were going to go on a boat?'

Lucy's forehead creased in concentration. 'Going to go, yeah I'm sure. They were both on speakerphone. Mum said something about a nice man with a boat, then Dad started talking about seeing some birds. Because you couldn't walk there. Something like that.'

'That's great. That will help narrow down the search area.' Meadows stood up. 'I'm going to speak to the search team, and we'll keep you updated.'

'I can't stay here,' Lucy said. 'If you think they could be at the reservoir then I'm going to look. Mum needs her insulin. She could be lying somewhere unconscious.'

'Your dad is likely to be with her. We are doing our best to find them. The reservoir is surrounded by forest and if you go off on your own, there is a danger that you'll get lost too. That will only hinder the search.'

'I'll stay close to the water. I can show their photo around. Please, I can't just sit here.'

Meadows thought of his own mother and how he would feel if she was missing. He wouldn't be able to sit around waiting for news.

'OK, but I'll get an officer to go with you.'

'Thank you.'

While Meadows made the call to search and rescue, Edris called the bailiff and arranged to meet him at the reservoir. It only took them a few minutes' drive to reach the water. They passed the search and rescue vans that were parked near the dam and followed the road down, across the bridge and up the other side, before parking next to the bailiff's Land Rover. Meadows got out of the car and looked across the reservoir. The smooth blue-grey water had an irregular shape, stretching beyond his vision, and was surrounded by trees and shrubs. To his left was the dam which dropped a hundred foot. Directly in front of him boats were tethered, and a few anglers sat watching their rods.

Edris came to stand next to him. 'If they were meeting someone here it's unlikely they would've taken the road. I would've thought they'd cut across through the trees and come out over there somewhere. Quickest route.' Edris pointed across the water.

'Depends on where they arranged the meeting,' Meadows said. 'What we need to know is, if they did arrange a boat ride, who with, and if they turned up.'

The bailiff approached them and introduced himself as Tom. He wore hiking trousers and a green sweater with the Welsh Water logo.

'I've arranged to open all the barriers but there's a lot of ground to cover that you can't access with a vehicle,' Tom said. 'A search and rescue vehicle went up this way just before you arrived.'

'Thank you.' Meadows watched as Lucy Wilson walked by with Hanes and approached a fisherman. He turned his attention back to Tom. 'We think that the missing couple may have gone out on a boat yesterday evening or arranged to meet with someone to take them out. Were there any boats out yesterday?'

'I didn't see any during the day but that doesn't mean someone wasn't out and up the far end. I clocked off at five, so if it was after that I'm afraid I can't be of much help.'

'Can anyone take a boat out?' Meadows asked.

'No, only private boats by prior permission with Welsh Water. If there was a boat out yesterday evening it would've been one of these.' He indicated the boats in front of them. 'They all have permits.'

'Would you be able to give me the details of the owners? It may be that one of them met up with the Wilsons and will be able to help us with where they were heading,' Meadows said.

'That's not a problem,' Tom said.

'What's the phone signal like here?' Edris asked.

'Sporadic,' Tom said. 'It also depends on what network you're on. If your missing couple were walking the tracks around the reservoir they would pick up a signal at some point. The track is well-defined, and you can download a map. We've never had anyone go missing on the main route. If they've wandered away from the track and into the woods on the other side then I doubt they would pick up a signal. It's very dense in parts. I'll go and get you that information.'

'Thanks,' Meadows said. He turned to Edris. 'Even if they did have a signal it would be no good to them. Neither of their phones are active. I'm guessing they ran out of battery.'

A few anglers were returning to their cars so Meadows and Edris showed the photographs of the Wilsons, but they were met with shakes of the head. Tom returned with a list and as Meadows was reading the information his phone rang. It was John from mountain rescue.

'We came across a distressed fisherman who claimed there was a body in the woods.' John paused. 'We checked it out and actually found two bodies who we believe to be Mr and Mrs Wilson. Both deceased.'

Chapter Four

Kitty didn't want to go through her mother's things so soon after the funeral, but her sister Lottie had insisted. Lottie was taking the clothes from the wardrobe and putting them in piles on the bed. There were those for charity shops, some for the recycling centre, and some which needed throwing out.

'It's better to do it now,' Lottie said. 'No point in putting it off, and I have to go back to work in a couple of days, so I won't be able to help you.'

'It's fine,' Kitty said as she folded clothes into a bag. 'I need to clear the place.'

'There's no hurry to move back to your cottage,' Lottie said.

'We don't know what might happen when the codicil is read tomorrow.' Kitty sat down on the edge of the bed.

'It could be that you get the house,' Lottie said.

'That wouldn't be fair.'

'No.' Lottie came to sit next to her sister. 'But it won't be fair on you if it all goes to Jac.'

'Maybe it won't be Jac. It could be split between us, or there's always the possibility that it could go to someone else.' Kitty grinned.

Lottie laughed. 'Not that again. Can you imagine?'

'It would be kinda funny. Anyway, the house isn't going to anyone at the moment. Uncle Madog has half the income from the farm and he owns the land.'

'Uncle Madog won't want to move into the house.'

'What about Jac?'

Lottie shrugged.

'He's your son,' Kitty said, 'he must've talked about it.'

'You know Jac, he has no interest in the farm.'

'That's what I'm afraid of.'

'Try not to worry,' Lottie said. 'Dad must have written the codicil for some reason, and he would want to protect the farm. I'm sure he wouldn't see me or you cut out.'

'No, but you know what he was like about the farm,' Kitty said.

Lottie smiled. 'Him and Uncle Madog both. Maybe it won't be a bad thing for you if the farm goes. You're not getting any younger and I think it's too much for you. You must think of your health. You haven't been happy for a while.'

'I love the farm. I'm happy here, it's just... never mind.' Kitty stood up and shoved another bunch of clothes into a bag.

'I don't know why you stay with him,' Lottie said.

The last thing Kitty wanted to do was get into a discussion about her marriage. She knew Lottie's feelings about Quintin, and she didn't blame her. Quintin could be difficult at the best of times. She tied off the bag and lifted it.

'I'll take some of these bags downstairs and I think I'll go and check on Uncle Madog. I didn't see him yesterday and I thought he might come over today.'

'I'm sorry,' Lottie said. 'I don't mean to go on about Quintin. But he seems to control everything you do. Him and that sister of his.'

'He doesn't control me.'

'When was the last time you left the farm? You have no life away from here. No friends. He's completely isolated you.'

Kitty sighed. 'I have everything I need here. Quintin may be a dick at times but he's all I have. He married me, if he hadn't I would've ended up an old spinster living alone.'

'You know that's not true,' Lottie said. 'I wish you could see yourself as others see you, and you'll never be alone.'

Kitty felt tears sting her eyes and turned away. 'I'll see you later. I won't be long.'

Kitty loaded the bags into the car ready for Quintin to take to the recycling centre. He had offered and it occurred to Kitty that Lottie was right. She seldom left the farm. Quintin took care of everything and lately he hadn't spent any time with her. As she walked over the bridge she wondered if he was seeing someone again. She was surprised that the thought didn't bother her. He had been happier over the past few weeks.

Kitty knocked at Madog's door before opening it.

'Uncle Madog.' She stepped inside. The first thing she noticed was the mess. All the kitchen drawers and cupboards were open. The plate of food she had left yesterday was still sat on the hob with the foil untouched.

She moved into the sitting room. It looked as if the contents from the Welsh dresser had been upturned on the table. There was a jumble of papers and odd knickknacks. Kitty felt an uneasy feeling creep over her. Madog was always tidy. She came in once a week to give the place a hoover and dusting and collect his washing, but she never had to put anything away.

The cottage was open plan and from her position she could see Madog's bedroom door was closed. She couldn't remember if it had been open yesterday. What if he was ill in bed when I came around yesterday? she thought. She approached the bedroom door and called out again before turning the handle. Holding her breath, she pushed the door open and was relieved to see the bed empty. It was made but like the other rooms the drawers were all open. The clothes inside had been stirred around and some had fallen to the floor.

Kitty hurried from the cottage with worry gnawing at her stomach. She felt the same way now as she had as a child when her beloved cat had gone missing. That same feeling of foreboding. The cat had been found dead two days later near one of the hedges. It had been Madog who found it and he'd been the one to tell her. He had comforted her by explaining that the cat was unwell. That it needed to go and find the place to cross over to where he would be free and well. He described a wonderful place that the cat would be, and she shouldn't be sad.

Kitty tried to push away those thoughts. Tried to calm herself. It's because Mum has just died, she told herself as she made her way to the lakes. She expected to find Madog standing on one of the banks fishing but there was no sign of him. She shouted out as she walked around. She went back to the farmhouse, grabbed her car keys, and drove down the lane. At the bottom she took a right, then a second right, and was thankful that she didn't have to open the gate to drive through. This track led to the dairy and as she pulled up outside the milking house she saw Quintin talking to their nephew, Pippa's son, Theo. They both turned when she got out of the car.

'What's up?' Quintin asked.

'I can't find Uncle Madog, have you seen him?'

'Not today,' Quintin said.

'What about yesterday?'

'Erm, no I don't think so.'

'Theo?'

'No, I don't think I've seen him since Friday.'

'He's not at home and he's not down by the lakes,' Kitty said.

'He'll be around somewhere,' Quintin said. 'Maybe he's gone up the Usk.'

'His Land Rover is still here,' Kitty said.

'So, maybe he went up with someone,' Quintin said.

'He would've said he was going,' Kitty said. 'I always make him a packed lunch and a flask if he's fishing for the day. The food I left him yesterday hasn't been touched.'

'Do you want me to have a look around for him?' Theo offered.

'If you wouldn't mind,' Kitty said.

'Oi, Luke!' Theo called.

A man came out of the milking shed. He was in his late twenties, with dark hair and a boyish round face. He wore wellies and blue overalls. 'What's up?'

'Kitty is looking for Madog,' Theo said.

'Haven't seen him,' Luke said.

'Wanna give me a hand to look for him? We can take the quads.'

'Yeah, no problem,' Luke said. 'We'll check around the fields.'

'Thank you,' Kitty said.

Kitty could see the annoyance on Quintin's face. He turned on her as soon as the other two men left.

'I don't know why you're making such a fuss. Luke's got work to do. We don't pay him to mess around.'

'He's not messing around. Weren't you listening to what I said? Uncle Madog didn't touch the food I left for him yesterday. No one has seen him since Friday evening. On top of that, his cottage is a mess. All the drawers have been tipped out.'

'Stupid old bugger has probably lost your father's letter and is hiding from us.'

'I don't care about the letter. I just want to make sure he's alright.'

'Well, you should care. Half the profit from the farm could be coming our way. That and half the money your mother has squirreled away over the years will be enough to get this place up to scratch. We can think of selling and getting out of here.'

'I don't want to leave the farm,' Kitty said. 'Besides, Uncle Madog owns the land.'

'Yeah, but who gets it when he kicks it?'

'Is that all you care about, the money?' Kitty asked.

'Yeah, and it's just as well. Where would you all be without me? You couldn't run this place. You've no idea how to balance the books. You just play around with your fish. Do you know how much it costs to run this place? How to deal with the labourers' wages?'

Kitty didn't answer. Maths had never been her strong point and Quintin had always been happy to take care of the finances. He was right, she wouldn't be able to manage without him.

'I'm going to look for Uncle Madog,' she said.

'Fine, some of us have work to do,' Quintin said. 'You might want to go and see Pippa. I bet it never occurred to you that he's up there drinking tea and chatting, while the rest of us waste our time. I can't finish the stock take until Luke gets back.'

Kitty got back in the car. The last person she wanted to see was Pippa, her sister-in-law always managed to make her feel inadequate. But again Quintin was right. Madog was fond of Quintin's mother, Eleanor. He often popped in for a chat.

There was no answer when Kitty knocked on the door to the manor house. She knocked again and called out as she opened the door. She found Pippa sitting at the kitchen table painting her long fingernails red.

'Well this is a surprise, darling,' Pippa said as she dipped the brush into the bottle.

Kitty looked down at her own short nails and put her hands behind her back. She knew Pippa had her nails done yesterday and wondered why she didn't get them painted at the same time. 'I was looking for Uncle Madog. I thought he might have popped in to see your mum.'

'No, haven't seen him.' Pippa kept her eyes down as she ran the brush the length of her nails. 'Mother is dozing in front of the television. Thank goodness. I'm exhausted looking after her.'

Kitty couldn't understand how looking after Eleanor could be exhausting. Most of the time she stayed in the sitting room. She was fully mobile and remarkably sharp for her age.

'Has Mum not been well?' Kitty asked.

'She's fine, but she gets up at nine every morning. She likes to go shopping so I have to take her a couple of times a week. It takes ages to get around the aisles. Then there're doctor's appointments and we have to go to the opticians in the morning. I don't think anyone understands how difficult my life is.'

'I can sympathise,' Kitty said. 'I was afraid to leave Mum's side towards the end.'

Pippa looked up. 'It's not the same though, is it? You have Quintin to help you.'

Kitty wanted to say that Quintin had been no help during her mother's illness. But Pippa wouldn't have a word said against her brother.

'Isn't Theo moving back in with you?' Kitty asked.

'Yes, but I can't expect Theo to help with Mother.' Pippa blew on her nails. 'He has his own problems and his back injury from work isn't helping his mental state.'

'Of course. It must be really hard for him,' Kitty said. She liked Theo. He was nothing like his mother. He never complained and he above everyone had reason to complain, she thought. 'I won't disturb you any longer. If you see Uncle Madog, can you let me know?'

Pippa nodded. 'Oh before you go, can you ask Quin to sort out my money?'

'I thought he did it last week,' Kitty said.

'No, well he dropped off a bit. Not the full amount. He does have a responsibility to Mother and me. It's the second month he's left us short. The bills must be paid, and it costs a lot to run this place. A little more would be nice. Even if it's just to have a treat now and again. I'd also prefer it if he did it by bank transfer. I know it helps you out as some sort of tax break but it's a nuisance to carry around cash. I'm sure you can find some other way.'

Kitty didn't have a clue what Pippa was talking about. She couldn't see how she benefitted by paying for Pippa and Eleanor to stay in this enormous house. As for the money, she'd seen a large amount go out of the account. Not what she'd call a bit of cash.

'I'll tell him.'

Kitty was glad to get away. When she parked outside the farmhouse Theo was waiting for her.

'We've checked around the fields and asked the boys if they'd seen Madog. There's no sign of him.'

'Thanks, Theo. I'll go back to his cottage and wait. If he's not back by dark I'm calling the police.'

Chapter Five

As much as Meadows wanted to go into the woods to inspect Mr and Mrs Wilson he knew he had to wait. Mountain rescue and a fisherman had already trampled over the crime scene. He knew it was a crime scene from the description. "Horrific" is what John, from mountain rescue, had said.

Meadows had told Hanes there had been a development and asked him to take Lucy back to the holiday cottage. He hadn't given any more details in case Lucy overheard. He called in scene of crime officers and uniform to assist, then cordoned off the entrance to the woods.

'I'm going to have a quick chat with the fisherman who found the bodies then talk to Lucy,' Meadows said. 'All sorts must be going through her mind. It's not fair to keep her in the dark.'

'I never expected this outcome,' Edris said. 'Poor woman. Go, I'll stay here until SOCO arrive. There's no one around but you never know who could be out for a walk. All this activity is bound to attract someone's interest.'

'I'll ask mountain rescue to cover any other entrances until help arrives.'

It was a long walk back to the car and the fading sun left a chill in the air. Meadows found the fisherman sitting on the edge of the boot of his car sipping from a plastic cup and talking to Tom the bailiff.

'This is Tony,' Tom said. 'Had a bit of a shock didn't you, mate?'

Tony nodded his head.

'I'll leave you to it,' Tom said.

'Thank you,' Meadows said. He turned to Tony. 'How are you doing now?'

'I'm OK. I couldn't stop shaking for a while. The bailiff gave me some tea from his flask. I think I'll need something stronger when I get home.'

'Have you been fishing in that spot all day?'

'Yeah, pretty much.'

'It's a fair walk from the car. Any particular reason you chose that place?'

'No, not really. It's quiet there, thought I'd have a bit of luck catching something.'

'Why did you go into the woods?'

'Got caught short.'

'You were quite a way in.'

'Yeah, well I didn't want to get caught with my trousers down and you sometimes get hikers that way.'

'Did you see anyone else near there today?' Meadows asked.

'No, haven't seen a soul all day.'

'Was there a particular reason why you chose that spot to relieve yourself. I mean is it somewhere you've used before and you knew you wouldn't be disturbed?'

'No, not really. You just go where you can. I've been in a couple of times today, well near that spot. All the while he was just lying there.' Tony shuddered.

Meadows guessed that Tony hadn't seen the second body. 'Did you touch the body? Feel for a pulse?'

'Oh God no. I'm afraid I made a fool of myself. I saw his boots when I crouched down. They were sort of poking out. I said something like, "Are you alright?" When he didn't answer I took a closer look. That's when I saw the blood. I screamed then ran. That's when I met up with the mountain rescue guy. I was blubbering like an idiot.'

'Don't worry about it,' Meadows said. 'You had a nasty shock. If you feel alright to drive then you can go home now. Just leave your details with the bailiff.'

'Thanks.' Tony stood up. 'I think it will be a while before I fish here again.'

'One more thing before you go. Were you here yesterday?'

'Yeah, I got here about eleven and left around five.'

'The same place?'

'No, I was fishing in the bay.'

'Did you happen to see a couple out walking? They would be in their sixties.'

Tony shook his head. 'There were a few out fishing.'

'Anyone out in a boat?'

'No, not that I saw.'

'OK, thanks. Someone will be in touch to take a formal statement. If you remember anything else, give us a call.' Meadows handed him a card.

Meadows caught up with Tom in the wooden information hut.

'Did you manage to round up the last of the anglers?' Meadows asked.

'Yeah, Tony is the last to go. Will we have to stay closed?'

'I'm afraid so,' Meadows said. 'It's going to take a while to clear the scene. I take it anyone fishing here yesterday, other than the private boat owners, would have to have a permit?'

'Yes, it's all done online now, but there are those who are season ticket holders.'

'Would you be able to provide names and addresses?'

'Not a problem for anyone on a day ticket fishing yesterday but there is no way to tell which of the season ticket holders were here. I'll print the list and highlight any names of the regulars I saw out yesterday.'

'That would be a great help, thank you.'

If it was just a case of eliminating anglers then they'd have a good chance of identifying the perpetrator, Meadows thought as he climbed into the car. But there were those who walked the area as well as those who risked fishing without a permit. Why here? He looked across the water as he drove past.

As he neared the holiday cottage his stomach started to churn. He wished he had better news to give Lucy. At least for the moment she would be spared the details, but that wouldn't last. When he entered the cottage Lucy was standing in the kitchen with a mug of tea in her hands as she talked to Hanes. She set the mug down and looked at Meadows.

'What's going on? It's Mum, isn't it. I knew it had been too long.' Her lips trembled.

'Lucy, I'm so sorry. The bodies of a couple matching your parents' description were found in the woods near the reservoir.'

'I don't understand,' Lucy said. 'What do you mean bodies? Are you telling me they are both' – Lucy sucked in air – 'they're both dead?'

Meadows saw the colour drain from her face. He put his arm under her elbow and led her to the sofa.

'There will need to be a formal identification but at this stage we are fairly certain it's your parents.'

'How? I mean, I was expecting the worse for Mum, but Dad as well.'

'I'm sorry I don't have the full details now. Your mum and dad will be taken to hospital, and we'll know more then. What I can tell you is that we are treating their deaths as suspicious.'

Meadows waited for Lucy's reaction, but she didn't seem to have taken in his words. He knew it was the shock. He'd seen it many times. People's thoughts seem to slow, and they got that faraway look. Questions would come later.

'Is there someone we can call for you?'

'My partner. He has the kids. I'm going to have to tell my brother. He's waiting for news.'

'We can do that for you,' Hanes said.

'No, I should be the one to tell him.'

'OK, I'm going to have a family liaison officer come to stay with you,' Meadows said. He felt there was nothing more he could do for Lucy now. What she needs is answers, he thought.

* * *

The light had faded by the time Meadows returned to the reservoir. He took his torch from the car and made his way alongside the water. It was quiet and eerie, the trees now shadows, and darkness stretched out before him. He was glad to meet up with Edris and he stepped past the cordon. He quickly put on a protective suit and covered his mouth. Edris yawned before pulling up his mask.

They followed the narrow dirt and stony path that had been cut through the grass by walkers then used the metal stepping stones laid out to preserve the scene. There were lights up ahead that had been placed by SOCO and white-covered figures could be seen scouring the ground. Just before they reached the point where the walkway branched off they were met by the head of forensics, Mike Fielding. Meadows recognised Mike despite the mask.

'Alright, Mike,' Edris said.

'Yeah, Daisy is in the first tent examining the male. We just finished erecting the second tent over the female. It's a bit of a nightmare. It looks like they were attacked on the path and dragged into the undergrowth. There's blood on the path as well as a blood trail leading to the bodies.

We've had to cordon off a large area. It's going to take days to process. We'll cover as much as we can to preserve the evidence. I just hope the weather holds.'

'OK, thanks, Mike,' Meadows said. 'We'll take a look and then get out of your way.'

He could feel the cold seeping through his latex gloves and didn't envy SOCO the task of combing the area through the night. He followed the path to the first tent and stepped inside. The smell of death filled the confined space, penetrating his mask. Edris was close behind him and Meadows could imagine his nose wrinkling and stomach turning over at the sight. Daisy, the pathologist and also Meadows' girlfriend, was crouched next to the body. She looked up and greeted him with a nod of the head.

Meadows eyes took in the scene. He recognised David Wilson although his features in death were a sharp contrast from the happy photo Lucy had shared. David lay on his back with his arms stretched out above his head, and his face tilted to one side. His fingers were curled, and his palms covered in dirt. His injuries were obvious. His dark grey hair was matted with blood which had dripped down his neck. There were two thin lines across his throat, the depth enough to cause bleeding but the wounds didn't gape. Above the lines, deep scratches ran vertically.

Edris stepped closer. 'Nasty,' he said. 'It's cramped in here. I think I'll wait outside, give you a bit more space.'

'What's up with him?' Daisy asked.

'He's got a toad of a hangover and hasn't eaten all day. He'll be OK.' Meadows crouched next to Daisy to get a closer look at David Wilson's wounds. 'Looks like a blade has been run across his throat.'

'Garrotted would be my guess,' Daisy said.

Meadows had an image go through his mind of gangsters and piano wire. 'I take it that's what killed him and not the head wound.'

'That would be my first thought although I couldn't tell you with certainty until I do the post-mortem. Head wounds do tend to bleed a lot, but he has been hit with some force and more than once.' She parted David's hair. 'See here, and here.'

'Any defence wounds?'

'His hands are dirty, and it looks like blood on the fingertips.' Daisy raised his hand. 'Nothing on the knuckles to indicate that he hit his assailant.'

'Time of death?'

'You know better than that,' Daisy said.

'We think they left the cottage around five yesterday.'

'It fits. Eighteen to twenty-four hours is my best estimate.'

'That will do,' Meadows said.

'He was moved after death.'

'That fits with what Mike told me. Killed on the path and dragged in after. Have you checked his pockets?'

'Mike has his phone bagged and ready to send to tech.'

'Good. Have you looked at Mrs Wilson?'

'Not yet. I'll take a quick look with you now then I'll finish up here.'

Meadows stepped back to let Daisy out first, then followed her to the second tent where Edris was waiting outside.

'I've taken a peek. Same as her husband,' Edris said.

Meadows nodded and stepped inside.

Anna Wilson was also on her back, but her arms were resting at her side. The obvious difference was the injuries to her face. Her left eye was swollen shut and there was a gash on her temple. Her shoulder-length ash blonde hair was tangled with dirt, twigs, and blood. Meadows knelt and looked at her throat. The markings were like David Wilson's, but she only had one line across her throat.

'Her hands are bloody,' Meadows said.

'Natural reaction is to put your hand to the injury,' Daisy said. 'She was facing her killer.'

'Or killers,' Meadows said. 'Not easy to kill them both at the same time. Although I'd imagine that's why they have head injuries. The killer wanted to incapacitate them first.'

Meadows felt around Anna's coat and found a phone in her pocket. Daisy handed him an evidence bag and he popped it inside. He tapped the screen through the plastic.

'Looks like the battery is dead.' He stood up. 'I'll leave you to it.'

'I'll get the post-mortems done as soon as they've been formally identified.'

'Thanks. See you later,' he said before stepping out of the tent.

'Ready to go?' Edris said.

'Yeah, I just want to give this phone to Mike.'

'It looks personal,' Edris said, glancing at the tent that covered David Wilson.

'What makes you think that?'

'It's vicious. Hitting them over the head and garrotting them. If he hit David Wilson more than once, why stop? He could've just finished the job.'

'Good question,' Meadows said. 'Unless they thought they would get too much blood over them. It looks like the killer came prepared. The other question is, was the killer waiting for them in that spot, or did they follow them? Either on the way to meet the boat owner or the way back.'

'More likely whoever owned the boat knew they were coming and waited for them,' Edris said.

'But why? From what Lucy said it sounds that the owner of the boat was unknown to them. Otherwise they would have said they ran into a friend or someone they knew. Until we find the person that had a boat out on the lake yesterday, we won't know. I can't see that someone was hanging around here waiting for the opportunity to kill two random strangers.'

'I guess not,' Edris said.

They found Mike, and Meadows handed him the phone.

'I'll put this with the other one and get it straight to tech,' Mike said.

'Have you found anything of interest?' Meadows asked.

'A rucksack. It was thrown into the trees. Nothing much inside. A couple of bottles of water, binoculars, tissues, Mr Wilson's wallet, and a packet of mints. I'll get the lot tested.'

'Not a robbery then,' Edris said.

Mike shook his head. 'There's money in the wallet as well as some credit cards, and a driver's license.'

'There's not much more we can do here,' Meadows said.

'Lucky you,' Mike said. 'It's going to be a long night. I'll let you know if anything comes up.'

'Thanks,' Meadows said. He turned to Edris. 'Come on, I bet you are longing for your bed.'

'Just a bit,' Edris said.

'I'll drop you home.'

They peeled off their protective clothing at the cordon and were walking the path back to the car when they met with Hanes.

'We've received a call about a missing person from Cwm Bach. As it's only seven miles from here I thought I better let you know. Missing person is a Mr Madog Jones, called in by his niece Kitty Eccleston.'

'Name sounds familiar.' Meadows put his hand into his inside jacket pocket and pulled out the list of boat owners the bailiff had given him. He read through the names. 'Madog Jones, he owns one of the private boats tethered here. Thanks, Hanes, we'll take this one.'

'Could be the man that offered the Wilsons a boat ride,' Edris said.

'That's what I'm thinking, but if that's the case, where is he?'

Chapter Six

Pippa Eccleston walked down the bridle path that led from her house to Madog's cottage. She could hear voices cutting through the darkness. People were out searching for Madog. Every now and then she caught a glimpse of a flashlight through the trees or in one of the fields. She kept her own beam trained on the ground. She had thought of keeping the torch switched off, but it was dangerous in the dark even though she knew the path well. There was always a tree root waiting to trip you up.

If I meet up with anyone, I can say I'm joining the search. Perfect cover, she thought and smiled to herself. It was the second night she'd been creeping around in the dark. The previous evening had been a disaster. She had timed it perfectly so the family would be with Kitty for dinner. She'd got as far as Madog's cottage door but had heard someone moving around inside. She'd scuttled away before being seen. On the other side of the bridge she'd waited behind a tree. She wanted to see if anyone came out of the cottage. They would have had to pass her. She must have waited for an hour. No one came. In the end, cold and angry, she had gone to the farmhouse and gave some excuse to Kitty for being late.

This evening she was going in, no matter who saw her. The lights were on in the cottage, but she expected that. She got to the door and listened. All was quiet. She opened the door, stepped inside, and closed the door quickly behind her. She could feel her heart thudding in her chest.

'Just popped in to check if he was back,' she said.

No one answered and she felt her breathing return to normal. She looked around; the place was a mess. All the drawers were open, and the dining table was covered in paperwork mixed with old batteries, pens, and other useless stuff.

Stupid old man, she thought. Probably forgotten where he put it. Another thought occurred to her, maybe someone else had got here before her and took it. She hoped it was Quintin. She couldn't bear it if Kitty or Lottie had got to it first.

She started in the kitchen carefully looking at every piece of paper she came across. Next the sitting room, then to the bedroom. She became more desperate and started upturning cushions and feeling under the mattress. Nothing. She felt like screaming as she threw the cushions back onto the sofa. She was about to leave when her eyes fell on the carriage clock on the mantlepiece. Pippa remembered her mother had one and used to keep the key to her jewellery box inside. She grabbed the clock and pulled open the door at the back. Inside she saw a piece of paper neatly folded to fit within. It didn't surprise her that it was hidden there. Why would he leave something so precious in a drawer for anyone to find?

She carefully unfolded the paper but instead of the letter she expected it was a picture drawn by a child. Two crude figures, one tall, the other small with triangular bodies. Both had wings. Fury rose in Pippa as she screwed up the picture into a ball and threw it onto the pile of papers on the table.

She left the cottage and walked back up the bridle path at such a pace she had to stop to catch her breath at the top. Inside the manor house, she had just taken off her boots when Theo came in.

'Kitty has called the police,' Theo said. 'She's going to wait in the farmhouse until they arrive. I'm just going to grab a cup of tea then I'm going out with Elsie to keep looking.'

'In the dark?' Pippa said. 'You should leave it up to the police to look for him.'

'You should come as well,' Theo said. 'Everyone else is out looking. You could at least pretend you care.'

'I do care,' Pippa said. 'I just don't see what good it will do for all of us to be searching around in the dark. Besides, I need to stay here for your grandma.'

'Grandma manages perfectly well when it suits you,' Theo snapped.

'What's wrong, darling?' Pippa asked.

'I'm worried about Uncle Madog, and poor Auntie Kitty is so upset.'

Bloody Kitty, Pippa thought. This is all going to be about her now. No one worries about me. They've no idea of the problems I've got.

'I'll get my coat on and come with you,' Pippa said.

'Don't bother if it's going to put you out,' Theo said. 'I don't think I'll have tea now. I'll have one at Auntie Kitty's later.' He left, closing the door with a little more force than necessary.

Pippa sat down at the table. Theo had been brooding all weekend. It wasn't like him. What if he knows? The thought made a coldness creep over her body. No, there is no way he'd have found out. She'd have to keep a watch on them all. Intervene if she had to. She didn't care what it took.

Chapter Seven

The track leading to the address Hanes had given them was rutted and seemed endless in the dark. The car rocked, and branches of trees reached out liked gnarled fingers.

'This really is the back of beyond,' Edris said. 'Who would want to live here?'

'Who wouldn't?' Meadows said.

'I guess it would appeal to you. Miles away from civilisation.'

Meadows laughed. 'Yeah, get myself a cow for milk, some chickens for eggs, and grow my own veg. Perfect.'

A house came into view with the front door lit by an outside light and Meadows could see the outline of two other cottages.

'I guess it's the one with lights on,' Meadows said as he pulled up the car.

They got out of the car and as Edris stretched his back, the door to the farmhouse opened and a woman appeared. She was petite. Meadows doubted she reached five feet. She had wild curly red hair which came down over her shoulders and was threaded with silver strands. She looked so delicate that she would shatter if she fell.

'Kitty Eccleston?' Meadows asked.

'Yes.'

Meadows made the introductions.

'Thank you for coming,' Kitty said. 'Please come in.'

She led them to the kitchen where a man sat at a scrubbed pine table, a glass of wine in one hand and a book in the other.

'This is my husband, Quintin,' Kitty said.

Quintin nodded at the detectives, set his glass on the table, and topped it up.

Meadows got the impression that Quintin wasn't happy with their presence. He was a heavyset man with receding grey hair, a beaky nose and thick jaw. He didn't offer a smile.

'Can I get you anything to drink?' Kitty asked.

'We'd love a cup of tea,' Edris said.

While Kitty was putting on the kettle Meadows and Edris took a seat at the table.

'You reported your uncle, Madog Jones, missing,' Meadows said.

Kitty turned around and leaned against the worktop. 'Yes, we've looked everywhere. I'm really worried about him. The rest of the family is still out looking, as well as some of the men who work on the farm. I didn't know what else to do. I thought it best to call you so that you can organise a search party and helicopter.'

'For God's sake, Kitty,' Quintin said. 'Give them a chance to have a cup of tea.' He rolled his eyes. 'I told her that Madog is an adult. If he's gone off somewhere, that's his business.'

'He wouldn't just go off,' Kitty said.

Meadows could see the worry in Kitty's eyes. 'We're going to take some details and assess your uncle's vulnerability. The more information we have at this stage the better the chances of finding him. Is that OK?'

Kitty nodded and turned to make the tea. Once it was set on the table she took a seat and Edris took out his notebook. In the forefront of Meadows' mind was the

Wilsons and the possibility that Madog Jones could be a person of interest.

'Does your uncle live with you?' Meadows asked.

'No, he has a cottage of his own here. I can show you.'

'We'll look once we've finished here,' Meadows said. 'When was the last time you saw him?'

'Friday evening,' Kitty said. 'I walked him back to his cottage.'

Last sighting was before the Wilsons went missing, Meadows thought. Could still fit the time frame of the murders. He could have gone to the reservoir early to wait for them. He gave a nod to Edris.

'Does Madog have a mobile phone?' Edris asked.

'Yes, but it's on the coffee table in his cottage. That's not unusual, he rarely takes it anywhere with him.'

'Can you give me a description of Madog?' Edris asked.

Quintin smirked. 'He looks a bit like a stickman.'

Kitty ignored the comment. 'He's seventy-four, six foot six, and thin. His hair is grey, he doesn't have much left, and he has blue eyes. He wears glasses. Thick lenses. He's short-sighted.'

'Do you have a recent photograph?' Edris asked.

'Yes.' Kitty stood.

Meadows looked at Quintin. 'Maybe you can get the photograph for us while we talk to Kitty.'

'Wouldn't know where to look,' Quintin said and took a gulp of his wine.

'Don't worry about it now. You can give us the photo when we've finished.' Meadows gave Kitty a smile and she sat down.

'Does Madog have any health issues?' Edris asked.

'He has a heart condition,' Kitty said, 'and some problems with his joints.'

Doesn't sound like a man physically capable of killing the Wilsons, Meadows thought.

'What about mental health?'

'He's not senile, if that's what you mean,' Kitty said.

'Any history of depression?'

'No.'

'Has he ever gone off without telling you his whereabouts before?' Edris asked.

'No, never,' Kitty said. 'This is so unlike him. I usually see him every day. I was just so busy yesterday.'

'When you saw him on Friday, how did he seem?' Meadows asked.

'He was OK; well, a little down. It was my mother's funeral, so it'd been an emotional day for us all.'

'Madog was your mother's brother?'

'No,' Kitty said. 'My dad's brother but he was very close to Mum, especially after Dad died. He looked after her. Made sure she had everything she needed, and they used to talk about Dad all the time. I know he's going to miss her.'

'Family funerals can be a difficult time,' Meadows said. 'Often emotions get the better of people. Were there any arguments?'

Kitty hesitated and he saw her eyes flick to her husband before she answered. 'No, we were all sad, but it was expected. The whole family came back here afterwards, and we lit a bonfire in the evening. The younger ones had a few drinks. They got a little loud. Uncle Madog left because he was tired. That's when I walked him home.'

'What did you talk about?' Meadows asked.

'Mum and Dad. He mentioned Mum's will. It's a little complicated and my dad left a codicil with Uncle Madog to be read after my mum died. He didn't seem overly concerned about it.'

'A codicil, what exactly is that?' Edris asked.

Quintin rolled his eyes. 'It's an addition to a will. A legal document, signed and witnessed, so it can modify parts of the will, or it could just explain certain terms.'

'So this was an addition to your mother's will?' Edris asked.

'No,' Quintin said. 'It's not that difficult to understand. Llew, Madog's brother, died years ago. He wanted his wife, Connie, to be taken care of but she couldn't inherit the farm. He made provisions for her, as a sort of caretaker. On her death it reverted to Llew's estate, and the codicil sets out the terms of who inherits. Have you got all that?'

Edris nodded. 'Could Madog have been worried about it? Maybe wanted a couple of days away from everyone?'

'No,' Kitty said. 'He wouldn't do that, and he has nowhere to go.'

'When you last spoke to him did he mention his plans for the next day?'

'No, not really. I asked him if he was coming to breakfast but he said he wanted some peace. I took him over some food about five, but he wasn't home. I left it for him, and it was still there today. Untouched. I've tried to think over what he last said to me. He said something like "I'll see you tomorrow."'

While Kitty was talking, Meadows was thinking how to phrase the next question. He needed to ask about Madog's boat and the possibility of him being at the Usk Reservoir. Before he had a chance to ask, the door opened and a young man and woman walked in with two sheepdogs. The dogs ran over to Meadows and Edris with wagging tails.

'Hello,' Meadows said, patting one dog as it put its head into his lap.

'Wagner, Elgar.' Quintin pointed to the corner. '*Cwtch*.'

The dogs headed to a basket in front of an Aga.

Meadows turned his attention away from the dogs and back to the man and woman. Both looked to be in their late twenties. The man was tall, lean and muscular with a boyish face and kind eyes. The woman was of average height with curly dark hair.

'No sign of him,' the man said.

'This is Quintin's nephew, Theo, and my daughter, Elsie,' Kitty said.

'We took a drive up the Usk, but we couldn't look around. There are police everywhere,' Elsie said.

Kitty looked alarmed as she turned to Meadows. 'Has something happened at the reservoir?'

'There's been an incident there but all those concerned have been identified. Do you have reason to believe that your uncle went to the reservoir yesterday?'

Kitty shook her head. 'His Land Rover is still parked here, and he would've told me if he was going.'

'Could someone have given him a lift?' Meadows asked.

'We've already asked everyone on the farm,' Elsie said. 'Uncle Lloyd and Auntie Lottie have gone to the pub to see if anyone has seen him. Jac and Celyn, that's Lottie's children, are checking Pant Teg.'

'Does Madog go often to the reservoir?'

'Less often now,' Kitty said.

'Madog's name came up on a list of boat owners. Does he still keep a boat tethered at the Usk?' Meadows asked.

'Yes,' Kitty said.

'Is it possible that he could've taken the boat out?' Meadows asked.

'Not on his own,' Kitty said.

'He'd need help to launch it,' Theo added.

'If he'd gone fishing he would be back by now,' Kitty said.

'Have you contacted friends and family he may be visiting?' Edris asked.

'He doesn't go anywhere,' Kitty said. 'He's either in his cottage, fishing on the lakes here, or occasionally up at the Usk.'

'If he had gone fishing then I guess he would've taken a rod and tackle with him,' Meadows said. 'Would you be able to check?'

'Yeah,' Kitty said. 'I never thought to look when I was in the cottage earlier. We can go there now.'

'If you could get that picture for us first then we'll take a look in his cottage.'

When Kitty left the room there was an awkward silence.

'Maybe we should take another look around the farm,' Elsie suggested.

'What for?' Quintin asked. 'It's dark so there's no point. Enough time has been wasted already today.'

'Do you think that Madog has gone of his own accord?' Meadows asked.

Quintin shrugged. 'Well he's not here. She's got most of the farm labourers out looking for him. If he was on the farm they would've found him by now. This is a working farm. We go to bed early and get up early. If the workers are tired because they've been up all night they'll be no good to me tomorrow.'

'I don't think we should be concerned about the farm. Mum is really worried; we all are,' Elsie said.

'It's not you that has to get up in the morning,' Quintin snapped. 'If you want to make yourself useful, go and tell the others to call it a night. The police will sort it out.' He stood up. 'If you'll excuse me I want some time to unwind before I go to bed.' He grabbed the remainder of the wine and left.

'I don't mind taking another look,' Theo said.

'Thanks,' Elsie said.

Kitty came back into the room with a couple of photos in her hand and placed them on the table. 'I'm sorry I can't find a recent one of him on his own.'

'That's fine,' Meadows said as he picked up a photo. It was taken by a lake with Kitty and Madog standing next to each other holding rods. They looked a comical pair, Meadows thought. Madog was so thin and tall he looked stretched, and Kitty was like a doll beside him.

'It was taken in May,' Kitty said.

'Lovely photo of the two of you,' Meadows said. 'We'll get it circulated. Given Madog's age and health I think it will be wise to call in mountain rescue. We'll also arrange for officers to search the surrounding area at first light. If you can show me the cottage now, Sergeant Edris will make the arrangements.'

'You're welcome to use the landline,' Kitty said. 'I doubt you'll get a signal here. You have to walk to higher ground.'

Edris took out his mobile phone and looked at the screen. 'Yeah, nothing. I'll take a drive up the road and come back and pick you up.'

'Me and Theo will check with the others and see if they've had any luck,' Elsie said.

'Thanks, love,' Kitty said. She picked up two torches from the worktop and handed one to Meadows. 'It's a bit of a trek to the cottage and there are no lights.'

'No problem,' Meadows said.

Edris pulled off in the car as Meadows left the light of the farmhouse and clicked on his torch.

'Do all the family live here?' Meadows asked.

'No, the farmhouse was Mum and Dad's. I moved in to help Mum when she got too ill to cope on her own. That's my cottage,' Kitty said as they walked past and took the path to the side. 'My sister's son, Jac, and his girlfriend are staying in that one.' She pointed to the right. 'They came down for the funeral. They'll be leaving tomorrow night, as will Elsie. She came to help me with the funeral arrangements, but she's got to go back to work. The other two cottages behind are empty. We rent them out in the summer. They are all self-contained with their own enclosed gardens. My sister Lottie, and brother-in-law, Lloyd, live in the village. This is Uncle Madog's Land Rover.' She shone the torch at the vehicle's window.

'Is it always parked here?' Meadows asked.

'Yeah, you can't drive any closer to Uncle Madog's cottage. It hasn't moved since Friday. He doesn't drive a lot now.'

They walked down a slope which led to a stream. Meadows' torch picked out the water tumbling over the rocky bed. He thought how easy it would be for the old man to slip but doubted the current was strong enough to carry him away.

'There's a bridge further up; we cross there,' Kitty said.

Meadows found Kitty easy company. She had a softness about her and radiated warmth. He guessed her to be in her mid to late forties, but she had a childlike quality. She talked as they walked, and he glimpsed the love she had for the farm and those around her.

'Did your mum and dad own all this land or just the farmhouse?' Meadows asked.

'It's complicated,' Kitty said. 'Uncle Madog owns the land. Mum owned the farmhouse but had fifty percent share of the farm profits. I own my cottage, the trout farm, and lakes, but not the land.'

Meadows laughed. 'Right, that does sound a bit complicated.'

'I just like to keep things simple,' Kitty said. 'I look after the fish and the cottages.'

Meadows had an image of the trout being carted off to supermarkets and landing on someone's plate for supper. Yet he got the impression that Kitty wouldn't breed the fish for that purpose. 'What do you do with the fish you breed?'

'They're used to stock the lakes; here, the Usk, and other reservoirs.'

They reached the bridge and Meadows stepped back to let Kitty cross first. The bridge was old, and the railings felt unsafe beneath Meadows' hands in parts. He stepped off the other side and followed Kitty through the trees until the lights of Madog's cottage appeared.

'Were the lights on when you called around yesterday?' Meadows asked.

Kitty stopped and thought for a moment. 'Yeah, in the kitchen and there was a lamp on in the sitting room. I turned on the main lights so it would be ready for when Uncle Madog got back.' She opened the gate and stepped through.

'Is it usual for him to go out in the daytime and leave the lights on?'

'It depends. If he's coming to my house for dinner then yes, as it's dark when he goes home.'

'Then I guess wherever he was going he intended to come back after dark,' Meadows said.

'Or he could have left early in the morning. The cottage doesn't get much light because of the trees. Uncle Madog usually eats his breakfast in the sitting room, with the lamp on.'

'Did you use your keys to get in or was the door unlocked?' Meadows asked.

'I don't have keys,' Kitty said. 'Uncle Madog never locks the door. None of us do. There's no one around here.' She pushed open the door.

Meadows stepped through the door into a kitchen. His first impression was one of going back in time. The walls were whitewashed stone. Old wooden kitchen cupboards separated the kitchen from the sitting room. There was a deep ceramic sink set into a wooden worktop and shelves held pots, pans, and dishes. A clothes rack hung above a blue enamel Aga and a foil-covered plate sat on top of the hotplate. All the drawers were open.

'It was like this when I came earlier,' Kitty said. 'The drawers in every room are open. Uncle Madog is usually very tidy. Quintin thinks he has lost the letter and was looking for it.'

'What letter?' Meadows asked.

'The letter my father left. It's supposed to be read tomorrow when the solicitor comes.'

'The codicil to the will you mentioned earlier?'

'Yeah.'

'What's in the codicil?'

'I don't know, no one does but Uncle Madog. I guess it has something to do with the farmhouse and what will happen to the profits. Dad was the oldest, so he owned the land, then when he died it went to Uncle Madog.'

'Right. Do you think he would've gone off somewhere if he couldn't find the letter?'

'No, he told me I shouldn't worry about the letter. If he'd lost it he would've said. Anyway, he wouldn't have kept it here in case someone found it.'

'Where would he have kept it?'

Kitty shrugged.

'It would be useful to know. If the letter was meant to be read tomorrow maybe he went off to get it.'

'It would be on the farm somewhere.'

This didn't make a lot of sense to Meadows. 'Are you saying someone has come in and upturned the drawers looking for the letter.'

'Madog wouldn't have left this mess. It's probably one of the family who can't wait to see what's in the letter. Anyway, it's not important. I just want to find him.'

Meadows thought Kitty was probably right. He was getting distracted by the letter and it may be the case that it had nothing to do with Madog's disappearance. What he needed to know was if Madog had been at the Usk Reservoir.

'Can you tell if anything is missing? Like his laptop,' Meadows asked.

Kitty laughed. 'Uncle Madog could barely send a text message. He doesn't own a computer of any sort.' She opened a kitchen cupboard and peered inside. 'There's money here. He didn't bother much with banks. He drew out his pension and put it in here. If he wanted any money from the farm he asked for cash. If someone came in here to steal something then the money would be missing.'

Meadows nodded. 'Where does Madog usually keep his fishing tackle?'

'Over there.' Kitty moved into the sitting room and opened a wooden panel.

While she looked inside, Meadows walked around the room. There wasn't much to see. A sofa with a floor lamp in the corner. A coffee table, a dining table with two chairs, and a Welsh dresser. It was clear to him that Madog liked to live a simple life. He moved to the fireplace and picked up a photo from the mantlepiece. It was of two men. One he could tell was a younger version of Madog, the other he assumed was Madog's brother, Llew. They looked remarkably similar. Both the same height, thin, with a small jaw and deep-set eyes. They were standing by a tractor, both smiling.

'His fishing bag and net are missing, and I think one of his fly rods. Oh, and his coat is not here. It's a green wax coat.'

'What does his bag look like?'

'It's an old canvas bag. If you look at the photo I gave you, you can see it on the ground.'

'Is there anywhere else he would go fishing other than here or the Usk?'

'No.'

'What about the stream?'

'I've walked the stream, besides there are only a few places that he would fish where it's deep enough and there aren't overhanging trees. It's his fly-fishing rod that's missing, so he would more likely be at one of the lakes or the reservoir.'

'Right, as you've searched around the farm, we'll concentrate the search at the reservoir. In the meantime, I'd like you to find out if anyone on the farm or in the village gave him a lift there.'

Meadows walked with Kitty back to the farmhouse where Edris was waiting. He wanted to tell Kitty not to worry but he knew his words would be empty.

He climbed into the car and filled Edris in on what he had seen at the cottage.

'It doesn't look good,' Edris said.

'No,' Meadows agreed. 'My concern is if Madog was up the Usk Reservoir fishing yesterday he may have witnessed what happened to the Wilsons. If that's the case, it's unlikely the killer would let him walk away.'

Chapter Eight

Meadows stood at the incident board waiting for the team to pull their chairs around. Edris and DC Valentine were already seated but with a noticeable gap between them. They usually sat together, and Meadows had observed a friction between them. He hadn't seen them exchange more than a "good morning" since they arrived. He had his suspicions that they had done something at Edris' party that they both now regretted. Maybe it's embarrassment, he thought. Valentine was usually bubbly and the only one who managed to tease DS Blackwell and get away with it. She was sitting now with her eyes downcast and her glossy black hair hanging forward, creating a barrier between herself and Edris. Edris was doing his best not to look in her direction.

DS Paskin pulled her chair past Meadows, mouthing "awkward" before plonking herself between the two of them. Meadows gave her a smile. Paskin was his go-to person for information. Whether it be social media, phone records, or background checks, her skills were invaluable.

Blackwell was the last in. He sat next to Valentine with a cup of coffee in his hands and his legs stretched out in front of him. Built like a bulldog, he had a thick triangular neck, shrewd eyes, and rarely smiled.

'You OK, Valentine?' Blackwell asked.

She looked at Blackwell and nodded.

Blackwell shot Edris a scathing look before turning his attention to the incident board. 'Looks like you had a busy weekend,' he said.

'You could say that,' Meadows said. 'OK, Mr David and Mrs Anna Wilson.' He pointed to the photos pinned to the board. 'Found in the woods surrounding the Usk Reservoir yesterday. They were staying in a holiday cottage nearby, home address in Bristol. Early indications show they died Saturday evening. Both sustained head injuries and were garrotted. We will be liaising with CID in Bristol. Paskin?'

Paskin flipped open her notebook. 'I haven't got a lot of background information yet. David Wilson was sixty-seven years old, and Anna Wilson sixty-five. Both retired. David worked for the council, and Anna was a schoolteacher, working with children with learning difficulties. Neither has a criminal record. Anna was active on Facebook. Lots of photos; family, holidays, that sort of thing. Their hobby appeared to be hiking.'

'We'll need a list of all their contacts, then cross-reference them, see if there is any connection to the area,' Meadows said. 'Bristol will conduct interviews from their end; they'll contact family and ex-work colleagues. DS Halliwell will be your main contact. I spoke to him this morning. He's going to the Wilsons' house to see if he can turn up anything there. Edris, do you want to fill the team in on what we know about the Wilsons' last movements?'

'Right.' Edris opened his notebook and read.

When he had finished Meadows said, 'So far we don't have a lot to go on. I've got a list of all the anglers who had tickets for Saturday as well as season ticket holders and boat owners. We need to speak to them all. See if anyone saw the Wilsons or someone acting strangely. We'll split the list between us. Paskin, can you put out an appeal on social media for anyone walking in that area over the weekend to come forward?'

Paskin nodded.

'We need to track down the person who offered to take the Wilsons out on a boat. Which leads me to Madog Jones.' Meadows pointed to the photo. 'Last seen Friday evening and he's one of the boat owners. I checked with the bailiff this morning. Madog's boat is missing. Edris?'

Edris read out the information they had on Madog.

'I would've expected him to be found by now,' Meadows said.

'So, he's our main suspect,' Blackwell said.

'Look at him,' Edris said. 'He's old and not in the best of health. I can't see him dragging two bodies into the woods.'

'He could've had help,' Valentine said.

'That's a possibility,' Meadows said. 'According to his niece, Kitty, he can't launch the boat alone, but what's the motive? Is there a connection between Madog Jones and the Wilsons? The other question is, where is the boat?'

'Could've taken it away,' Paskin said.

'You'd need a trailer,' Blackwell said.

'Madog's vehicle is still parked at the farm,' Edris said. 'We don't know for sure he did go to the Usk. Maybe someone stole the boat.'

'Mountain rescue and a search team are still at the Usk. If the boat is there, they will find it. It's not something you can easily hide,' Meadows said.

'What if it sank?' Paskin said. 'The boat and Madog Jones could be at the bottom of the reservoir. Madog and his accomplice kill the Wilsons, the accomplice kills Madog and sinks the boat.'

'Don't think it's that easy to sink a boat,' Edris said.

'Of course it is,' Blackwell said. 'You just punch a hole in the bottom. Just need the right tool.'

'At the moment we don't have enough evidence that Madog was at the Usk, other than missing fishing tackle, let alone in the water. I can't justify sending divers in or dragging a stretch of water that size,' Meadows said. 'Any thoughts?'

'It sounds like a vicious attack,' Blackwell said. 'Personal.'

'Whoever killed them would have to know they would be there at a certain time,' Valentine said.

'Which leads us back to Madog Jones and his offer of a boat ride,' Paskin said.

'If it was Madog that offered them a ride. It doesn't sound like the person with the boat was known to the Wilsons,' Edris said.

'So, the person who wants to kill them persuades Madog to take the boat out with them, offers the Wilsons a ride later that day, waits for them and kills them. They then have to kill Madog as he is a witness,' Valentine said.

'I don't see it,' Blackwell said. 'Why wait to the last day of their holiday? Cutting it a bit fine. If someone followed them from Bristol they would've been hanging around for a week, with a risk of being spotted. Sounds like they hiked to all sorts of remote areas. Plenty of opportunity. Why bother with a ruse of a boat ride?'

'He's got a point,' Edris said.

'Then we're left with a random killing,' Valentine said.

'I can't see someone hanging around in the woods of the Usk waiting for some unsuspecting tourists to kill off,' Blackwell said.

'Not impossible,' Meadows said, 'but highly unlikely. I think the most logical explanation is that there's a local connection to the Wilsons. Either that connection is Madog and an accomplice, or Madog was a witness and is either afraid and is hiding as he knows the killer, or he himself has been killed. The latter doesn't explain the missing boat. Edris and I are visiting Lucy Wilson, then attending the post-mortem. Valentine, Blackwell, I'll leave you two to make a start tracking down the anglers. Thanks, everyone.'

* * *

Edris chattered away as Meadows drove over the mountain. An early night had seen him returned to his well-groomed and quirky self.

'Whatever is going on between you and Valentine, you need to sort it,' Meadows said.

'Oh, I didn't think anyone would notice.'

'Really? You've gone from being best friends with occasional flirting to not being able to look at each other.'

'At the party we both had a lot to drink. We went back to my flat and—'

'Whoa there,' Meadows said. 'I don't want details. I just don't want an atmosphere at work. The two of you need to talk it out.'

'I don't know how to,' Edris said. 'I thought we had a good time but what if she didn't? I was drunk. What if she's said something to Paskin? Oh,' Edris groaned. 'Everyone's going to be laughing at me.'

'What do you mean by "thought she had a good time"? I hope you didn't take advantage of her.'

'No! Honestly, I think it was the other way around. Not that I'm complaining but she didn't even hang around. She took a taxi home.'

Meadows laughed; he couldn't help himself.

'It's not funny,' Edris said.

'It is a bit. How many women have you left dangling? How do you think they felt when you didn't call them the next day?'

'That's different. I never make any promises.'

'Oh, so Valentine did?'

'No, but we're friends.'

'Well, that's your problem. You've both crossed the line. Now you have to work out how to get back into the friend zone.'

'I suppose,' Edris said.

When they arrived at the holiday cottage they found two other people with Lucy. One she introduced as her bother Mark, the other a cousin, Dean, who had come down to drive back the Wilsons' car. Both Wilson children looked weighted down by grief. Lucy was pale and her eyes red and puffy. Mark had a distant look, as if he had switched off his emotions to deal with the situation.

Lucy sat down in an armchair. Meadows suspected she didn't have the energy to stand for too long. He sat on the sofa alongside Edris, and Mark remained standing.

'I'll pack the car,' Dean said.

'Do you want a hand?' Mark offered.

'No, you stay with Lucy. There's not that much to take out.'

'We've packed up Mum and Dad's things,' Lucy said. 'Unless you need us to stay, I'd like to go home. Mrs Perkins has been great letting me stay but I think she'd like the cottage back now.'

'That's fine,' Meadows said. 'We can arrange a family liaison officer from Bristol to keep you up to date.'

'Before we go I'd like to see where they died and lay some flowers,' Lucy said.

'I told her that's not a good idea,' Mark said.

'You can take some flowers to the cordon but I'm afraid we are still processing the area,' Meadows said. 'I can arrange for someone to take you to the location if you like.'

'We can come back, Luce,' Mark said. 'Why put yourself through that now? They're not there.'

Lucy nodded. 'I know, it's just that I keep expecting them to call. I should've gone in to see them.' She looked at Meadows. 'Mark went in to identify them alone. I couldn't do it.'

'That's understandable,' Meadows said.

'Now I won't be able to say goodbye.'

'You will get another chance to see them,' Meadows said. 'I know this is a very difficult time for the two of you, but we do need to ask you a few questions.'

'OK,' Mark said.

Lucy nodded.

'I need to tell you that after our initial assessment we will be treating the death of your parents as a murder investigation.'

'You mean someone killed them?' Lucy asked.

'Yes,' Meadows said.

'Does she have to hear this now?' Mark said.

Meadows guessed that Mark had seen his parents' injuries, particularly the ones to his mother's face. He doubted he'd shared this information with his sister.

'There will be media coverage,' Meadows said. 'It's better to be prepared. Details will not be given to the press, but I can't guarantee that there won't be speculation. Can you think of anyone who would want to harm your parents?'

'No, absolutely not,' Mark said.

Lucy shook her head.

'Any problems in work before they retired?'

Another shake of heads.

'We understand that your parents stayed here on a previous occasion. Did they have any connection to the area?'

'No, they just liked the place,' Lucy said.

'No friends or relatives in the area?'

'No.' Lucy looked at Mark. 'Did you ever hear them mention that they knew anyone from around here?'

'No,' Mark said.

'Do you know when they stayed here last?' Edris asked.

'It would've been last September,' Lucy said. 'Since they retired, they take holidays out of season.'

'Do you know how they came about renting this cottage the last time they were here. Was it a recommendation?' Edris asked.

'I don't think so,' Lucy said. 'They usually find places online. They sometimes go back to the same place if they enjoyed it or haven't finished exploring the area.'

'Did they have any financial concerns?' Meadows asked.

'The mortgage was paid,' Mark said. 'Both had good pensions.'

'If they had any money worries, I'm sure they would have said,' Lucy added.

'I have to ask, who benefits from your parents will?'

'There is just the two of us,' Mark said. 'Mum and Dad said everything would be split equally if anything was to happen to them. I'm not sure if either of them made a will. They wouldn't have expected to go together.' Mark put his fist to his mouth as if to stem a sob.

Meadows glanced at Edris indicating that he should proceed.

'I'm sorry to have to ask, but I will need accounts of your whereabouts on Saturday.'

'You can't think that we... that we would...' Lucy wrapped her arms around her body.

'It's just procedure,' Edris said. 'We have to eliminate you from our enquiries.'

'I was out shopping with my partner and kids in the morning. We had some lunch, that's when I spoke to Mum and Dad. We went swimming in the afternoon. We went home after that.'

'Did you leave the house at any time after?'

'No. I cooked, then we all watched a movie together before the kids went to bed.'

Edris scribbled in his notebook then looked at Mark.

'I was working Saturday. I'm a carpenter. I had a job in Bath fitting a kitchen. I got home about six.'

'Do you live alone?' Edris asked.

'No, with my wife and two boys.'

'Can you give me the address of the property you were working at, and contact details of anyone who was there at the same time?'

Mark gave the details which included an apprentice, two builders, and a plumber.

'Thank you,' Edris said and closed his book.

Meadows stood. 'We'll leave you to finish packing. Once again I am very sorry for your loss. We will do everything we can to find the person responsible. If you do think of anything, or a name comes to mind that your parents may have mentioned, please let us know.'

Lucy saw them to the door and watched as they got into the car.

'Do you think they are telling us everything?' Edris asked.

'Unlikely. Everyone has disagreements. There are very few that are loved by all. I don't get the impression they would deliberately withhold information that would lead us to the killer. But there has to be some connection.'

'Unless one of them did it,' Edris said.

'There is that. We'll have to wait for Bristol to check out their alibis.'

Meadows' phone trilled and he hit answer. It was John from mountain rescue.

'No luck finding the old man, but we've found his boat.'

Chapter Nine

Kitty carried the tray of tea through to the sitting room and placed it on the table. Elsie carried in a second tray with milk, sugar, and biscuits, set it down next to the tea and stepped back.

There was an air of impatience in the room as the family watched Kitty pour the tea and Elsie hand it out. Kitty was grateful for her daughter's help. Her hands felt unsteady and the last thing she wanted to do was pour scolding liquid on someone's lap. Her sister Lottie and brother-in-law Lloyd sat on the sofa with their two sons, Jac, and Arwel, and daughter Celyn. They were squashed so close together there was barely room to move their arms to take the tea. Quintin was sitting in one armchair, and his sister Pippa in the other. Mr Howells, the family solicitor, was standing by the fireplace.

Kitty didn't want to be there. She couldn't care less what the solicitor had to say. Madog's absence gnawed at her stomach, and her body felt taut with hysteria bubbling beneath the surface. She wanted to scream. To tell them all to get out. She wanted to be back outside looking for Madog, not politely drinking tea and listening to how her mother's money would be divided. She couldn't care less.

She had convinced herself that Madog had had an accident and was lying somewhere cold and alone. The thought was unbearable. It had kept her awake most of the night and now her eyes burned with fatigue.

With the last of the tea served, she sat down next to Elsie on one of the dining room chairs that had been dragged in from the kitchen. She didn't mind that the others had taken the comfy chairs. Being forced to sit upright would at least keep her awake.

Mr Howells cleared his throat and looked around the room. He was a stout man in his sixties, with thick white hair and rimless glasses.

'Firstly, Kitty and Lottie, I want to express my deepest sympathy for the loss of your mother. I met Connie on several occasions, and she was a lovely lady.'

'Thank you,' Lottie said. 'We appreciate you coming out to see us.'

Mr Howells smiled. 'I think it would've been a little cramped in my office. I take it there is still no news on Madog.'

'No,' Kitty said. 'The police are still searching, and we are hopeful.'

Mr Howells nodded. 'Well, I won't keep you too long. Madog's absence does change things. As you will all be aware, Connie didn't own property or any part of the land. She inherited fifty percent of the farm's profits from your father, Llew, and was entitled to live in this house for the remainder of her life. She left some personal effects to her daughters and grandchildren. There is also a considerable amount of money.' Mr Howells picked up a leather folder and took out a piece of paper. 'I have a copy of her will here. The money in its entirety is to be retained by the estate.'

'What!' Quintin leapt out of the chair. 'The money was Connie's to spend as she wished and nothing to do with the farm.'

'Yes, that is correct, however these are her final wishes.'

'Can I see?' Quintin asked.

Mr Howells handed Quintin the will.

Kitty watched as he scanned the document. His lips were set in a hard line, and you could almost see the anger radiating from him. She hoped he wasn't going to cause a scene. She hated any sort of confrontation.

'Do you want to read it?' Quintin held the paper out to Kitty.

Kitty shook her head.

Quintin turned to Lloyd and thrust the paper at him.

'I don't want to read it,' Lloyd said. 'We all heard what Mr Howells said. The money goes to the farm. Getting angry about it isn't going to change things.'

'Don't act like you don't care about getting your share of the money,' Quintin said.

'It's Lottie's money,' Lloyd said.

'Yeah, but you benefit,' Quintin said.

'Don't be a dick, Quintin,' Lottie said.

'There's no need to be rude, darling,' Pippa said.

Lottie turned to Pippa. 'You can butt out. I don't know what you're doing here. It's supposed to be just family.'

'I am family,' Pippa said. 'I'm here to support you all.'

Kitty heard Elsie snort beside her. She looked at Lottie's children. They were watching the exchange with bemused expressions. She glanced at Pippa who looked like she had been slapped across the face. She wished they would all be quiet and let Mr Howells finish. Lottie had a point, she thought. Pippa shouldn't be here. She guessed that her sister-in-law wanted to see if Quintin was about to come into money, which would be to her benefit.

'Why don't you sit down, Quintin. I'm sure Mr Howells will explain things to us,' Kitty said.

Quintin shot Kitty a dirty look before handing the will back to Mr Howells. 'It doesn't really make a difference. Kitty and Lottie will inherit the fifty percent shares and therefore the money.' He plonked back in the armchair.

'Not necessarily,' Mr Howells said. 'Madog still owns the land and fifty percent interest. The remaining fifty percent reverts to Llew's will and the codicil he left with his brother. Connie understood this.'

Quintin huffed. 'Well don't drag it out. What does the codicil say?'

'I've no idea,' Mr Howells said.

'How can you not know? These things have to be witnessed,' Quintin said.

'Yes, however it was some years ago. I wasn't the one to witness the signature, it was my late father.'

'But you must hold a copy,' Quintin said.

'No, both Madog and Llew were in agreement that the only copy would be held by Madog.'

'Well, Madog isn't here so there is no codicil,' Lloyd said. 'Can't we just ignore it?'

'It's not that simple,' Mr Howells said. 'We know it does exist so we can't proceed with probate at this time.'

'What if Madog is dead?' Quintin asked.

Kitty heard herself take a sharp intake of breath. It felt as though someone had doused her in ice water.

'Dad!' Elsie said.

'I'm only saying what everyone is thinking,' Quintin said.

'What happens if the codicil is not found?' Lloyd asked.

'That depends. Madog knows what's written in the codicil. If it's the case that erm...' Mr Howells folded his hands. 'If the current situation is not resolved happily then we will be dealing with the whole estate. That will make things more complicated.'

'I don't see how,' Quintin said. 'If Madog has, er, passed away, then the whole estate should be split between Kitty and Lottie. Kitty would get the land as she is the oldest.'

Kitty saw a ghost of a smile on Quintin's lips.

'We would need to revert back to the terms of the original will. I cannot speak for Madog. He left no instructions with me. If there is no will then it may be the case that the estate goes to the oldest male heir, which would be Jac. I would imagine fifty percent shares would go to Arwel. I need to look at the terms of the original will left by Kitty and Lottie's grandfather.'

'I'm cool with that,' Jac said.

A smile lit up Arwel's face.

'I don't know what you two are grinning at,' Quintin said. 'It's not going to happen. That will is archaic and sexist. Kitty and Lottie can't be cut out because they are women.'

'I'm afraid a will can't be void based on being discriminatory,' Mr Howells said. 'A person is entitled to leave their estate to whom they please.'

'I can't see Llew or Madog cutting out Lottie and Kitty,' Lloyd said.

'There may have been provisions made for them in the codicil,' Mr Howells said. 'I'm sorry I can't be of more help today. I'll await news of Madog and in the meantime I will look at the terms of the original will. I'll also confer with my partners.'

Kitty stood up. 'Thank you, Mr Howells, I'll see you out.' She led the way to the front door where Mr Howells touched her on the arm.

'I hope Madog is found safe and well. I know he means a great deal to you.'

Kitty felt her emotions constrict her throat. She managed to say thank you before closing the door. When she walked back in the room she found Quintin had poured himself a large whisky.

'Lot of use he was,' he said before taking a gulp.

'It's not his fault,' Kitty said.

'We're not going to take his word for it. We'll get our own solicitor. Fight it,' Quintin said.

'Fight what?' Lloyd asked.

'For a start, the release of Connie's money. It's just sitting there in the bank, and no one can access it.'

'Mum's money has nothing to do with you,' Lottie said. 'With a bit of luck Kitty's share will have a proviso that states you can't touch it.'

'I don't know what you lot are arguing about, it might be all mine,' Jac said.

'I'll make sure it doesn't go to you,' Quintin said.

'I think you've said enough, Quintin.' Lloyd stood up. 'If the estate is Jac's then you better be careful. You are standing in his house.'

'Get out, all of you,' Quintin said.

'We'll leave when we are ready,' Lottie said. 'It's not your place to ask us to leave.'

'I can't listen to any more of this,' Kitty said.

She left the house and walked down to the fishing lakes. She took a deep breath and let it out before sitting on the grass. Dampness crept through her jeans, but she didn't care. The one person who could make her feel better wasn't here and she didn't want to think about a life without him.

'Kitty!'

Kitty looked up and saw Lottie walking towards her. She gave her a smile before she sat down next to Kitty with her legs outstretched and looked out over the water.

'I'm sorry,' Lottie said. 'It got out of hand. It's just Quintin winds me up sometimes.'

'Sometimes?' Kitty asked.

Lottie laughed. 'OK, most of the time.'

'You know I won't fight the terms of the will if it all goes to Jac,' Kitty said.

'I know but I doubt you'll stop Quintin. He wants control.'

'It's just because he cares what happens to the farm. He's looked after the finances for years. Even Mum trusted him, that's why she left the money to the estate. Probably to pay back some of the loans.'

'What loans?' Lottie asked.

'For the new dairy equipment. I know Mum paid some towards it.'

'When was this?'

Kitty could see suspicion in Lottie's eyes. She wished she hadn't said anything. 'I don't know. About a year ago.'

'She never said anything to me. Did Uncle Madog know about it?'

'I don't know. You know what he's like with money. As long as he has food, and the animals are cared for, the rest means nothing to him. Dad was the one to take care of all that stuff.'

'Yeah, you and Uncle Madog are too alike,' Lottie said. 'Maybe we should have a look at the accounts. We have a right to see them, especially now.'

'You see them every year,' Kitty said.

'It's just a summary that Quintin gives to Mum and Uncle Madog along with their share of the profits. It doesn't show all the details.'

'Why do you want to see them?'

'Just interested, that's all.'

Kitty didn't think that Quintin would be happy for Lottie to look at the accounts. It would just cause another argument.

'They go to an accountant, don't they? You could ask for a copy.'

'An accountant would only give that information to Mum or Uncle Madog. I'm not even sure Quintin uses one. Lloyd says Quintin handles everything now.'

Kitty had a vague memory of a discussion about finances. There was a lot of talk about tax and liabilities, most of it had gone over her head. She'd signed some papers for the trout farm.

'I guess that makes sense, Quintin knows what he's doing with money. I just don't think it's a good time to ask him about it.'

'Don't worry about it now,' Lottie said. 'And don't worry about the farm. Even if Jac inherits he'd never make things difficult for you. You own your cottage and you've got the trout farm. You pay rent on the land now so it will be no different.'

'Unless Jac sells.'

'Come on, sitting here worrying isn't going to do you any good.'

'You're right. I'm going to go to Uncle Madog's cottage, tidy up, and change the bed. I want it ready for him when he gets back.'

'That's the spirit,' Lottie said.

Kitty could see the pity in her sister's eyes despite her smile. She didn't know why everyone felt the need to protect her. It was as though they thought she couldn't handle the truth. She was sure Lottie was keeping something from her. All these questions about money. It was only last week that Madog asked about the accounts, she thought. Maybe he was worried about money. Quintin had said the farm was struggling and the trout farm was only breaking even. She'd have to tell the police next time she spoke to them.

Chapter Ten

Lloyd was livid. He couldn't believe that Quintin had the nerve to speak to him or Lottie as he had, and in front of the whole family. He would make damn sure it didn't happen again. With what he knew, Quintin would have to show him a bit of respect from now on, he thought.

He walked to the milking shed and sat on one of the chairs near the door. He didn't feel like working. All he wanted to do was go home and get a few hours' sleep. He knew Quintin would turn up at the dairy at some point. If he didn't keep the office locked Lloyd would have gone in and found out exactly what Quintin got up to. There would be evidence somewhere. If he had that he could threaten to take it to Kitty. The thought made him smile. He'd love to see Kitty lose her temper and chuck Quintin out. He'd help her pack his bags. The only downside would be seeing Kitty hurt. He didn't want that. He loved her like she was his own sister.

It didn't take long for Quintin to show up. Lloyd stepped out of the milking shed.

'We need to talk.'

Quintin looked around. 'Not here, come up to my office.'

'Your office?' Lloyd laughed. 'It's *the* office, or maybe we should call it *our* office.'

Quintin ignored him and turned to walk to the dairy.

Lloyd followed. 'Maybe we should arrange for me to have my own space. I am manager here.'

'Shut up,' Quintin snapped.

Lloyd followed Quintin into the dairy and up the metal staircase where Quintin unlocked the door to the office and stepped inside.

Lloyd walked over to the large leather sofa and plonked down.

'I bet you get a good sleep on this,' Lloyd said.

Quintin shut the door. 'What do you want?'

'I've changed my mind. We have to stop. The police are all over the place looking for Madog. You don't know where they will turn up next. I can't keep this up.'

Quintin huffed and sat in the chair behind the desk. 'You wanted to be part of it.'

'You didn't give me a lot of choice,' Lloyd said. 'I didn't think it would be like this.'

'What did you expect?'

'I don't know, you made it sound as if—'

'Don't you dare,' Quintin said. 'You knew well enough what was involved.'

Lloyd wanted to argue but Quintin was right. He should never have got involved. He should have known better. 'Three nights is not enough and I'm bloody knackered.'

'Well go and get some sleep,' Quintin said. 'I've got better things to do than listen to you bitching.'

'I'll be missed,' Lloyd said. 'It's OK for you. You can hide away in here, no one notices if you're asleep or not. You don't have to face anyone and pretend everything is OK.'

'Everything is OK. Or will be if you keep your head.'

'We need help,' Lloyd said.

'No. If we do that it will increase the risk. Not to mention we'll have to give a cut to someone else.'

'That's your problem – greed,' Lloyd said.

Quintin laughed. 'And you think you are any better. You've had a taste now so you're not going to stop.'

'Yes I will,' Lloyd said. 'It's too dangerous. Madog not being here to read the codicil has only brought us a little time.'

'We need the codicil, you bloody idiot,' Quintin said. 'Once we have complete control we–'

'Complete control?' Lloyd cut him off.

'You know what I mean.'

Lloyd wasn't sure he did, but he didn't want to ask about it. 'Kitty and Lottie will have control.'

'Yeah, well I can handle Kitty. She hasn't a clue what goes on.'

'I wouldn't be too sure about that,' Lloyd said. 'Anyway, Lottie will want to be hands-on. I don't want her to find out.'

'Man up,' Quintin said. 'You let Lottie walk all over you.'

'No I don't. We're partners. Our relationship is based on mutual respect. Something you know nothing about.'

'Just go,' Quintin said. 'Be ready Wednesday morning.'

Lloyd stood up. He would have liked to smack Quintin in his smug face, but it wasn't his style. He left the office wishing he'd never got involved. If he could turn back time to that morning he would walk away and not look. But he hadn't and he let Quintin persuade him to do something he never dreamed he would.

Chapter Eleven

John from the mountain rescue team was standing next to his Land Rover when Meadows parked by the dam.

'How close to where the Wilsons were found did you find Madog Jones' boat?' Meadows asked.

'Nowhere near,' John said. 'It's over the other side of the reservoir. We can drive some of the way but then we'll have to walk. Hop in, I'll take you.'

'Has the boat been identified?' Meadows asked as he stepped up into the vehicle.

'Yeah, we asked the bailiff to look before we called you. No sign of Madog but we're concentrating the search in that area. In case he's wandered into the woodland. I'm afraid I don't hold out much hope of finding him alive. The area has been cleared, and the helicopter hasn't picked up anything on the thermal imaging. Either way I would've expected to find him by now.'

'Then that just leaves the water,' Edris said leaning in between the passenger and driver's seat.

'How far from the water was the boat found?'

'Far enough that it didn't land itself if that's what you're thinking. It's been dragged into the trees and some attempt made to conceal it.'

John parked up just beyond the water tower and Meadows jumped out. A strong wind rippled the water and the trees danced in union.

'How far do we have to walk?' Edris asked as he pulled up his hood.

'Twenty minutes if we set a good pace,' John said.

They followed a well-defined path that ran parallel to the bank that sloped down to the water. It was steep in some places with bracken, yellowing trees, and shrubs. Across the stretch of water the rugged mountain peaks met with steel grey skies. Meadows drank in the beauty of the landscape, his skin tingling with the cold air. This should've been a safe place for the Wilsons to explore. Now it's forever corrupted with the brutality that took place here, he thought.

'Down here,' John said. 'Watch your footing, the grass is slippery.'

They followed John until they came to a small clearing between the trees. The boat was leaning on its side and covered with branches.

'We haven't touched it,' John said.

Meadows snapped on a pair of latex gloves and moved closer. There was a fishing bag, a rod, and a pair of green wellies lying on the bottom. He picked up the bag and saw a pair of glasses beneath.

'Looks like Madog's bag,' Edris said. He took his phone from his pocket and called up a copy of the photo Kitty had given them. 'Yeah, look.' He held out the phone for Meadows.

Meadows nodded. 'Same glasses. We need to get forensics to take a look.'

'No signal,' Edris said.

'They're still over the other side. Easier to just go and talk to Mike, we can see if they've found anything of interest. Keep an eye on the phone. As soon as you get a signal, get Blackwell to pick up the bag and take it to Kitty to identify and check the contents.' He turned to John. 'I would imagine it would take some strength to drag the boat this far up.'

'Yeah, can't see someone of Madog's age moving it on his own. Should we step down the search? I think it will be fruitless continuing here.'

'Keep it going for now. I'll organise the cadaver dogs. If he is in the woods somewhere I don't reckon he went in voluntarily and he could be well hidden. Right, let's go and find Mike.'

'I hope you are not expecting me to walk all the way round,' Edris said.

'We could probably walk around the top, It'll be quicker,' Meadows said.

'I wouldn't recommend going that way,' John said. 'It's marshy in parts, I don't want to have to come and rescue the two of you. I'll give you a ride back to your car and wait for your guy to come to collect the tackle bag. You can drive to the first bay from there.'

After leaving John at the dam they trekked up the other side of the water and through the cordon where they found Mike and his team still working.

Meadows filled him in on what they had discovered on the other side of the reservoir.

Mike nodded and yawned. 'I'll send someone over.'

'Hope you haven't been here since last night,' Meadows said.

'No, we laid sheeting over as much as we could and came back at first light.'

'Have you found anything of interest?' Edris asked.

'We've got some good casts of footwear. Lot of footfall in the area but only a handful of prints that are fresh. It looks like the Wilsons were heading in this direction towards the water when they were attacked and hit from behind. We picked up a set of footprints mixed with the Wilsons' and coming off the side of the path, as well as leading to and from the direction of the water.'

'So, you reckon one person attacked the Wilsons?' Meadows asked.

'It appears that was the case.' Mike beckoned them towards a heavily marked area. 'Those are the Wilsons' prints' – he pointed – 'and those are unidentified ones. Mainly concentrated in this area. Size ten. I'll send you the details. There were a couple more. One set I guess belong to the fisherman. They come off the path just before this area and into the trees where the Wilsons were found. The other set is the same and I would think from mountain rescue. We'll get impressions from them in order to eliminate them from our enquiries. Blood on the ground and trailing into the woods.'

'Looks like there was a struggle,' Meadows said.

'I would say so given the disturbance. Then there's this over here.'

Meadows and Edris followed Mike into the trees on the opposite side of the path to where the Wilsons were found. Mike crouched down and pointed a gloved finger.

'What's that?' Edris asked.

'Looks like fishing line,' Meadows said.

'It's been wrapped around the trunk a few times and knotted. It could've been placed here at any time before the attacks, or the killer used it as some sort of marker. It's in line with where the Wilsons were attacked,' Mike said.

'Why would the killer mark the spot?' Edris asked.

'Maybe they picked this location so they wouldn't be seen,' Meadows said. 'Plenty of cover so they could ambush the Wilsons. It's also enough distance from the water so they wouldn't be seen.'

'There are some marks on that tree.' Mike pointed. 'The bark has been indented, and the same on two trees opposite but no fishing line. I'll cut this one off and send it in for testing. Nothing else to show at the moment.'

'OK, thanks,' Meadows said. He turned to Edris. 'We better get going. See what we can find out from the post-mortems.'

* * *

It had only been that morning that Meadows had kissed Daisy goodbye before they both left for work. Yet in this environment they remained professional. She led them now into the mortuary where David and Anna Wilson lay side by side on metal gurneys, both covered to the neck by a sheet. The smell of formaldehyde mixed with other chemicals assaulted Meadows' nostrils. It was a smell he'd come to associate with violent death. He switched to breathing through his mouth, a trick he'd learnt early on in his career.

'Shall we start with Mr Wilson?' Daisy asked and stepped up to the table. 'As you saw at the crime scene, he sustained two blows to the back, right side of his head.' She parted the hair.

'With what?' Edris asked.

'I'm good but I'm not a psychic,' Daisy said with a smile. 'Something hard?' she teased. 'Blunt force trauma, no defining shape to the wound, or fibres found in or around the area.'

'Enough force to knock him out?' Meadows asked.

'Possibly, he would certainly have been dazed. One of the blows fractured the skull. Cause of death, strangulation. If you look here' – she pointed to the side of David's neck – 'the skin is torn, and further up it's not broken. Some sort of fine cord. No fibres, so my guess would be nylon.'

Meadows thought of the trees at the crime scene. 'Fishing line?'

'That would do it,' Daisy said, 'it would have to be strong.'

'You see rods bending with the pressure of reeling in fish and the line doesn't snap,' Edris said. 'I reckon a ten-pound line would do it.'

'You've been fishing?' Meadows asked.

'Don't sound so shocked. My father used to take me. Didn't like it much,' Edris said.

'That doesn't surprise me,' Daisy said. 'So we're going with fishing line. Looks like the killer doubled it up and it separated, causing the second mark on the neck.'

'Or he managed to free himself and the killer had to wrap it around again,' Meadows said.

Daisy nodded. 'The second one is deeper. Likely the one that killed him. The scratch marks running down to the line would have been caused by him clawing at his neck to try and free himself. Some are deeper than others.'

'Poor man,' Meadows said. 'Any defence wounds?'

'No bruising or broken skin on the knuckles, but damage to the skin on the fingertips and under the nails on both hands from where he tried to loosen the bind on his throat. There are scrapes to the palms of his hands.' Daisy turned David Wilson's hand. 'There was a couple of tiny stones embedded in the skin.'

Edris peered at the wounds. 'There was evidence of a struggle on the ground. So, I'm guessing he was hit from behind, fell forward and put his hands out to break his fall,' Edris said.

'If you were hit hard enough to knock you out then your legs would buckle,' Meadows said. 'As he was hit on the right side of his head, I would expect him to fall to the left and have some bruising.'

'There was no bruising to the arms or shoulders,' Daisy said. 'Marks on his back are consistent with being dragged.'

'What if the blow didn't knock him out?' Edris asked.

'My natural reaction would be to put my hand to my head and turn to see what hit me,' Meadows said. 'In either case I can't see him putting out both hands to break his fall.'

'Maybe the killer jumped on him from behind, got him on the floor then hit him before choking him,' Edris said.

'That's a possibility. Any other injuries?'

'There's some marks on his ankles.' Daisy moved to the bottom of the gurney and lifted the sheet. 'See the line here?' She pointed.

'Similar to the ones on his neck,' Meadows said.

'Looks like he was bound,' Edris said.

'I don't think so,' Daisy said. 'The marks run across the front but not around the sides and back.'

A scenario was playing in Meadows' mind but he wanted to hear about Anna Wilson's injuries before he voiced them.

'There were no drugs or alcohol found in his system,' Daisy said as she replaced the sheet. 'He was fit and healthy for his age. His medical records show he visited his GP for regular check-ups but had no ongoing complaints. Shall we move on to Anna Wilson?'

Meadows nodded.

'Blunt force trauma to the head. Two separate wounds on the right side. Then you can see additional trauma to the left of her face.' Daisy indicated the area. 'She was hit with enough force to fracture her cheekbone and there is substantial damage to her eye socket. Same ligature marks to the neck, but only one line. Again, scratch marks on her throat and damage to her fingertips and nails indicate that she tried to free herself. She also has scrapes to the palms of her hands.'

'Does she have the same marks on the ankles?' Meadows asked.

'Yes and bruising to her right shoulder.'

'Maybe Mrs Wilson was the target,' Edris suggested. 'Given the additional injuries.'

'I don't think so,' Meadows said. 'Remember the fishing line tied to the trunk of the tree at the crime scene?'

'Yeah.'

'I think the killer lured them there and tied the line to trip them up. Two victims, one killer. It would make it easier to attack if they were on the ground and account for the marks on their ankles and scrapes to their hands. If they tripped they'd put out their hands to break the fall. The killer then comes up behind them. Hits David Wilson first as he is the biggest threat, then hits Anna on the back of the head. Anna would've been dazed. The killer then moved back to David and wrapped the line around his neck. He or she would know that David would fight to protect his wife. As the killer is strangling David, Anna gets up and tries to help her husband. There were deeper scratches on some areas of David's throat. Anna had long nails. The killer releases David and hits Anna in the face. David would've been fighting for breath and unable to help Anna. The killer put the line around David's neck a second time, this accounting for two lines visible on David's throat. Once David is dead, the killer moves to Anna and strangles her. They move Anna first, she was furthest in and had her arms resting at the side. Next they have to move David. It wouldn't be easy. I think the killer dragged him as far as they could, then left him. David's arms were stretched above his head when he was found. Less care was taken with him.'

Edris nodded. 'Yeah, I can see that working. I'm impressed.'

'I'm not saying that's what actually happened, but it seems to be the most likely scenario. As for the who and why, I have no idea.'

'I've sent scrapings, taken from under their nails, to the lab. One of them may have clawed at the attacker's hands,' Daisy said.

'Thank you.' Meadows turned away from the gurneys. 'We'll leave you get back to work.'

'I haven't finished yet,' Daisy said. 'I kept the most puzzling part till last.' She walked over to the worktop and picked up a sample dish and handed it to Meadows.

Meadows peered into the dish and saw two small hooks brightly decorated. One resembled a fly with bright orange and yellow wings and a tail striped black and yellow leading to a feathered end. The other looked like a bug with a pink ring around a brass head and a multicoloured body.'

'Fishing flies,' Edris said looking into the dish.

'Where did you find them?' Meadows asked.

'Impaled in the victims' tongues. The pink one for Anna Wilson and the yellow for David Wilson.'

'Tongues, *ych a fi*,' Edris said.

'Post-mortem?' Meadows asked.

'Yes.'

A cold feeling crept over Meadows. This was a statement, and when a killer left a calling card it was usually the start of things getting worse.

'I think we better start tracking down those anglers,' he said.

Chapter Twelve

Meadows was sitting at his desk with his eyes fixed to the computer screen. He'd been the first in the office as he wanted a head start before the morning's briefing. Edris had come in next and now he could hear the rest of the team talking over a coffee. He continued to scroll through pictures of fishing flies hoping to match the ones found on the Wilsons.

'Any luck?' Edris asked.

'No, there're hundreds, probably thousands of them. Then there're different categories. Wet flies, dry flies, river flies, and salmon or trout flies. Not to mention nymphs, lures, buzzers, and a whole host of other strange names. It shouldn't be this difficult. Are you fairing any better?'

'No, I've called a few fishing shops. They all say the same. There are too many of them and if I can give them a name, they can supply one. Honestly, if I had a name I wouldn't be calling.'

'We'll have to leave it there for now. Let's get on with the briefing.'

Meadows walked over to the incident board and called the team around. He noticed that Valentine and Edris were still sitting as far apart as they could manage. He quickly ran through the post-mortem results although they had all seen the gruesome photos pinned to the board.

'Blackwell, Valentine, how did you get on with the list of anglers yesterday?'

'We got through about a third of the ticket holders. Only one we spoke to thinks he remembers seeing the Wilsons. The couple had stopped and asked if he had any luck then went on their way. He wasn't sure about the day. He'd been fishing on Friday the 17th as well so it may have been then,' Blackwell said.

'Most of them were too busy trying to catch fish to notice anything around them. No one was that far up the reservoir on that side,' Valentine added.

'What about vehicles parked on Saturday?'

'Very vague. Some said about five near the dam. Others thought there were more. Problem is there is more than one parking place. All depends on what side you are fishing. There is no CCTV at the reservoir and no cameras on the roads leading to it. I don't think we are going to get much more.'

'Given the connection with the fishing flies and line I think it's our best line of inquiry,' Meadows said.

'Yeah, but how are we going to eliminate them?' Blackwell asked. 'They are already admitting to being there.'

'One of them might have seen something,' Edris said.

'We need a map of the reservoir to place the anglers at the spot they said they were fishing and cross-reference it with the other accounts,' Meadows said. 'There's not that many of them.'

'It could've been someone poaching,' Blackwell said.

'The bailiff does regular checks,' Edris said.

'At the moment they're all potential witnesses. While you're talking to them, see if anyone can identify these flies,' Meadows said.

'Putting hooks in someone's tongue is an odd thing to do,' Paskin said. 'It's like the killer wanted to silence them.'

'Yes, it does appear to be symbolic, but stop them saying what?' Meadows asked. 'Anything from Bristol CID?'

'I spoke to Halliwell this morning. Both Lucy and Mark Wilson's alibis check out. Nothing out of the ordinary in the Wilsons' house. He also spoke to ex-work colleagues of both Anna and David's as well as the neighbours. All said the same. They were a nice couple, no problems.'

'Well, someone didn't like them,' Blackwell said.

'There were a few responses to the social media appeal,' Paskin said. 'A couple of anglers who are on the list and two hikers. I've spoken to them all. They didn't see anything out of the ordinary and not one of them saw a boat out on the water. Lot of comments on Anna Wilson's Facebook page. People expressing their shock and sympathy. I've looked back at most of her posts. There's been no malicious comments.'

'Nothing back from forensics on Madog's boat yet,' Meadows said. 'Blackwell, did Kitty Eccleston identify the bag and contents?'

'Yes, she was clearly distressed about the discovery, but she looked. Nothing missing apart from his priest,' Blackwell said.

'His priest; that's a new one,' Paskin said.

'It's what anglers use to whack the fish,' Edris said.

'According to Kitty, Madog's priest was old and made of wood,' Blackwell said. 'Could be what was used to attack the Wilsons. I reckon that could give someone a nasty bash on the head.'

Meadows nodded. 'If you've got a good description, can you find a picture of one similar?'

'Yeah, no problem,' Blackwell said.

'I've put in a request for Madog Jones' phone records, both landline and mobile,' Paskin said. 'I haven't managed to find a connection between him and the Wilsons. I'll keep looking.'

'Maybe there isn't one,' Edris said. 'Madog could've been fishing on that side of the lake and witnessed what happened to the Wilsons.'

'Yeah, but why go to the trouble of hiding him and the boat?' Valentine asked. 'The killer just left the Wilsons to be discovered.'

'Not really,' Edris said. 'Their bodies were dragged into the undergrowth. If Lucy Wilson hadn't mentioned that they were meeting someone for a boat ride then we wouldn't have been looking in that area.'

'That doesn't work either. They could've just left Madog with the Wilsons,' Valentine said.

Meadows was watching the interaction between Valentine and Edris. It wasn't a case of bouncing off ideas. It was more of a case of discrediting each other's theories.

'There's a simple answer to that,' Blackwell said. 'Madog Jones killed the Wilsons and has done a runner. Just because we haven't found a connection it doesn't mean there isn't one. It was his boat found hidden, and his priest that is missing. He's only ten years older than David Wilson. If it was someone younger and fitter, they wouldn't have had to use fishing line to trip up the Wilsons before attacking them. That's if we're going with your theory.' He looked at Meadows. 'The old boy could be fitter than we give him credit for. He may have known the Wilsons from years ago. Had some long-held grudge. He sees them when he's fishing, offers to take them out on the boat later. That gives him time to set up. Then he waits and kills them.'

'Why bother hiding his boat?' Edris asked.

'Obviously he couldn't risk being seen putting it back,' Valentine said. 'I think it's a good theory.'

'Then explain to me how he got there? His car is still parked at home,' Edris said.

'Well, he got there somehow. Maybe he walked,' Valentine said.

Blackwell and Paskin's heads were swivelling back and forth as they listened to this exchange, both looking amused.

'So, he just happened to be out fishing when he bumps into the Wilsons who he hasn't seen for years and kills them,' Edris said. 'All this without telling anyone where he is going. Just in case he wants to murder someone that day. On top of that he hides out because so far no one has seen him, and leaves his wellies in the boat and runs off in his socks.'

'You got any better theories?' Valentine snapped.

Meadows was glad to see Chris Harley from tech walking in. Chris was tall and wiry with a mop of wild hair and spoke with a gentle voice.

'Hi, Chris, how are you liking the new office?' Meadows asked.

'S'OK,' Chris said as he pushed his glasses up the bridge of his nose. 'More space, better equipment.'

'Good, what you got for us?'

'Some files from the Wilsons' phones I thought you may be interested in.' Chris put his laptop on the nearest desk and sat down.

The team gathered around the screen.

'OK, this is the list of last calls from Anna Wilson's phone. You can see the last call made was to her daughter, Lucy, on the afternoon of Saturday, 18th of September.' He closed the file and opened another one. 'There's a whole pile of photos, but I thought you'd be interested in the ones from the day of the murder.'

The first photo filled the screen. It was of David Wilson looking out over the reservoir with binoculars. Meadows recognised the area. David was standing on the opposite bank to where Madog's boat had been found.

'This is from Saturday?' Meadows asked.

'Yes.'

'Do you have a time stamp.'

'Eight-fifteen in the morning.'

'Is that a boat he's looking at?'

Chris clicked the mouse and the photo enlarged. He moved the cursor and the boat came into view. It was sideways on and a figure was bent forward looking away. A black coat and woollen hat could be made out but nothing else.

'Shame we can't see the face,' Edris said. 'But it looks like Madog's boat.'

'It doesn't look like Madog though,' Meadows said. 'He's tall and thin.'

'Difficult to tell,' Blackwell said, 'the coat may be really thick.'

'Yes, but it wouldn't make him smaller. Look.' He pointed to the screen. 'Madog is six foot six, this person looks broad and not that long in the body. Besides, Kitty said that Madog's coat is green. Can you enhance the photo?'

'Yeah, I'll do my best, but I don't think it's going to be that much clearer.'

'You got some program that can match Madog's photo to the person in the boat?'

'I'll see what I can do,' Chris said. 'Maybe if we have more photos I can try and work on some measurements.'

'Thanks. Any other photos from that day?'

'Yeah.' Chris clicked through them all. There were some of David in the woods and then Brecon town and cathedral. They worked back through the snaps that catalogued the Wilsons' holiday. There were several taken at the reservoir on different days but no more that showed a boat.'

'Any photos on David's phone?' Meadows asked.

'Yes, but not as many. I showed you these ones as they have shots of the reservoir. I'll send the files to you.'

'Thanks,' Meadows said.

'No problem.' Chris shut the laptop.

Meadows returned to the board. 'Right, we need to identify the person in the boat. This may be when they met up with the Wilsons.'

'If it's not Madog Jones on the boat then where is he?' Blackwell asked.

'Probably dead and the killer stole his boat,' Edris said.

'Or he is the killer,' Valentine said. 'Just wearing a different coat.'

'OK let's get on with tracking down the fishermen,' Meadows said. 'Edris and I will make a start on the season ticket holders. Blackwell, Valentine, can you carry on with the day ticket holders and see if any of them can identify the flies? Maybe the names of the flies will give us something to go on. So far we don't have much else.'

* * *

Meadows and Edris were sitting in the dentist waiting room waiting for a patient to finish treatment. The dentist, Andrew Clark, was a keen fisherman with a boat moored at the Usk Reservoir.

'I hate dentists,' Edris said.

'No one likes going to the dentist,' Meadows said.

'Yeah, it's the smell. It makes me feel sick. I associate it with terror. My mother used to bribe me to come. Then there'd be the wait, followed by the walk to the chair. It was like walking the green mile.'

Meadows laughed. 'It's not that bad.'

'Have you ever had an extraction or a root canal filling?'

'No.'

'Lucky you.'

'I don't eat sweets, well not often.'

Edris sat back and stretched his arms back before folding them across his chest. 'I hope this one isn't going to regale us with tales of fishing. I've heard enough about how many fish were caught, the weight, and what bait was used and not one of them could identify the flies.'

'Mr Clark will see you now,' the receptionist called.

Meadows followed the dental assistant into the room where Mr Clark was sitting in a swivel chair. He was dressed in green scrubs with a matching cap.

Edris scuttled over to the chair in the corner of the room and took out his notebook. Meadows guessed he was getting as far away from the dentist chair and the tray of tools as he could.

'Thank you for seeing us,' Meadows said. 'I appreciate that you are busy.'

'I'm happy to help if I can. I heard on the news about the couple found at the reservoir. Awful business.'

'Were you fishing at the Usk last Saturday?' Meadows asked.

'Yes, I was there all day. I didn't see the couple.'

'What time did you arrive?'

'About seven, I like to get there early and make a day of it.'

'Were there many cars parked there?'

'Oh, I don't know. There were some, yes, maybe three or four. I couldn't give you any specifics. I think there was some parked on the other side as well.'

'You have a boat moored on the Usk. Did you take it out?'

'No.'

'Whereabouts on the reservoir did you fish that day?'

'Near the dam. I moved further up during the day.'

'Did you go up the top end?' Meadows asked.

'No, I didn't go that far up.'

'We have a map of the area. Would you mind pointing out exactly where you fished that day?'

Edris stood up and showed the dentist the map on a tablet.

'I started off about there,' – the dentist pointed – 'and moved up around there.'

Edris marked the locations. 'Did you see anyone else fishing?'

'Yes, there were some at the dam. Then one I passed around there.' He touched the screen. 'He was still there when I made my way back. There could've been more fishing further up.'

'Did you see anyone take a boat out when you were there?' Meadows asked.

'There was only one out. It was heading up the far end of the water when I arrived.'

'Did you see who was on the boat?'

'No, they were too far away.'

'There was more than one person on the boat?' Meadows asked.

'Yeah, two of them. They were too far out to see their faces. Could've been a father and son. One looked small.'

'Did you see the boat come back? Or anyone return to a car?' Edris asked.

'No, I stayed until dark. I was concentrating on the water. If someone walked the path behind me I probably wouldn't have noticed.'

'Just one more thing, could you look at a couple of fishing flies to see if you recognise them?' Edris asked. He loaded up the photo.

The dentist looked closely. 'That might be a mayfly, looks like one I have.' He pointed to the yellow one. 'It could be a yellow drake, but I can't be certain. If I had my fly box with me I could've taken a look.'

'Thank you, you've been very helpful,' Meadows said. 'We'll leave you to get back to your patients.'

While Meadows started the car Edris googled the yellow drake and compared it to the fly found on David Wilson. 'It's not the same,' Edris said. 'It doesn't have the black and yellow stripes.'

'Try googling mayflies and look at all the yellow ones. You might find a match,' Meadows said.

His phone trilled in his pocket. He took it out and saw "Mike SOCO" flash across the screen.

'Hi, Mike, you got something?'

'Yeah, I'm still up at the Usk. We've just pulled a body out of the water.'

Chapter Thirteen

A mist of fine drizzle made the view of the reservoir opaque as Edris and Meadows took the path up the right side of the dam. They'd been directed to turn off the path just before the location of where Madog's boat was found. It wasn't difficult to find because a cordon had already been set up and a damp-looking PC Hanes was waiting for them.

'He was spotted floating in the water by the bailiff. Lucky SOCO were here organising the removal of the boat. They pulled him out. He's just down the bank.' Hanes pointed.

'Thanks,' Meadows said.

They picked their way down through the tall wet grass and trees until they came to a clearing where they put on protective clothing. A little further down a forensic photographer was snapping shots of the body which lay on black plastic sheeting as Mike collected samples.

'Think we may have found your missing man,' Mike said as they approached. 'He wasn't weighted down; I imagine he's been in a few days and body gases have brought him to the surface. The wind was up yesterday which would have caused movement in the water so there's no telling with certainty exactly where he went in.'

Meadows stepped closer and his eyes travelled the length of the bloated body. One foot was bare, the other covered in a sock. Waterproof trousers were still held in place by the elasticated waist. The coat looked like the one Kitty had described as Madog's. The zip was ripped open but held together at the neck. His jumper had risen, showing mottled flesh beneath.

'The right height to be Madog,' Meadows said looking at his face. 'And facial structure.'

'Not many around here that are that tall,' Edris said. 'It's gotta be him.'

Meadows crouched to take a closer look. He couldn't see any obvious head trauma, but across the neck he could see a thin line similar in size to the one he'd seen on the Wilsons.

'Look at this,' Meadows said.

Edris stepped closer. 'It looks like our theory was right. Madog was up here fishing and witnessed the murder of the Wilsons, so the killer went after him.'

'But the dentist saw two people in the boat. Father and son he thought. Next to Madog most men or women would appear child-size,' Meadows said.

'Then Valentine is right. Madog and another killed the Wilsons. The other then kills Madog. Chucks him off the boat and hides it.'

'There was only one person in the boat when Anna Wilson took a photo that morning.' Meadows looked down at Madog's hand and saw the strap of a watch. 'That person as far as we know wasn't Madog.'

'OK, the killer needs the boat to tempt the Wilsons into going out on the water. He goes out with Madog and kills him so he can steal his boat.'

'Don't see it,' Meadows said as he undid the buckle on the wristwatch. 'He could have taken any boat. Besides, if he was just using it as an excuse to get the Wilsons back that evening, he could just say he had a boat he was taking out later. Why go to the trouble of stealing one he then has to hide?'

He held up the watch and turned it over. There was an inscription, "Happy 60th all my love Kitty" and what looked like an engraving of a butterfly.

'Got a bag, Mike?' Meadows asked as he stood up.

Mike handed Meadows a clear evidence bag and he dropped the watch in.

'Looks like there is no doubt it's Madog,' Meadows continued. 'The watch stopped at seven forty-five; well, just after. I imagine it happened when he went into the water. What time did Anna Wilson take that photo?'

'Eight-fifteen,' Edris said.

'Right, so Madog was dead before the Wilsons,' Meadows said.

'The watch could've stopped at quarter to eight that evening,' Edris said.

'No, the Wilsons were killed on their way to the water. It gets dark at seven-thirty. They wouldn't have been walking through the woods at nightfall. And where was Madog when the photo was taken?'

'Yeah, I guess. Then we're back to Madog being killed for the boat.'

'No, I don't think Madog was a witness,' Meadows said. 'I think it's the other way around. I think Madog was the target. Along come the Wilsons with David Wilson looking out at the water with binoculars. He would be able to identify the killer.'

'Then why stick flies in their tongues?'

'To stop them talking; well, in the killer's mind. Mike, is there anything in his mouth?'

Mike took a torch and shone it inside Madog's mouth. 'Difficult to tell with the bloating,' Mike said. 'Best wait until the post-mortem. Are you happy for him to be moved?'

'Yes, the closest you're going to get to a crime scene is the boat. Did you find anything of interest?'

'We lifted a lot of prints. Minute traces of blood. As it's a fishing boat you would expect that. I've sent it off for analysis to see if it's human. We kept the boat covered and should be able to get it moved today.'

'That's great, thanks.' He turned to Edris. 'We better go and see Kitty Eccleston. We need to find out who had a reason to harm Madog. That person has killed three people, so I think we're dealing with a very dangerous individual.

* * *

The drive up to the farmhouse was a different experience in the daylight. To the left and down an embankment Meadows could see a large lake with a wooden pavilion overlooking the water. The view was interrupted by trees, with autumn leaves of gold, red, and brown, some fallen and carpeting the ground. Through the trees glimpses could be caught of a second and third smaller lake.

They reached the farmhouse which had two potted hydrangeas each side of the door, the last of the blooms browning at the edges. Meadows got out of the car and looked around. He could see a single-story stone cottage set back among the trees. Another cottage lay further up the track, this one he remembered Kitty pointing out as hers, as they walked to Madog's cottage. The final dwelling in view was behind wooden gates. He took a deep breath as he approached the farmhouse door. It had only been a couple of days since he delivered the news of the Wilsons' death to Lucy, now he was about to bring another person's world crashing down. It wasn't Kitty though that answered the door but her daughter, Elsie, who Meadows had met on Sunday evening.

'Is your mother home?' Meadows asked.

'She's down by the lake fishing. I persuaded her to go for a couple of hours to take her mind off things. If you go behind Mum's cottage there's a path past the fishery that leads to the lake.'

'Perhaps it would be better if you come with us,' Meadows said.

Realisation dawned on Elsie's face. She gave a little gasp. 'You've found him, haven't you?' She shook her head. 'If you're gonna tell her that he's... that... I can't... I can't watch.'

'I'm afraid it isn't good news. It will be better for your mother if you're there,' Meadows said.

Elsie nodded and stepped outside. She had only walked a few steps when she stopped. 'I feel sick.' She touched her stomach. 'You don't understand what this will do to Mum. She's very close to Uncle Madog, they see each other every day. It will kill her.'

'She'll be OK,' Meadows said, 'but she's going to need your support.'

Elsie nodded and wiped the tears that tracked down her face. She was quiet as they walked past the cottage, so Meadows picked up the conversation to try and distract her.

'So, your mum likes to fish?'

'Yes, both she and Auntie Lottie learnt to fly-fish when they were girls. Uncle Madog used to take them out all the time.'

They came to a concrete structure which was divided into long troughs. Fish of various sizes could be seen darting through the water.

'So, this is where you breed the fish,' Edris said.

'Yeah, well Mum and Uncle Madog take care of them.'

The nature of Kitty and Madog's relationship was clear. They were a big part of each other's lives, Meadows thought. Sometimes he despaired at the cruelty that humans inflicted on each other, and the devastation left in its wake.

'That's the pod,' Elsie said as they passed a small round pond. 'You can see the baby brownies.'

'Oh yeah,' Edris said as he peered into the water.

Elsie appeared a little calmer as they walked past the first two lakes. Each one had a boathouse with one or two rowing boats tethered to wooden posts. They found Kitty on the bank of the third lake. She was so immersed in her fishing that she didn't notice the three of them approaching. Elsie put up her hand to indicate they should stop. The reason became apparent when Kitty started to cast. Any closer and they risked getting hooked.

Meadows watched Kitty's graceful movements, the rod almost an extension of her arm. She flicked forwards and the line propelled through the air, but before it hit the water she flicked back extending her arm behind her. The line whipped back in a loop following the trajectory of the rod, and with precise timing she flicked forward again with a swish. Meadows found it mesmerizing as he watched her complete around four casts before the line finally landed about twenty foot out into the water. With her other hand she started pulling in the line in a figure-of-eight movement. She looked so peaceful Meadows was loath to disturb her.

'Mum,' Elsie said.

Kitty jumped, the rod jerking in her hands. 'Oh, you gave me a fright,' she said. She looked from Elsie to Meadows and Edris.

'Why don't you pull your line in and we can go up to the house,' Elsie said.

Elsie's voice had a quiver and Meadows saw the fear in Kitty's eyes.

'You've found him, haven't you? Please just tell me.'

'I'm so sorry, Mum,' Elsie said.

'No. Oh please no.' The rod fell from Kitty's hand.

Elsie moved forward and wrapped her arms around her mother.

'I've got that,' Edris said as he grabbed the rod and reeled in the line before setting it down on the bank.

'Come on, let's go,' Elsie said.

She seemed to be holding her mother up. Kitty looked so tiny wrapped in Elsie's arms that it was difficult to tell who was mother and who was the child.

In the farmhouse kitchen, Kitty cradled a mug of tea that Elsie had placed in her hands. Meadows noticed that she had also given her mother two tablets, but he didn't ask what they were for. Kitty was deathly pale with a sheen of perspiration across her forehead. He was worried that she would faint from the shock, or worse.

'I've called Auntie Lottie,' Elsie said. 'She's on her way.'

'Kitty, we're going to have to ask you a few questions. Would you like us to wait until your sister arrives?'

Kitty shook her head.

'I'd like you to look at something for me and tell me if it's Madog's,' Meadows said.

Kitty nodded.

Meadows took the plastic bag with the watch from his pocket and laid it on the table.

Kitty ran her finger over the watch with a trembling hand. 'Yes, it's Uncle Madog's; where did you find it?'

'I have to tell you that a man matching your uncle's description was pulled out of the Usk Reservoir this afternoon, he was wearing this watch.'

A sob escaped Kitty's mouth. Elsie took her hand and squeezed.

'He always wore the watch,' Elsie said. 'Mum gave it to him for his birthday.'

'Was it his heart?' Kitty asked.

'We don't think his death was natural or accidental,' Meadows said.

Kitty seemed to take a moment to absorb this information. 'What do you mean? Are you saying someone hurt him?'

'We will have to wait for the post-mortem but I'm afraid that does seem to be the case,' Meadows said.

'I want to see him,' Kitty said.

'I don't think that is a good idea,' Meadows said gently. 'He's been in the water for a few days. There will need to be a formal identification, but we can do that from his dental records.'

'I don't care what he looks like,' Kitty said. 'I just want to be with him. I can't bear the thought of him being alone.' Tears flowed freely down her face.

'Let's leave it a few days and see how you feel then,' Meadows said.

Kitty nodded and took the tissue that Elsie offered before she wiped her eyes.

'I guessed from the moment that I saw he hadn't touched the food I left him. I should've gone back to check on him, started searching sooner. I saw him every day from as long as I can remember. It was just Saturday, with Mum's funeral and things to sort out. I should've gone back.'

'It wouldn't have made a difference,' Meadows said. 'You're not to blame. What you can do now is help us to find the person responsible.'

Kitty nodded.

'Did Madog ever mention a David or Anna Wilson?' Meadows didn't think now that there was a connection between them, but it still needed to be clarified and Madog cleared of any involvement in the Wilsons' deaths.

'No but I heard the names somewhere.' Kitty's brow furrowed as she thought, then realisation dawned on her face. 'The news yesterday, they were the couple found at the Usk. Everyone on the farm has been talking about it.'

'Yes,' Meadows said.

'Was Madog there when they died? He would've tried to help and... no.' She put her hands to her face.

Meadows knew Kitty's imagination would take her to a dark place. 'We don't know what happened. He wasn't found with the Wilsons, but we have to look at all possibilities. The Wilsons came from Bristol, did Madog ever visit there, or have family or friends in that area?'

'No, it was just my dad and Uncle Madog. They lived here all their lives. The last holiday they took was in the seventies and that was to Ireland. I don't think he has left Wales since.'

Meadows nodded at Edris.

'As you are aware, we found Madog's boat pulled up on to the bank. It would appear that he was out fishing,' Edris said. 'We have a witness who saw him with someone else out on the water. Do you know who that may have been?'

Kitty shook her head. 'No, but if he was on the boat he would've had someone with him. He couldn't manage the boat alone anymore.'

'When was the last time Madog was out on the boat?' Edris asked.

'Erm, Thursday. He went fishing with Quintin, Lloyd, that's my brother-in-law, and our nephew Theo. I'm not sure who went on the boat. I think they may have taken it in turns.'

'Did anyone else use the boat?'

'Some of the boys on the farm. Sometimes Uncle Madog went out with Roy, his friend. He's lives at Pant Teg Farm.'

'I'm going to show you a photo taken on Saturday morning of a boat on the Usk Reservoir. I want you to confirm, if you can, that it is Madog's boat and if it's Madog or someone else you recognize on the boat. It's taken from a distance and has been enhanced so it's a bit pixelated.' Edris showed the screen to Kitty.

'It looks like his boat,' Kitty said, 'but it's not him.'

'Are you sure?' Edris asked.

'Yeah, it's not his coat for a start and erm, not his shape.'

'Have you any idea who it might be?'

'No, I'm sorry.'

Elsie looked at the screen and shook her head.

'OK, now we know Madog was at the Usk, do you have any idea how he got there?' Edris asked.

'No, we've asked everyone on the farm,' Elsie said.

'Could he have walked?'

'No, it's too far. Besides, why would he? He has his jeep, or he could've asked one of us to take him,' Kitty said.

'Then someone must have driven him,' Edris said. 'A friend, someone from the village?'

Kitty shook her head. 'He went to the pub sometimes.'

'The local?'

'Yeah, the Fly and Trout. Maybe he met someone there. All the locals know him.'

'Auntie Lottie asked in the pub,' Elsie said.

'Kitty, can you think of anyone who may have wanted to harm Madog?' Meadows asked.

'No, everyone likes him,' Kitty said.

'He treated everyone that works on the farm like family,' Elsie said. 'He watched most of them grow up. They all turned out to look for him.'

'He couldn't work very much on the farm, but he was always around,' Kitty said. 'He'd help with feeding or cleaning equipment, just not the heavy work.'

'You mentioned last time we were here that Madog attended your mother's funeral and that he was upset,' Meadows said.

'Yes,' Kitty said. 'He was very close to my mum.'

'Was there anyone at the funeral you didn't expect to see, or someone you didn't know but Madog seemed to know?'

'It's all a bit of a blur,' Kitty said. 'I couldn't tell you who was there.'

'There were a lot of people,' Elsie said. 'Most of the village, everyone that works here at the farm, or has worked in the past. Some of Gran's family came over from Ireland. They didn't hang around.'

'Did you see Madog talking to anyone in particular?' Meadows asked.

'No,' Kitty said. 'He was very quiet. He rode in the funeral car with me and Lottie to the church. He sat in the front with me and Quintin. We had refreshments in the church hall. Uncle Madog sat at the table with me. People came over to talk to us.'

'What about after? When you came back here. You mentioned before that a few of you gathered around a bonfire.'

'Yes, but that was just close family.'

'How many?' Meadows asked.

The kitchen door opened and a woman who Meadows guessed to be Lottie came in and went straight to Kitty. Lottie had the same hair colouring as Kitty but that was the only similarity between the sisters. Lottie looked to be about five foot seven with a curvaceous figure.

As Elsie filled her in on the conversation, she pulled a chair close to Kitty and put her arms around her. All three were crying. Meadows wished he didn't have to ask them any more questions. Kitty and Lottie are already grieving for their mother, he thought, and a violent death on top is a lot to deal with.

'The detective was just asking about who was here on Friday evening,' Elsie said.

'Me, my husband Lloyd, my son Jac, and his girlfriend Nia. My other son Arwel, my daughter Celyn, and her husband Kai,' Lottie said. 'Actually no, Kai took the kids home.'

'Me, Mum, Dad, and Uncle Madog, Auntie Pippa and Theo,' Elsie said. 'I think that was all.'

'And Theo is whose son?' Edris asked.

'Pippa's,' Lottie said.

'Did Madog argue with anyone?' Meadows asked.

'No,' Elsie said. 'He never argues, he is… he was a real softy.'

Lottie nodded. 'I don't think I ever heard him raise his voice.'

'Kitty, you said you walked Madog back to his cottage that evening. Was he the first to leave?' Meadows asked.

'I think so,' Kitty said. 'I'd gone to get some snacks and when I came back he wasn't sitting by the fire. Jac said he had left.'

'Had anyone else left?'

'Celyn and Theo,' Elsie said.

Meadows saw a look pass between Lottie and Elsie, but he let it go.

'Pippa wasn't there,' Kitty said. 'When I went to catch up with Uncle Madog she was with him.'

'Pippa is your sister-in-law?' Edris asked. He'd been scribbling away in his notebook and Meadows suspected that he was losing track of the family members and their relationship to Madog.

'Yes, Quintin's sister,' Kitty said.

'What were they doing when you caught up with them?'

'They were standing by my cottage in the dark, talking.'

'Did you hear what they were talking about?' Meadows asked.

'No, not really. She sounded angry. She went off as soon as I got to them.'

'Did she go back to the others?'

'No, she went ahead of us, across the bridge. She lives in Bryn Glas Manor. There is a bridle path that leads there. It's a shortcut.'

'Did Madog say what they'd been talking about?'

'No, I asked him what she wanted, and he said something like "you know what Pippa is like".'

'What did he mean by that?' Meadows asked.

'She can be… well—'

'A bitch,' Lottie cut in.

'Lottie!' Kitty said.

'She is kinda,' Elsie said. 'She's bossy and controlling. I was terrified of her when I was a child.'

'Pippa is a strong character,' Kitty said. 'She may not have been arguing with Uncle Madog.'

'You said Madog was to read the codicil to your father's will. Would that have had an impact on your late mother's estate?' Meadows asked.

'Well Mum left all her money to the farm if that's what you mean,' Lottie said. 'She didn't own any property.'

'Is there a copy of the codicil with a solicitor or held in a secure location?'

'No, there isn't and only Madog knew what was in that letter,' Lottie said.

'Did he talk to you about it?' Meadows addressed Kitty.

'No, he just told me not to worry, he said I'd be OK. But it's not OK.' Kitty sobbed and rubbed her hand over her chest.

'I think Kitty's had enough. Maybe we should do this another time,' Lottie said.

'Of course,' Meadows said. 'We'll leave you to get some rest.' He stood and pushed the chair beneath the table. 'I'm so sorry for your loss.'

Elsie walked them to the door. 'Mum isn't well,' she said. 'She doesn't like to make a fuss about it.'

'We will need to talk to her again,' Meadows said. 'We'll try not to distress her.'

Elsie nodded and closed the door.

'They're an odd family,' Edris said as Meadows started the engine.

'How so?'

Edris shrugged. 'All their lives revolve around the farm. They don't seem to have a life away from it. Then there's Kitty's relationship with Madog. It's like they were dependant on each other. You heard what Elsie said. They see each other every day. It's odd. Are you that close to your uncles and aunts?'

'I don't have any,' Meadows said.

'Oh, no family other than your mum and brother?'

'Not that I know of. Mum and Dad met when they joined the commune. I suppose they left their families behind. They never mentioned them. It was one big family anyway, so I guess I had more uncles and aunts than the average person.'

'I've got one set on my father's side and two on my mother's. We get together on special occasions, but we don't see each other all the time. Do you think there may be more to Kitty and Madog's relationship? She appears very fragile.'

'I don't get the impression anything sinister was going on. Lottie doesn't strike me as someone who would hold her tongue. Still, like you say, all their lives are tied to the farm and that includes their livelihoods. We need to look at the family dynamics.'

'Did you notice the look Lottie gave Elsie when she said that Celyn and Theo had gone off together?' Edris asked.

'Yes, Celyn is Lottie's daughter and Theo is Pippa's son, so they are only related by marriage. There could be something going on there.'

'What if Madog saw them at it in the woods? He might have decided to go back to the party. Celyn is married so she wouldn't want anyone to know.'

'I suppose people kill for less, but I get the impression the family would protect their own. My gut feeling is that there is someone who didn't want the codicil read. Let's go and see Pippa Eccleston. I want to know what she and Madog were talking about the night before he went missing. Kitty didn't go into the cottage with Madog. Maybe Pippa was waiting there to continue their conversation. After that we'll call in to the pub, I'll buy you a pint and we'll have a chat with the locals. I doubt anyone can keep a secret around here.'

Chapter Fourteen

Bryn Glas Manor was a Georgian house with a stone-pillared porch and ivy creeping up the walls. Meadows used the heavy iron knocker which echoed around the courtyard.

'Doesn't look like anyone is in,' Edris said. 'No lights on.'

'Could be in one of the back rooms.' Meadows gave the door another thud.

A light came on and a few moments later the door opened. A woman with sleek dark grey hair looked them up and down but didn't offer a smile.

'Pippa Eccleston?'

'Yes,' she said.

Meadows introduced himself and Edris. 'We'd like to ask you a few questions about Madog Jones.'

'Right, well it's not convenient right now.'

'It won't take long,' Meadows said.

'I suggest you call to arrange a suitable time,' Pippa said and closed the door.

Edris raised his eyebrows but didn't comment until they were back in the car. 'I think Lottie's description of Pippa was pretty accurate.'

'She wasn't in a hurry to help us,' Meadows said.

They drove into the village and parked in front of the Fly and Trout where a couple of smokers were standing outside with pints of beer in their hands. Meadows gave them a smile as he walked past and opened the door.

'Bar, I think,' Edris said as he pushed open the inner door on the right.

A silence fell over the room when they entered, and all eyes looked their way.

'Evening, gentlemen, what can I get you?' the landlady asked.

Meadows ordered the drinks then asked about Madog.

The smile faded from the landlady's face. 'She shook her head. We're all so worried about him. I hope he's OK. I've known him for years. He's a real gent.'

They would learn of the news soon enough, Meadows thought, but without a formal identification he wasn't willing to divulge the information.

'We are asking everyone if they saw Madog on Saturday or gave him a lift somewhere. Maybe to the reservoir,' Meadows said.

'Lottie has already been in asking. Listen up!' she called. All eyes turned her way. 'These two are police and need your help. They want to know if any of you saw Madog or gave him a lift anywhere on Saturday.'

There was a general murmur and shaking of heads.

'Thank you,' Meadows said. 'We'll be staying for a drink so if any of you have any information that you think will help please come and talk to us.'

Meadows chose the nearest table to the door and sat down. No one approached them but occasionally someone would look over. Slowly the chatter resumed.

'I don't think they want to talk to us,' Edris said.

'We'll finish our drinks and I'll drop you home.' Meadows took a sip of his orange juice.

'Any news from your brother?' Edris asked.

'He's arrived in London and is spending some time with friends before making his way down here. Any day now.'

'I bet you can't wait to see him.'

'No, it's been a long time since we were last together. He'll spend a few days with me then go up the commune. I'm hoping I can join him there for a week.'

As Meadows sipped his drink, he saw a man approach. He looked to be in his seventies with a bald head and jolly face.

'I wasn't sure if I should come over,' the man said. 'It's probably nothing.'

In Meadows' experience this sort of statement often led to something. 'Any information you can give us will be helpful, have a seat.'

'Thanks, I'm Roy.' He held out his hand.

Meadows and Edris shook hands with him. He sat between them.

'I've known Madog all my life, and his brother, Llew. We all went to school together. I hope he's OK. Poor Kitty must be out of her mind.'

'Do you know all the family well?'

'Yeah, it's a small community, see, and we all know each other. You don't get many strangers here.'

'When was the last time you saw Madog?'

'Thursday night I think, yeah because it was Connie's funeral the next day. Connie was Kitty and Lottie's mother. Madog had been out fishing with Lloyd, Theo, and Quintin. That's what I wanted to talk to you about. He wasn't himself.'

'In what way?' Meadows asked.

Roy shrugged. 'I know it was Connie's funeral the next day, but it was more than that. He'd asked me a couple of weeks ago, it could've been longer, I can't remember. Anyway, he asked me what I know about accounts. I've run my farm all my life and kept the books, so I told him if he wanted a hand I'd be happy to help. He said he just wanted someone to look over them. Make sure everything was in order. He was going to ask for them.'

'Ask who? His accountant?' Edris asked.

'I don't know, he didn't say.'

'Do you think he was worried about money?' Edris asked.

'I don't think so. I didn't get the impression the farm was in trouble. Bryn Glas is the biggest farm in the area. They have a lot of livestock, the dairy, not to mention crops and the trout farm. He said it was for Kitty.' He leaned in close. 'He thought she was being taken advantage of, by that husband of hers.'

'Quintin,' Meadows said.

'Yeah.'

'How?'

'I don't know. He's not well liked around here. None of the Ecclestons are. He asked me not to say anything.'

'Did he give you the accounts?'

'No, Connie died. When I saw him on Thursday, I asked him if he still wanted me to take a look. He said he had more important things to worry about and he did look worried.'

'Did he give you any idea what he was worried about?' Meadows asked.

'No, he said he couldn't talk about it. It must've been bad for him not to say. We've shared many things over the years. I mean he asked me to look at his finances. That's how much he trusts me. He knows I can keep things to myself. I wouldn't be telling you this, only I thought it might help.'

'Do you think that whatever was troubling him arose after Connie's death?' Meadows asked.

'Yeah, I mean of course he was upset when Connie died, but it didn't come as a shock. We all knew she didn't have long.'

'Do you think he was concerned about what would happen to the farm after Connie died? Ownership would be passed down. Did he talk about that?'

'No, but I can't see him being worried about that. He owns half of it. Oh, do you mean that the girls could sell up? That can't happen. There's something in the old man's will that stops that happening.'

This piqued Meadows' interest. Maybe Madog had talked about the codicil, he thought. 'You mean Madog's brother, Llew's will?'

'No, their father. I can tell you what I know. I don't suppose Madog will mind, most of it is common knowledge.'

'Go on,' Meadows said.

'Bryn Glas Farm and Bryn Glas Manor used to be all one estate. Tenants lived in the cottages and worked on the land. When the owner died there was some fallout. I don't know the full details. Some say it was debts, others say the wife was greedy, but the manor and some land was sold. After that an agreement was drawn up that the land couldn't be controlled by one person, and it couldn't be passed on to anyone who married into the family. It must be a blood relative. So, Connie had no rights to the farm. She controlled Llew's fifty percent when she was alive but now that will go back to the family so it will depend on the terms of Llew's will. One thing is for sure, the sons-in-law won't be able to inherit but they'll benefit if their wives do.'

'Lloyd and Quintin?' Edris asked.

'Yeah, but there are grandsons that could inherit.'

'It does sound like it's complicated and could've caused worry for Madog,' Meadows said. 'So Madog inherited the land and his brother had fifty percent interest. Surely, it's down to Madog to say who inherits. He has no family of his own, so I guess he has to choose wisely who he leaves the land to.'

'No, it was Llew who inherited the land. He was the oldest, Madog had his fifty percent interest and the cottage. Both were happy with the arrangement and the farm did well. They took a holiday to Ireland and Llew met Connie. We all thought it would upset things, but she was a lovely woman. She looked after Madog like he was her own brother. Then she had Kitty and Lottie. Madog adores those girls, especially Kitty. She was always with him. When Llew died the land reverted to Madog and Connie had the fifty percent interest, but Madog didn't move to the farmhouse. He thought it was right that Connie stayed there.

'They were a happy family.' Roy smiled. 'Then the Ecclestons bought the manor house. Bryn Glas Manor was run-down. It'd been empty for a good few years. Hugo and Eleanor Eccleston moved down from London with the money to fix it up. Quintin and Pippa were kids at the time. They went to boarding school and came home in the holidays. Too good to mix with the locals. The family didn't fit in well. The Ecclestons didn't bother with Madog and Llew until they wanted to buy some land. Quintin and Pippa had left university and Hugo wanted to build a housing estate on the land that runs behind the manor. He was all talk. Quintin was working in London and had some interest from investors. Plans were drawn up, but they needed access. The land behind the manor is locked in by Bryn Glas Farm. Hugo wanted to buy two of the fields.'

'Let me guess, Madog and Llew wouldn't sell,' Edris said.

'Yep, both brothers agreed on that. Hugo was confident that they would take the money eventually. He even started work prepping the land. Had all sorts of trucks and diggers driving through his garden. I think if he could have gained access that way, he would have. Highways wouldn't grant permission from what I heard, and the manor would lose the garden and have no privacy.'

'Right, so Hugo lost out on an opportunity and probably lost money,' Meadows said.

'It was worse than that. The bottom fields in Bryn Glas Farm flooded. Madog and Llew were convinced that Hugo had messed with the stream further up where it crossed his land. Hugo offered to do remedial work to help divert the flow and stop the flooding.'

'If the brothers sold the land,' Meadows said.

'Yeah, but they wouldn't budge. Then Granny Irish died and left money to Kitty and Lottie. I think she didn't want the money to go into the farm. I don't know how much money, but Lottie bought a house in the village and Kitty started the trout farm. The flooded bottom fields worked to her advantage, and they were turned into lakes. Then Quintin took an interest in Kitty. I suppose she was flattered by the attention. She was never a confident girl. They got married. Llew wasn't happy. I can't say I blame him. Everyone thought that Quintin did it so he could get in with the family and persuade them to sell the land. He's not well liked. He quit his job when he married Kitty and worked on the farm. Not manual labour – as a manager. Now if Kitty was to inherit Connie's share as the oldest then Quintin will probably persuade her to sell. That would worry Madog. He'd be torn between splitting the farm and giving into Kitty.'

With Madog out of the picture Quintin would have a better chance, Meadows thought.

'So, Hugo Eccleston still wants to build the estate,' Edris said.

Roy laughed. 'Hugo Eccleston is well dead, and Eleanor is frail from what I hear. It's Pippa and Quintin who will benefit from building the estate. Pippa lives with Eleanor and controls her mother from what I hear.'

Meadows thought of the argument Kitty had witnessed between Pippa and Madog. 'Did Madog get on with Pippa or was there animosity between them?'

'I don't think anyone gets along with Pippa Eccleston. She's… I'm not sure how I can put it politely.'

'That's fine,' Edris said. 'We're used to hearing all sorts. You can't shock us.'

Roy smiled. 'She's a domineering, self-centred, arrogant bitch.'

'In what way?' Meadows asked.

Roy shrugged. 'It's difficult to explain. She's very close to Quintin. Growing up they were given everything, but money couldn't buy her a family of her own. She wasn't pleased when Kitty and Quintin got together. She got up to all sorts of tricks to split them up. Then they got married and she somehow even made herself centre of attention that day. When Kitty got pregnant with Elsie, Pippa got herself pregnant with Theo. Everything Kitty had, Pippa wanted. It's like she's jealous of Kitty and would be happier if it was just her and Quintin. Very odd if you ask me.'

'What about Pippa's partner?' Edris asked.

'She doesn't have one, she didn't stay with Theo's father, he lives in London. Poor Madog must've been worried about all this. He knew Kitty wouldn't be able to stand up to Quintin and his sister. They would bully her into selling the land. Maybe he thought he'd get away from it all for a few days. Only I'm sure he wouldn't worry Kitty like this. I hope you find him soon.'

'Thank you for talking to us,' Meadows said.

Roy went back to his own table and no one else came to talk to them so they left.

'Information overload,' Edris said.

'Yeah but some interesting family history.'

'It's gotta be about money. If Quintin married Kitty to get his hands on the land, it didn't work. Now he has an opportunity if Kitty gets the land from Madog.'

'Yes but she's not the only one in the running. It depends on what was in the codicil. Lottie is also in the running for fifty percent. If her son Jac was to inherit the land then her family would have the majority interest. Lottie may not want the codicil found, especially if she thought Kitty would get the land. In any case it sounds as though there has to be an equal split. I also don't get the impression that Kitty would sell, even under pressure from Quintin.'

'Well, whoever took Madog to the Usk is our killer,' Edris said. 'I can't see anyone driving up to the farm; they'd have to go past the farmhouse and risk being seen. He could've walked up the bridle path to meet Pippa. She argued with him.'

'But what motive would she have for killing him? She's not a blood relative so won't inherit.'

'No but she'd do it for her brother by the sounds of it.'

'There is still the possibility that he walked into the village to meet someone. It's mainly farming in this area and an early start for most. I would've expected someone to see something. Maybe we'll get a bite on our social media appeal,' Meadows said.

'Most of them are probably not on social media. The internet is so bad here it's like living in medieval times,' Edris said.

Meadows laughed. 'I remember a time when there was no internet.'

'That says it all.'

Chapter Fifteen

The next morning Meadows watched as Blackwell marked the map of the reservoir with red dots representing anglers.

'We've now completed the interviews with everyone who was fishing on Saturday, 18th of September,' Blackwell said. 'The accounts are consistent only in the fact that they saw bugger all except rising fish. Some were fishing together. Others saw each other or walked past. The only one up the top end of the left-hand side of the water was the fisherman who found the Wilsons and that was on the Sunday. No one was at the top of the right-hand side on Saturday where Madog's boat was found, here.' Blackwell pointed to the map. 'Considering the weather conditions, expert opinion is that Madog went in the water somewhere around here.' He indicated a spot on the map. 'This area would've been obscured from view of the anglers dotted around this area.'

'But not from the Wilsons who were walking the area that morning,' Meadows said. 'That and the fact that only one person can be seen in the photo, taken by the Wilsons, adds weight to the theory that the Wilsons were killed because they witnessed what happened to Madog Jones and not the other way around. They just happened to be in the wrong place at the wrong time. That's going to be hard for Lucy and Mark Wilson to hear.'

'If the dentist's account of seeing two anglers in the boat at seven is correct, then the photo of the person in the boat taken by the Wilsons at eight-fifteen is our killer. How did the killer persuade the Wilsons to come back? We know they didn't die until later that day,' Valentine said.

'He offered them a ride on the boat,' Edris said. 'We know this from Lucy Wilson's account of when she talked to her parents that afternoon.'

Valentine's eyes narrowed. 'Yeah but if you had witnessed a killing you wouldn't come back.'

'They probably didn't witness the actual killing,' Edris said. 'But they saw the killer with the boat. They would've been able to identify him, or her.'

'Paskin, what have you got for us?' Meadows asked before Valentine and Edris could get into another argument.

'Nothing from Bristol. I've informed them of developments our end. Analysis from the samples taken from under the Wilsons' fingernails has come back. No DNA from their attacker.'

'Most likely the attacker wore gloves,' Blackwell said.

Paskin nodded. 'Dental records confirmed the identity of Madog Jones. I've put in a request for his phone and financial records. So far nothing more on social media. No connection between Madog Jones and the Wilsons but I guess we are not expecting to find one now. Chris from tech ran an analysis on the photo of the figure on the boat compared to photos of Madog. He's fairly certain that it's not Madog on the boat. Mike ran some tests on the fishing line. It's known as monofilament, this particular one is ten-pound strength, fairly common. There were no cells or any other forensic evidence found.'

Meadows nodded. 'We need to concentrate our efforts on the Joneses and Ecclestons and anyone connected to them and the farm. I want to know all there is to know about the family.' He filled the team in on Edris' and his conversation with Roy. 'It appears that the terms of the late Llew Jones' will are complicated; and why the codicil? Paskin, see if you can get hold of the family solicitor. He's likely to dig his heels in on Llew's will because of client confidentiality but he may be able to tell us the terms of Madog's will, particularly who the beneficiaries are. Blackwell and Valentine, can you organise a search of Madog's cottage then talk to Lottie's children, Jac, Celyn, and Arwel? They should be still around. Edris and I will talk to the rest of the family. Then we need to get a list of everyone that works on the farm. They would've all been up early on Saturday morning. One of them might have noticed something. Also, we can find out what they know about the family. According to Madog's friend Roy, Quintin is not well liked. I want to know why.' Meadows checked his watch. 'OK, Edris and I have to get to the hospital for the post-mortem results. We'll meet you at the farm after we have the pleasure of interviewing Pippa Eccleston.'

'You should've left her to me,' Blackwell said.

Meadows laughed. Blackwell took no nonsense from anyone, but he might well meet his match with Pippa. 'That's very tempting. If we get any problems, I'll let you know.'

* * *

Daisy was sitting at her desk writing up the report on Madog when they arrived.

'Good timing,' she said. 'I've just finished. I'll take you through.'

Madog had been washed and lay with his arms at his side but looked anything but peaceful. It wasn't a sight that Meadows would wish upon anyone, let alone Kitty and her family. He hoped that they'd make the decision not to see him. There was only so much they could do in the morgue to make him look presentable.

Edris stepped closer and looked at Madog's hands. 'Did the water do this?' he asked.

'Do what?' Daisy asked.

'His fingers.'

'Your skin wrinkles if you stay too long in the bath. Imagine how it would look if you stayed in the water for three days,' Daisy said. 'It's the same effect. I've seen worse. They call it "washerwoman changes".'

'I didn't mean the skin. His fingers look, well, alien-like,' Edris said.

Meadows looked. 'They are very long.'

'Oh that,' Daisy said. 'I've read through his medical records. Madog had Marfan syndrome.'

'Never heard of it,' Edris said.

'It's a rare genetic disorder,' Daisy said. 'It affects the connective tissue, skeleton, and organs. Madog had the classic characteristics. Tall, long-limbed, with long fingers and toes. He also had a problem with his heart and took beta blockers. I won't overload you with details. There would've been several other problems. Poor guy wasn't in the best of health.'

'His brother had a similar appearance, but I've met the rest of the family. None of them are particularly tall. In fact one of them is the opposite.'

'I think it's about a fifty percent chance of getting passed down. Symptoms vary widely, some only get mild symptoms. It doesn't skip a generation. So, if it wasn't passed down to the children then the grandchildren would be in the clear. Anyway, it wasn't Marfan syndrome that killed him,' Daisy said.

'I noticed the line across his throat when they pulled him from the water,' Meadows said.

'Yes,' Daisy said. 'Similar to the Wilsons, only no head injuries. There's bruising on his back. I imagine he was sitting down and the attacker used a knee for leverage as he pulled the ligature. He was dead before he went into the water. Tearing to the tips of the fingers. He struggled. Bruising to the arms probably from impact with the side of the boat.' Daisy shook her head. 'Given his age and condition he was defenceless. Pensioners and children always get to me.'

Meadows understood the feeling too well. He couldn't imagine what Madog had done to deserve this end.

'I've got another one of these for you.' Daisy grabbed a sample dish from the counter and handed it to Meadows. 'Same size as the flies found on the Wilsons, this one is white.'

'In his tongue?' Edris asked.

'Yes,' Daisy said.

'Can you email Edris a photo?' Meadows asked.

'I'll do it right away,' Daisy said.

'One more thing. We are working on the assumption that Madog died first, probably before eight on the Saturday morning. We think his watch stopped when he went into the water,' Meadows said.

'The time of death fits but if you're asking me to tell you one hundred percent that he died before the Wilsons, you're out of luck. They died on the same day; you're talking hours. If it had been days it would be a different matter. The Wilsons had eaten lunch, that was evident, whereas Madog's stomach was empty. He could've not eaten all day. There are other markers which would lead me to conclude that it's highly probable that Madog died first.'

'That's good enough for me,' Meadows said. 'Thanks, I'll see you later.'

'If the flies in the Wilsons' tongues were supposed to be a symbol of silence, then why one in Madog's tongue?' Edris asked. 'What did he have to keep quiet about?'

'He knew what was in the codicil and I'm guessing he wasn't the only one. Then again they could have a different meaning altogether. Let's go and have a chat with Pippa Eccleston, then we'll go and see Kitty. Maybe she can throw some light on these flies.'

Chapter Sixteen

Everyone that worked on Bryn Glas Farm had been asked to gather at the dairy. Quintin had wanted to be the one to make the announcement, but Lottie insisted that it should be Kitty as she was now head of the family. Kitty could see Quintin watching her, she knew he would be waiting for her to make a fool of herself. The thought of speaking in front of the group terrified her. She didn't want to embarrass the family and wished she had let Quintin do it. She wasn't sure she'd be able to get the words out. She still felt dazed. It was as if she was detached from her surroundings. The clock kept ticking but her world had come to a standstill. It didn't seem right that people should be carrying on with life all around her.

A hush fell over those crowded around. Even the dogs lying at Quintin's feet looked sombre. Kitty could feel her mouth go dry and a lump form in her throat. It felt like she would choke. Lottie, who was standing next to her, grabbed her hand and gave it a squeeze.

'I can't,' Kitty said.

'It's OK,' Lottie said. 'I'll do it.'

Kitty's mind drifted as Lottie made the announcement. She thought back to her childhood, sitting inside the dairy on a wooden stool. Madog handing her a cup, the taste of unpasteurised milk. He had told her it would make her strong, help her grow. It didn't work, she thought.

People were talking to her now, coming close and crowding her.

'I'm so sorry,' Luke Henry who worked in the dairy said. He gave her a hug. 'Madog was a lovely man. We're all going to miss him.'

'Thank you,' Kitty said, 'and thank you for everything you did to try and find him. I know you gave every spare minute of your time. You must be exhausted.'

'I just wish there'd been a better outcome,' Luke said.

One by one they came to offer their condolences. Some just patted Kitty on the arm. She guessed some felt there were no words they could give.

Kitty saw Luke and Theo chatting before they were interrupted by Quintin who seemed to be indicating to Theo that it was time to go.

'Let's go back to the house,' Quintin said as he passed Kitty. 'I asked Pippa to make some tea so we can discuss what happens next. Wagner, Elgar, come.'

The dogs jumped up and followed Quintin.

'I don't mind Theo being here but why has he asked Pippa to be at the house?' Lottie whispered.

Kitty shrugged. 'I expect she doesn't want to miss out on anything.'

'It's nothing to do with her. If she opens her mouth, I'm going to sling her out,' Lottie said.

Kitty smiled. 'I don't know why you let her wind you up.'

'I don't let her, just her presence is enough. All that "darling" and air-kissing, and she always has a smug smile on her face. It's like she's having a private joke with herself at your expense.'

'She's not that bad,' Kitty said.

'Is she still taking money from Quintin?'

'Yes, but I guess she looks after Eleanor, and they can't manage the expenses in that big house.'

'It's your money that's being used,' Lottie said. 'Why should you pay for them to live in that house? They could sell up, buy a smaller place. They'd have plenty to live on then.'

'I can't see that happening,' Kitty said. 'I suppose I wouldn't like to leave my home.'

'That's different. You work hard. I don't think that one has ever done a day's work in her life. Yet she always finds something to complain about.'

They arrived at the farmhouse and entered through the kitchen. Pippa was sitting at the table reading a book. She put the book down and stood up. 'I put out the cups ready for you.'

'Thank you,' Kitty said.

'I'll give you a hand,' Lottie offered. She turned to Pippa. 'Why don't you go and take a seat in the sitting room.'

'Yes, I think I will. I'm exhausted,' Pippa said.

'Why, what have you been up to?' Lottie said.

'It's all this business with Madog. I had to tell Mummy this morning. It's so upsetting for her.'

'Poor you,' Lottie said. 'I'll bring you a cup of tea.'

The sarcasm in Lottie's comment forced Kitty to turn away so Pippa wouldn't see her smile. She flipped the switch on the kettle and kept her back turned.

'Right,' Pippa said. 'I'll go and join the others.'

Lottie closed the door behind her. 'I don't want anyone to hear us.'

'Why?' Kitty asked.

'I want to talk to you about what the police said yesterday. I didn't want to say anything in front of Elsie. Then Quintin came back.' Lottie took the lid off the teapot. 'All those questions the police asked. Wanting to know where everyone was on Friday night. They think someone here killed Uncle Madog.'

'No,' Kitty said. She grabbed a handful of teabags and threw them in the pot. 'No one here would hurt him. Why would they?'

'Did he talk to you about what was in Dad's letter?'

'No. Honestly, he never told me what Dad wrote. I never asked him, it wouldn't have been fair. Do you really think that someone hurt him because of that?' Kitty asked as she picked up the kettle. 'I don't think we should even be talking about it.' She poured the boiling water into the pot.

'Think about it,' Lottie said. 'Why would Dad write that letter? Why bother adding a codicil to the will to be read after Mum died?'

'Because he would've been worried about the farm. He wouldn't have known Mum would die before Uncle Madog. More likely he would've thought it was Mum left and he wanted to be sure once she was gone that the farm fell into the right hands.'

'That doesn't make sense, Kitty. I think he knew something. Knew that Uncle Madog had other ideas about who should get the farm.'

'I don't know what you are talking about,' Kitty said. 'Why would Uncle Madog go against Dad's wishes?'

'You know why.' Lottie lowered her voice. 'You said that Uncle Madog—'

'Don't,' Kitty said. 'I'd had too much to drink.'

'What if you were right?'

Kitty didn't even want to think of the possibility. 'No, he wouldn't.'

'We need to find the codicil,' Lottie said.

'Then we'll search Uncle Madog's cottage. I didn't look at anything when I tidied up. I just put everything back into the drawers.'

'I've already looked.'

Kitty shook her head. 'You shouldn't have gone in there looking through his stuff. What if the police had seen you?'

'I went in early this morning before they arrived. I wanted to do it before anyone else had a chance.'

'What if someone's already taken it?' Kitty asked. 'The place was a mess, every drawer opened.'

'I thought of that this morning. What if he didn't keep it in the cottage? Something that important, he wouldn't take the risk of someone finding it. It was the last letter from his brother. He would have treasured it,' Lottie said.

A memory stirred in Kitty's mind. Madog sitting at the farmhouse table. A younger Madog. She had been twirling around in a dress. It was her tenth birthday.

'Are you ready, Kitty?' Madog asked.

'Yes,' she squealed jumping up and down in excitement.

'Get your wellies, it's treasure hunting time,' Madog said.

'And for Lottie?'

'Yes, of course for Lottie.'

'You'd better get going,' Connie said. 'Daddy will be back for lunch then we can all have cake.'

'Yeah, and you never know who else might be out looking for treasure,' Madog said. 'Pirates.'

Madog had got some of the farm workers to dress up and they'd run around the farm. Hiding from pirates and hunting treasure.

The memory faded.

'The jars,' Kitty said.

'Yeah, I've been thinking that.'

'I can't see him doing that,' Kitty said.

'He was always burying jars for us to find. Birthdays, Easter, Christmas. Any special occasion he could come up with. Even if it was just to cheer one of us up.'

'Yeah, but we were kids.'

Lottie laughed. 'No we weren't. He made me hunt for my present on my twenty-first birthday.'

'Oh yeah, the keys to your new car.'

'Your thirtieth birthday,' Lottie said.

'But he wouldn't have buried something that important and risk it being lost forever,' Kitty said.

'Yeah he would. It would be just like him. He'd want to keep it safe.'

'We should tell the police. If he's buried it then it could be anywhere on the farm. We'll never find it.'

'It would be somewhere special. Maybe a place that meant something to him and Dad, or a place he used before. Perhaps he thought if anything happened to him we would know where to look. It's worth a try,' Lottie said. 'I don't think we should tell the police. We don't want them knowing our business. If Dad wanted to protect Uncle Madog then we should do the same. If we find it and you were right, then we'll decide what to do. We'll start tonight. Try and think of all the places it might be. If we do a few places each we're bound to find it.'

'And probably a few jars he's forgotten over the years,' Kitty said.

'Don't tell Quintin what we're doing. I won't say anything to Lloyd.'

'OK.'

There was a noise outside the door. Lottie flew across the kitchen and yanked open the door.

'Came to see what was taking you so long,' Quintin said. 'Everyone is waiting. We've all got things to get on with.'

'We were having a chat,' Lottie said. 'We'll be there in a minute.' She grabbed the pot of tea. 'Put the cups on a tray. They can pour their own.'

Kitty carried the tray into the sitting room and looked around. Celyn and Elsie were sat together, both with puffy eyes. They had both kept it together in front of her but couldn't hide the fact they'd been crying when out of her sight. She wished they didn't feel the need. It was their grief as well as hers, she thought. They had all loved him. Jac and Arwel sat next to Lloyd, all three quiet. Pippa was talking to Quintin.

'Where is Theo?' Kitty asked.

'He left about five minutes ago,' Pippa said. 'He wanted to stay but he was in a lot of pain. This has been very hard on him.'

'It's been hard on all of us,' Lloyd said.

'It's got to be worse for him,' Lottie said. 'All this has got to have stirred up bad memories. We all know he is struggling.'

Kitty was glad to hear Lottie standing up for Theo. She was right. If anyone needed protecting it was him.

'Thank you, darling,' Pippa said.

'But Lloyd is right, it's hard on all of us. Arwel, I think you should go back to uni; Celyn, you've got the kids to worry about and, Jac, you need to go home,' Lottie said.

'No,' Arwel said.

'Your mum is right,' Lloyd said.

'Uncle Madog wouldn't want you all sitting around crying,' Kitty said. 'He was always one to keep moving. His motto was "Keep busy, less time to think." That goes for you, Elsie. You've got to get back to work.'

'I can take more time off,' Elsie said. 'There's the funeral to plan.'

'We don't know when that will be,' Lottie said. 'It'll depend on the police. You'll all want to be back for that.'

'Now that's sorted we need to discuss what will happen with the running of the farm,' Quintin said.

'We just carry on as normal,' Lloyd said.

'Things have changed,' Quintin said. 'We don't know yet who will inherit the land from Madog. I called the solicitor this morning and–'

'Who gave you permission to do that?' Lottie cut in.

'Someone had to do it and inform him of what has happened,' Quintin said. 'I'm just trying to be helpful. You and Kitty have enough to deal with.'

'Mr Howells already said he doesn't have Madog's will,' Kitty said. 'We don't even know if he wrote one.'

'I was just arranging for him to come and see us. We need to know what happens now. He said he would call either you or Kitty to confirm an appointment. In the meantime I'm happy to keep things running. I already pay all the invoices and run payroll. It makes sense for me to make any financial decisions in the meantime.'

'I don't think it should be down to one person,' Lloyd said.

'Do you know how to run the finances, Lloyd?' Quintin asked.

'No, but I think that any decisions about money should be made jointly,' Lloyd said.

'Fine,' Quintin said. 'If you want me to ask you about every order and every payment, be my guest. You'll spend more time in the office than doing your own job.'

'I'm not talking about the day-to-day running, just the big decisions,' Lloyd said.

'Fine,' Quintin huffed.

'My brother has run this farm for years,' Pippa said. 'I think you should trust his judgement. Do you know how much you'd have to pay for his expertise?'

'He hasn't run the farm,' Lloyd said. 'He keeps the books.'

'I do a lot more than that,' Quintin said. 'If we are going to be partners then—'

'What do you mean partners?' Lottie said.

'I mean all of us,' Quintin said.

Kitty felt like the tension in the room was wrapping itself around her. She didn't know why they all couldn't agree to just carry on as normal. No one needed to be in charge. The farm had been running smoothly for years without any arguments.

'It should be me and Kitty that make any decisions,' Lottie said. 'Perhaps we should ask Mr Howells if Uncle Madog appointed executors. If not then maybe we should think about doing it.'

Kitty saw a look of worry flit across Quintin's face, but he quickly regained composure. 'We really don't need to do that,' he said. 'They might put things on hold until probate is complete. We could lose a lot of money.'

'I'm inclined to agree with Quintin,' Lloyd said. 'I'm sure we can keep things running smoothly between us. What do you think, Kitty?'

'I'm fine with that,' Kitty said. 'Now that's sorted I need to get on. I haven't seen to the fish yet.'

'I have to go,' Pippa said. 'The police are coming to talk to me.'

'What for?' Quintin asked.

All eyes turned towards Pippa. Kitty had stood up, but she stayed still. She wanted to hear what Pippa had to say.

Pippa shrugged. 'I expect they're talking to everyone in the family. Haven't they called on you yet?' She looked at Lloyd and Lottie.

'No,' Lloyd said.

'I spoke to them yesterday,' Lottie said. 'Strange how they want to talk to you first.'

'I expect they will get around to everyone,' Pippa said.

Kitty remembered her comment to the detectives about Pippa being alone with Madog and the possibility of them arguing. Pippa will know it was me, she thought. She's going to be furious.

'I better go,' Kitty said.

She rushed out of the house, glad to be away from everyone. The pain in her chest had spread to her stomach making her feel nauseous. It wasn't a pain that could be dulled with a pill but a raw pain that gnawed constantly. She knew it was grief, but worse than that was the images that went through her mind. Madog in the water, someone holding him under the surface as he struggled to breathe. The police had said he was in the reservoir, so drowning had seemed the logical explanation. There were other scenarios, far worse, that tortured her mind. She tried to block these thoughts, but they wouldn't be silenced.

The police had also put the idea in her mind that someone close could have killed Madog. Then there was Lottie and her talk of the codicil. She thought now of her family, and she couldn't imagine any one of them hurting Madog. She was so wrapped up in her thoughts that she didn't notice something was wrong until she reached the troughs. It was the smell that hit her first, then she screamed.

Chapter Seventeen

Pippa Eccleston opened the door wearing a black turtleneck jumper over grey trousers. Her make-up was pristine – smoky grey eyes and ruby lips. Her dark grey hair was cut into a sleek bob, and she held herself in a manner of self-importance.

'Come in,' Pippa said. 'I'll take you through to the drawing room as I don't want to disturb my mother. She's had a very difficult morning. The news of Madog has shaken her.'

Pretentious was Meadows' first impression of Pippa. He half-expected her to say she was going to ring for tea. He followed her into a room where dark wooden panelling covered the lower half of the walls and met sage green paint. The furniture was upholstered in chintz with nests of tables positioned around the room. It had an old-worldly look but lacked authenticity. There wasn't that smell of old wood.

Pippa perched on the edge of a high-backed chair and crossed her legs at the ankles. Meadows noticed her flick her eyes towards Edris as he took a seat and pulled out his notebook.

'Is it just you and your mother that live here?' Meadows asked.

'Yes, and my son, Theodore. He's in the process of moving back.'

'Is he home?'

'Yes.'

'We will need to speak with him once we've finished talking to you,' Meadows said.

'He's up in his room having a lie-down and I don't wish to disturb him. It will have to be another time. He's been through a difficult time and now this.'

'Unfortunately this is a murder inquiry so we will need to talk to him today,' Meadows said.

Pippa pursed her lips. 'Very well. If you insist, I'll call him down. We may as well do this together. It will waste less of our time.'

Pippa left the room and Edris raised his eyebrows. They didn't hear her call out. Meadows assumed she must have gone upstairs because it was some time before she returned.

'He'll be down presently,' Pippa said resuming her position on the chair. 'Now what is it you need to ask me?'

'We understand that you are related through marriage to Madog.'

'That's correct. My brother Quintin is married to Kitty.'

'Given that you live so close you must've known him very well,' Meadows said.

'I wouldn't describe it as being a close relationship. I saw him occasionally when I visited my brother. He did call at the house to see Mummy but that was only after Daddy died. I think he had a soft spot for her. Other than that, it was at family gatherings, special occasions.'

Theo came into the room and smiled at Meadows.

'Detectives Meadows and Edris,' Pippa said.

'We met briefly at Auntie Kitty's on Sunday,' Theo said. He lowered himself carefully into a chair.

Meadows noticed that Theo had a pinched look as if he was in pain. There was also a sadness in his eyes. Something deeper-rooted than the recent tragedy.

'Yes,' Meadows said. 'You'd been out looking for Madog with Elsie. We were just asking your mother how well she knew Madog. Did you spend a lot of time with him?'

'I've known him all my life,' Theo said. 'He taught me to fish when I was a boy.' He smiled.

'So you knew him very well,' Meadows said.

'Yes, I spent a lot of my childhood on the farm. Elsie and I are the same age. We were close growing up. Uncle Madog and Auntie Kitty were always together. I hadn't seen that much of him lately. I've been living in Cardiff.'

'You went fishing with Madog last Thursday,' Meadows said.

'Yes, Uncle Quintin and Lloyd came with us.'

'Did you go out on the boat?'

'Yes, Uncle Quintin and I went out in the morning. Then we switched in the afternoon.'

'How was Madog?'

'He was OK. A little quiet. I think he was still upset by Auntie Connie's death.'

'Was everything alright between Madog, Lloyd and Quintin?'

Theo shrugged. 'I suppose.'

'No atmosphere between any of them?'

'What are you implying?' Pippa asked.

'I'm not implying anything,' Meadows said. 'I'm just trying to establish if there was any upset within the family.'

'Uncle Quintin wanted Uncle Madog to go out on the boat with him, but he said that he would stay with me and have a chat. Uncle Quintin said I should go with him.'

'Did you get the impression that Madog wanted to talk to you alone?'

'Maybe but he seemed OK to stay with Uncle Lloyd.'

'You both attended Connie Jones' funeral last Friday, is that correct?' Meadows asked.

'Yes, the whole family attended,' Pippa said.

'Did either of you talk to Madog?'

'He was with Kitty most of the time,' Pippa said.

'He was sitting in the front pew,' Theo said. 'Mum, Granny and me sat two rows back.'

'After the funeral did you both go to the church hall?' Meadows asked.

'Yes, we didn't stay long though,' Pippa said. 'We had a cup of tea then came back with Mummy. She was tired.'

'But you went to the farmhouse later that day,' Meadows said.

'Yes, Lloyd lit the fire, and everyone had a few drinks,' Theo said.

'Was Madog drinking?'

'I'm not sure,' Theo said.

'I think he was just drinking tea,' Pippa said. She made a show of looking at her watch. 'Is this going to take much longer?'

Meadows ignored her question. 'Who was the first to leave?'

'I don't know,' Theo said. 'I went for a walk with Celyn. She was a bit upset.'

Meadows noticed the look Pippa gave Theo. Her reaction was like Lottie's when Elsie had mentioned that Theo and Celyn had gone off alone together.

'If I recall, it was Madog who left first. He said he was tired,' Pippa said. 'I left shortly after.'

'Did you walk with Madog?'

'Part of the way.'

'What did you talk about?'

'We just exchanged pleasantries. Talked about what a nice service it had been for Connie.'

'Did you argue with him?' Meadows asked.

'No.' Pippa smiled. 'What on earth would I be arguing with Madog about?'

'We had a different account of your conversation with Madog,' Meadows said.

Pippa's eyes flashed. 'Kitty came along and interrupted our conversation. I expect we looked serious because we were discussing the funeral. She must have misinterpreted our talk for something else. I assure you, we were not arguing.'

'Where did you go when you left Madog?'

'I came home. I used the bridle path. Mummy had been on her own all evening. I don't like to leave her too long.'

'When was the last time you saw Madog?'

'That was the last time I saw him,' Pippa said.

Meadows turned his attention to Theo. 'Where did you go when you went for a walk with Celyn?'

'Down by the lakes.'

'Did you see anyone else?'

'No, only Uncle Madog on our way back.'

'With Kitty?' Meadows asked.

'No, he was on his own.'

'What time was this?'

'I'm not sure, about nine, nine-thirty,' Theo said.

'Where exactly did you see him?'

'By the fishery, he was heading towards the lakes.'

'Did you talk to him?'

'He asked if I was going back to the party. Then he asked me to have a word in private. He said he wanted me to keep an eye on Auntie Kitty.'

'Did he say why?'

'No, he just asked me not to mention it. I asked if he wanted us to walk him home. He said he had something to do. That's the last time I saw him.'

'Didn't you find it odd that Madog was walking to the lakes after dark?'

'Not really, he had a torch and his head torch. He liked to walk. I thought he might have wanted some peace.'

'Did you go back to the bonfire?'

'Yes.'

'Who was there?'

'The cousins and Uncle Lloyd. Kitty and Lottie were in the house I think.'

'What about Quintin?'

'I don't know. Maybe he'd gone to bed. Uncle Lloyd took Celyn home. I stayed and talked to Jac for a while then I walked home on the bridle path.'

Meadows gave Edris a nod.

'We have to ask both of you where you were early last Saturday morning and Saturday evening. To be clear that's Saturday, the 18th of September.'

'This is ridiculous,' Pippa said. 'You can't think that we would have anything to do with what happened to Madog.'

'We will be asking everyone connected to Madog so we can eliminate them from our enquiries,' Edris said.

'I was here,' Pippa said. 'Mummy gets up around eight every morning. We had breakfast about nine together, or thereabouts. Wasn't it?' She looked at Theo.

'Yes, something like that. I wasn't taking much notice of the time. I went for a walk around the farm. I saw Luke, that's Luke Henry, at the dairy and stopped for a chat. I came back here and that was it. My back was killing me. I had an injury in work, so I've been trying to rest up.'

'And you?' Edris looked at Pippa.

'I went out to do a bit of shopping then came back here to make some lunch. I didn't go down to the farm until later. I thought they'd all want a bit of peace. Kitty invited the whole family for dinner, so I went down around seven and was home no later than ten.'

'Did you go to the family dinner?' Edris asked Theo.

'No, I stayed with Granny.'

'We'll have to talk to her to confirm the times,' Edris said.

'Not today,' Pippa said. 'As I already told you she's had a shock and she's very frail. Now I think we've answered all your questions and you've taken up enough of our time.' She stood up.

'One more thing,' Edris said. 'What size boots do you both wear?

'Twelve,' Theo said.

Edris looked at Pippa.

Pippa huffed. 'An eight. Now, is that all?'

'For now,' Meadows said. 'We may need to talk with you again.'

'I'll see you out,' Pippa said.

She followed them out and closed the door behind them without a word.

'She couldn't wait to get rid of us,' Edris said as he fastened his seatbelt.

'No,' Meadows agreed. 'The question is, was it because we were an inconvenience or something more? She seemed to be leading Theo on some of the answers. There was also her reaction to him taking a walk with Celyn.'

'Yeah, I noticed that,' Edris said.

'Let's go and see Kitty. Hopefully she'll be feeling up to answering a few more questions. She knew Madog better than anyone. She may also be able to identify the flies.'

Chapter Eighteen

Pippa closed the door on the detectives and walked towards the kitchen. She needed a drink. She felt it was a bit early to open a bottle of wine but reasoned a shot of whiskey would do the trick. She was surprised to find Theo sat at the kitchen table.

'I thought you'd go back upstairs for a lie-down,' she said.

'I'm feeling a bit better now. It was entertaining watching you lie to the police and trying to decide whether to contradict you or not.'

'I didn't lie. What makes you say that?' Pippa didn't want to hear the answer, but she had to play along.

'I heard you were late getting to Auntie Kitty's dinner. You blamed me. Said that you had to wait for me to get back from seeing to the horses so I could sit with Grandma. Who you said wasn't feeling well. She wasn't ill. The police will know what time you got there. Kitty would've told them. They'll know you lied.'

Pippa got the feeling that Theo was enjoying her discomfort. 'I saw to the horses before I left. I didn't feel like getting there early. I didn't want to tell the police that. What would they think?'

'That bullshit about us having breakfast together on Saturday morning?'

'It sounded better if we were both here together.'

'They'll be back, and they will talk to Grandma,' Theo said.

'She doesn't know what day it is half the time,' Pippa said.

'Don't be too sure about that. She knows when the soaps are on. She also knows a lot more that goes on here than you give her credit for.'

'Don't worry about it,' Pippa said.

'I'm not.'

'Look, darling, you've had a hard time and I know you're not too happy about moving back here. Things will get better.'

'Will they?' Theo stood up. 'I think I will go back to my room.'

Pippa put her fingers to the bridge of her nose and applied pressure. She could feel a headache brewing. She didn't like to be at odds with Theo. He was all that she had. She couldn't even run to Quintin, not this time. He had got her into most of the trouble, but he didn't know the half of it. She was going to have to go and see him. If he could take some of the burden away, she could deal with the rest.

She walked into the sitting room where Eleanor was sitting in the armchair watching a film.

'I need to go out for a while,' Pippa said. 'Do you need anything?'

'Where are you going?'

'Get my nails done.'

'You've had them done already this week,' Eleanor said.

'No I didn't, it was last week, remember. It's Thursday today.'

'No it's not. It's Wednesday.'

Pippa watched her mother trying to count back the days. If I keep changing the days she won't know where she is, Pippa thought. All I need is the police to doubt her reliability. 'It is Thursday, Mother. You're just getting confused with everything that's been going on. I broke a nail when I was making us breakfast on Saturday morning. Remember? I showed you. I was annoyed because I had just got them done. All this business with Madog has upset you.'

Eleanor nodded. 'It's not that I had a great deal to do with him, but he did call around to see me now and again.'

'Yes, so the police will want to talk to you.'

'To me? Well I can't tell them anything.'

'They're just talking to everyone that knew Madog.' Pippa hoped that this was the case. No one else at the farmhouse that morning was expecting a visit. She hoped she hadn't been singled out. It's because Kitty saw me arguing with Madog, that's all, she thought.

'If there is nothing you need then I'll go. I might call and see Quintin on my way.'

'That's a good idea. Poor darling, he's going to need some support.'

Pippa tried not to roll her eyes. It was always about Quintin with her mother.

Eleanor went on. 'He'll probably have to sort out the funeral as well as Madog's affairs. You know what that lot are like down there.'

'I'll see you later.' Pippa hurried out of the room. She didn't want to hear any more.

A few minutes later she was sitting in Quintin's office.

'You've spoken to the police then?' Quintin said.

'Yes, they just left.'

'What did they ask?'

'They wanted to know where I was on Saturday morning and evening. Bloody Kitty told them I had been arguing with Madog on Friday night.'

Quintin smirked. 'That's not going to look good for you.'

'I'm glad you find it amusing,' Pippa said. 'Wait until they start looking at you.'

'Let them look,' Quintin said.

'How can you sit there like you haven't got a care in the world? This is your mess. You've got to sort it out.'

'What do you think I have been doing?'

Pippa sighed. 'I can't keep covering for you.'

'You won't need to for much longer.'

'Do you know what's in Madog's will? Did the solicitor tell you? He did, didn't he, and you haven't told the others.'

'No, he didn't.'

'The codicil? That's what you've found, and you've destroyed it,' Pippa said.

'No, what makes you think I have it?'

'You need to find it and destroy it, especially if it isn't in Kitty's favour. And Madog's will. You promised everything would be OK.'

'I told you I'm working on it. Just give me a couple of weeks. I have a plan.'

'You've always got a plan, but it never works out. You're not the one who is going to suffer.'

'You don't know what you're talking about. If Kitty finds out…'

'You better hope she doesn't,' Pippa said.

'Are you threatening to tell her?'

'Just do as you promised. I'm sick of making excuses for you.'

'You're not in a position to judge me,' Quintin said.

'What's that supposed to mean?'

'You know what I'm talking about. Do you want me to spell it out?'

A silence grew between them. Pippa was furious but she didn't dare push him. She didn't know how much he knew.

Quintin stood up and came around to Pippa's side of the desk. 'Let's not argue,' he said. 'We need to stick together. It will be OK. Just hang on a little longer.'

Pippa nodded. He was right. She had to keep it together, not just for herself but for her mother and Theo.

Chapter Nineteen

Meadows and Edris found Kitty standing in one of the troughs surrounded by dead fish. Her hair was tied back but clumps had come loose and were clinging to the side of her face. As she was netting the fish and tipping them into a bucket, a man was emptying them onto a trailer lined with plastic sheeting. The smell of fish mingled with the acrid smell of bleach.

'What happened?' Meadows asked.

'I don't know,' Kitty said. 'I came to feed them, and they were all dead. Someone has done this.'

'Chlorine or bleach,' the man said.

'And you are?' Meadows asked.

'Luke Henry. I'm taking the fish up to one of the fields. Lottie is up there sorting out a pit so we can burn them.'

'You better get out of the water, Kitty,' Meadows said.

'I've got waders on,' Kitty said.

'Even so. We don't know for sure what's in the water. I'll arrange to get it tested. This is criminal damage, so we'll need to get forensic officers out here. I suggest that no one else comes near the fishery for now.'

'Once we get a phone signal,' Edris said, looking at his screen.

'Come on out, Kitty,' Luke said. 'I can deal with this. Once I get the fish out I'll get a couple of the boys to help me deal with them up the field. You've enough on your plate. If that's OK?' He looked at Meadows.

'Yes, just leave a couple of fish for testing.'

'We do need to ask you a few more questions, Kitty,' Edris said. 'Maybe it's better you leave that to Luke while you talk to us.'

'OK.' Kitty stepped out of the trough. 'Thank you, Luke.'

'No problem,' Luke said.

Meadows smiled at Luke then followed Kitty to a shed where she changed out of her waders and scrubbed her hands.

'Why would someone do this?' she said as she dried her hands.

'We're going to try and find out,' Meadows said, 'but you're going to have to help us.'

Kitty nodded.

'When was the last time you checked the fish?' Meadows asked.

'Yesterday. In the evening before it got dark. I'm usually down here first thing in the morning, but after yesterday...'

'Did you hear anything out of the ordinary last night?'

'No.'

'Who was here yesterday?'

'The whole family came after you gave us the news about Madog. Jac and his girlfriend are still staying in the cottage, but they are leaving today. We were all in the farmhouse. Pippa came down with Theo. I don't know what time everyone left. I went to bed. I wouldn't hear anything from the house, it's too far away. The only ones who would've noticed anything were Pippa and Theo when they walked home. If there was anyone down here Theo would've checked it out.'

143

Unless it was one of them, Meadows thought. 'Have there been any threats made against you or any concerning the farm?' he asked.

'No.'

'Any financial problems. Unpaid bills, disputes over money, that sort of thing?'

'No, nothing like that,' Kitty said. 'The farm is doing well.'

'Any arguments in the family, or with anyone that works here?'

'No, we're a close family. We have the odd argument but nothing serious. Everyone that works here is like family. Most of them have worked here for years. No one has been sacked or left suddenly. I just don't understand why this is happening to my family.'

'Who profits from the fishery?' Meadows asked.

'I suppose I do, and Quintin. Rent is paid to the farm as I don't own the land, but the rest is mine.'

'But that will change now?' Meadows asked.

Kitty shrugged.

'Who's the beneficiary of Madog's will?' Meadows asked.

'I don't know. We have to wait for the solicitor to come and see us.'

'I see. What would happen if you don't benefit from Madog's will? If the land is owned by another member of the family. What happens to your fishery and cottage?'

'Nothing. I still own them. Dad made sure everything was in order. I will always have to pay rent for the lakes and fishery but it's for my use only. The land can't be used for anything else unless I volunteer to give up the use. The cottage is different. No land rent. It's my home for life and mine to pass on to Elsie.'

'Do you think that someone may be wanting you to give up the fishery?' Edris asked.

Kitty looked shocked at the idea. 'No, why would someone want that? No one can benefit from the land or lakes other than family.'

'Kitty, you have to think of the possibility that it may be the case.' An idea came to Meadows. 'We did hear that plans had been made for houses to be built on the land of Bryn Glas Manor and access through the land of the farm would be required.'

'That was years ago,' Kitty said. 'The land here is no good for access. It would need to be the top field. It's too steep to do anything from here and you've got the stream.'

'What about the old bridle path?' Meadows asked. 'If a bridge was built over the stream couldn't that be used as a road?'

'You'd have to drain the lakes and build them up. The bridle path is steep and narrow. I can't see that it would be easily converted to a road. The only person who would benefit from that is Pippa and…'

'Quintin?' Meadows asked.

'He wouldn't have done this. We're going to lose a lot of money as it is. Quintin hasn't talked about the new builds for years.'

'OK,' Meadows said. 'What about the rest of the family? Who would benefit from you giving up the land?'

Kitty shook her head. 'No, there's no one in my family that would do this to me, and no one would hurt Uncle Madog.'

Meadows nodded. 'I'd like you to look at some photographs of fishing flies and tell me if you can identify them and if they mean anything to you.'

Edris called up the first photo of the white fly and showed it to Kitty. Her reaction was immediate. She stepped back and her eyes filled with tears.

'Why are you showing me this?'

'Do you know what it is?' Meadows asked.

'Yes. It's a white moth.'

'Did it mean something to Madog?'

'It's special to me, well to both of us. It's the first fly that Uncle Madog gave me. It caused an argument with Lottie and it's one of the few times I saw Uncle Madog cross.'

'Can you tell us about it?' Meadows asked.

'It's just kid's stuff.'

'All the same it might be important.'

'Lottie and me were always fascinated by Uncle Madog's fly boxes when we were girls. All the pretty colours, I suppose. We were never allowed to touch them. After he taught us to fish we were allowed to choose one from his box. I chose the white moth. To me it was the best one. It was not only pretty but looked perfect, which was the opposite of what I felt about myself at the time. So I had the white moth, but Lottie wanted it. She cried so much that in the end I let her have it. When Uncle Madog found out, he was upset. He made Lottie give it back. He said he had given it to me, and I should never give away a gift, especially as he had wanted me to have it. I said I thought Lottie should have it as she was pretty and, like I said, it was just childish. The white moth meant a lot to me at a difficult time. Uncle Madog gave me this.' She pulled a necklace from inside her jumper. It was a silver chain with an opal pendant in the shape of a moth. 'I never take it off. What has it got to do with what happened to Uncle Madog?'

'We found this particular fly with him,' Meadows said.

'Uncle Madog wore one on his fishing jacket. He also had boxes of flies. I imagine he'd have a white moth among them.'

Meadows didn't want to cause Kitty distress by telling her where the fly had been found. 'It was left with Madog for us to find. It wasn't the case that he was using that fly or could have placed it himself. There are a couple more for you to look at. These were found with the Wilsons, the couple murdered at the Usk, we believe the same person that killed them is responsible for Madog's death.'

Edris swiped the screen and showed the photo to Kitty. 'The yellow one we think is a drake mayfly,' he said.

'It's a Thomas yellow mayfly; the other one is a pink squirrel.'

'Are you sure?' Edris asked.

'Yes,' Kitty said. 'These were found with the other couple?'

'Yes,' Meadows said. 'They weren't fishing and as far as we know have never been fishing. Do these flies mean anything to you or Madog?'

'I'm sure the Thomas yellow was last year's winner,' Kitty said.

'Winner?' Edris asked. 'Like a competition for best fly?'

'No.' Kitty smiled. 'The winner of the White Moth Cup, it's a fishing competition we hold here each year. The winner gets to keep the cup and hold the title for a year, as well as a cash prize and an assortment of tackle. Uncle Madog and me started it years ago. It started off small and just grew. It's held over a week in May with a ceremony on the Saturday evening. We get people from all over the UK, some from abroad. The tickets get sold out in minutes of going on sale.'

'So, these flies are used in the competition,' Meadows said.

'Yeah, but they're not the only ones. There are rules on the types of flies. I won't bore you with the details. The winner's name, weight of the fish, and the fly used to catch it are displayed in a frame in the summer house. It's where I keep my white moth. Would you like to see? I can check which year the pink squirrel won and tell you the names of the winners.'

'That would be useful, thank you,' Meadows said.

They made their way to the first lake and Kitty talked about the setup of the competition. Meadows noticed that she relaxed as she talked about fishing.

'We were talking to Pippa earlier,' Meadows said as they passed the first boathouse.

'She said you were going to call on her,' Kitty said. 'Did you ask her about arguing with Uncle Madog?'

'Yes, she said that they were just talking.'

Kitty sighed. 'She isn't going to be happy with me.'

'I wouldn't worry,' Meadows said. 'It is best to be honest. Pippa said that she had been discussing your mother's funeral with Madog and they probably looked like they were having a serious talk. Do you think that was the case?'

'I couldn't hear what they were saying but I could hear Pippa's voice. Her tone was, well, sharp. I couldn't hear Madog's voice. She was standing very close to him.'

'You mean like up in his face?' Edris asked.

'It was difficult to get up in Uncle Madog's face,' Kitty said with a smile. 'But yeah, that's what it looked like. Like she was having a go at him.'

'And Madog just brushed it off?' Meadows asked.

'Yeah, but he didn't like confrontation.'

'If they were arguing, what do you think it was about?' Meadows asked.

'I've no idea.'

'We also talked to Theo while we were there. He seems like a nice man.'

'Yeah, Theo is lovely.'

'Pippa said he's had a hard time lately.'

Kitty nodded and it was clear she didn't want to talk about it.

'He seems to be doing OK,' Meadows said.

'He tries. This back injury has put him out of work and then the split with his wife. I think the divorce has just come through; it's a shame. His wife, Ffion, was nice. Now he can't afford the rent on his flat, so he has to move back in with Pippa. I not sure he's so happy about that.'

'What about his father? He couldn't live with him for a while?'

'Theo's father has never been involved in his life. Quintin told me once that Hugo had paid off Theo's father because Pippa didn't want anything to do with him. Pippa usually gets what she wants. Can you imagine taking money in place of your own son?' Kitty shook her head. 'That's why he spent so much time with us as a child. Hugo didn't bother with him much. Uncle Madog was more like a grandfather to him and Quintin and Lloyd sort of stepped up as father figures. Poor Theo, losing Uncle Madog must be really hard for him.'

'Hard for you all,' Meadows said.

'To be honest none of this feels real. It's like I'm talking about someone else. Maybe I'm losing it.'

'It's a natural reaction,' Meadows said. 'You're going to feel detached for a little while. It's our mind's way of dealing with things. It will get better.'

'Or worse. I don't want to think about Uncle Madog never being around again.'

'Tell me a little more about the family. Elsie, and Lottie's children are all a similar age. They must've had a lot of fun growing up here,' Meadows said.

'Yeah, and you always knew they were safe. With Uncle Madog or helping Lloyd or someone on the farm. I thought they'd never want to leave but they've all got lives of their own now. I don't think any of them want to step in to take over the running of the farm.'

Likely they'll want to sell it, Meadows thought. 'As Theo grew up here he must have been close to his cousins.'

'Yeah, they all get on well.'

'I got the impression that Lottie wasn't too happy about Theo and Celyn taking a walk alone on Friday evening. Pippa didn't appear so happy about it either.'

'Celyn is married, and I don't think she's that happy with Kai. People talk and I don't think Lottie wants gossip about Theo and Celyn. It would cause problems with Kai. I wouldn't read too much into it.'

They reached the summer house at the third and largest lake. A white wooden moth was mounted on the side of the building. Kitty opened the door and let out a gasp. Meadows could see past her to the broken glass and frames on the floor.

'Don't go inside,' Meadows said.

Kitty didn't seem to hear him. 'Oh no,' she cried as she started to shift glass and broken wood, and plastic. 'They're all gone. All the flies. My white moth.'

'Come out, Kitty,' Meadows said. 'We will need to check for prints. The less you touch the better.'

'What's happening?' Kitty exclaimed. 'Uncle Madog, the fish, and now this. It's like someone is trying to destroy us.'

'It does look like the farm is being targeted,' Meadows said. 'Particularly the fishery.'

'How much money is involved in the business?' Edris asked.

'I don't know exactly, but we've done well. The competition brings in a lot of money from tickets, and sponsors. We give out a cash prize but it's the title that everyone wants.'

'When was the last time you were in the summer house?' Meadows asked.

'I don't know. Not since before the funeral. We don't use it that often. It's mainly at competition time.'

'Do you keep it locked?' Edris asked.

'No.'

'Were there any problems with the competition this year?' Meadows asked.

'Not really, there was one incident. We had to disqualify one of the anglers, Rhodri Morgan, for illegal baiting.'

'That sounds serious,' Edris said.

'It's a big no-no,' Kitty said. 'It gives a huge advantage over the other anglers. All tackle is checked, including bags. We found salmon paste – it's made from salmon eggs – in Rhodri's bag.'

'Did he cause a scene?' Meadows asked.

'Yes, Uncle Madog found it and Rhodri denied it was his. He said someone must have slipped it in his bag. Rhodri is one of the top competition winners. We never had a problem with him before. We had no choice but to disqualify him.'

'Did he make any threats?'

'No, he was pissed off though.'

'We're going to need a list of anglers that attended the competition that day. We also need a list of all the farm workers.'

'Quintin will have all the names for you. We'll have to go back to the house so I can call him. He'll be up at the office in the dairy. Good signal and faster internet connection up there.'

'OK, there are a couple more questions that Sergeant Edris needs to ask you. It's standard procedure in a case like this to ask anyone connected to the victim for their whereabouts on the day in question. It helps build a picture of everyone's movements. You understand that this does not mean that you are a suspect?'

'Yeah.' Kitty nodded.

'When we spoke to Theo, he said when he got back from his walk with Celyn, on Friday evening, it was just Jac, Elsie, Arwel, and Lloyd left at the bonfire. Jac's girlfriend had gone back to the cottage. Where were you at this time?' Edris asked.

'I was in the house with Lottie for a while, then she went home, and I went to bed.'

'What about Quintin?' Edris asked.

'He was still outside with the others, I think. He must've been because he wasn't in the house when I went to bed.'

'What about Saturday morning?' Edris asked.

'I was out of the house by six. I let out the chickens and collected the eggs.'

'Both you and Quintin?'

'No, he'd already left by the time I got up.'

'Did you see anyone else around the farm at that time?'

'Aled and James were just coming in. They get the second batch of cows down from the field. They are milked in two batches.'

'What about Quintin or Lloyd?'

'No, they were probably inside the dairy.'

'What about the rest of the family?' Edris asked.

'Lottie doesn't work on the farm. She's a hairdresser but she would've been at home. The kids were all sleeping.'

Meadows smiled. He knew the kids Kitty referred to were the cousins who were all in their twenties. Any one of them could've taken Madog to the Usk, he thought.

'What about Saturday afternoon and evening?' Edris asked.

'Elsie helped me prepare dinner for the family. I wanted to get it done early. I took a plate over to Uncle Madog, then they all turned up. Well, they were all later than they were supposed to be. Lottie got here first bringing Celyn and Arwel with her. Quintin got back about eight. Lloyd was last to come, oh and Pippa arrived about the same time. Elsie went to fetch Jac. They all left before ten.'

'That's great, thanks,' Edris said.

They reached the farmhouse and Kitty made a call to Quintin then let Edris use the phone to call forensics.

'He asked if you could meet him at the dairy,' Kitty said. 'It's easy to find. Down the track, turn right and right again, then the first gate.'

'Officers will come shortly to take prints from the fishery and summer house,' Meadows said. 'As the summer house hasn't been used recently they may get lucky. In the meantime I want you to think about security. You need to start locking the door, especially at night. Maybe padlocks on the sheds and animal pens.'

'Do you think my family is in danger?' Kitty asked.

Meadows thought it more likely that Kitty was the one that should be worried, but he didn't want to frighten her. 'You don't want a repeat of what happened to the fish. If gates and doors are locked it makes it harder for someone to get in. I'll have an officer come and talk to you. They can give you advice on how best to secure the farm.'

Meadows doubted this would help, there were too many entrances, but he wanted Kitty to take the threat seriously. If it was one of the family then she would need more than padlocks to keep her safe, he thought.

Chapter Twenty

The dairy was a modern structure which was attached to what Meadows guessed to be the original building. Quintin's office was inside the newer part and reached by a set of metal steps. It overlooked what appeared to be a small factory. Large stainless-steel drums dominated the room and storage units were fitted across one wall and steel worktops ran along the other length.

'What goes on down there?' Edris asked looking out of the window to the floor where figures in white coats and wearing hairnets moved around.

'Cheesemaking,' Quintin said. 'We started producing our own cheese about five years ago. Those are cheese kettles.' He pointed to the stainless-steel drums. 'State of the art. I have the lists for you and have highlighted the day that we had to disqualify an angler. There's also the list of farm workers. I hope you're not going to interrogate everyone. There's work to be done and now we have a shortage of fish to contend with.'

Unlike the rest of the farm workers, Quintin was dressed in a pair of jeans with a shirt and jacket. On his wrist he wore a heavy-looking gold watch. Meadows guessed that like his sister, Pippa, he was used to getting his own way and liked to feel in charge.

'Given the circumstances I doubt anyone will mind a few questions,' Meadows said.

'Right, well, if there's nothing else then I need to get on with work.' Quintin sat down behind his desk.

'While we're here we'd like to ask you a few questions,' Meadows said.

'Can't it wait?'

'No.' Meadows plonked down in a chair and Edris followed.

'We need to go over your movements last weekend,' Edris said. 'Starting on Friday.'

'That's easy enough, I was here,' Quintin said.

'Friday evening the family got together for a few drinks after the funeral,' Edris said. 'What time did you leave?'

'I didn't leave. I live here,' Quintin said.

'What time did you go into the house?'

'Sometime after nine.'

'With Kitty?' Meadows asked.

'Yes, we had a cup of tea and went to bed.'

Edris flicked through his notebook. 'Kitty said she went into the house with Lottie, then went to bed after she left. She was under the impression that you were still outside with the others at that time.'

'Oh yes, Friday night I slept in the cottage. I wasn't in the mood for Lottie.'

Meadows sat back in his chair, his hands resting on his knees as he watched the exchange with interest. He's lying, he thought. Why? Did he go and see Madog to make arrangements for Saturday morning?

'What about early Saturday morning?' Edris asked.

'I was here. I would have arrived about six-thirty.'

'Did you see anyone?'

'Luke was down on the floor.'

'Did you speak to him?'

'No. I was already in when he got here. I saw him through the window.'

'Did he see you?'

'The light was on so, yes, he would've known I was here.'

Not the same thing, Meadows thought.

'What about Saturday evening?' Edris asked.

'Dinner at home with the family at about seven. I had a lot to catch up on because of the time I had to take out for the funeral.'

Another inconsistency with the time, Meadows thought. Kitty said he got back at eight. A long day if he started at six-thirty.

'When you went fishing with Madog last Thursday he wanted to go out on the boat with Theo, but you took Theo out instead. What was the reason for that?' Meadows asked.

'I just wanted to spend some time with my nephew.'

Meadows nodded. 'What size boot do you wear?'

'Ten. Why?'

'OK, that's all, for now.' Meadows stood up. 'We'll see ourselves out.'

Outside they met up with Blackwell and Valentine. Meadows filled them in on the poisoned trout and break-in at the summer house.

Blackwell frowned. 'So, you think this is revenge for some angler being disqualified?'

'If it was just the fish, then yes it would fit,' Meadows said, 'but the murder of Madog Jones must be about more than that. We'll talk to the angler involved just to be sure.'

'You never know,' Edris said. 'These people take these competitions seriously. A ruined reputation may be enough to drive someone to murder. I heard of people getting killed for less.'

Blackwell laughed. 'A psychopathic fisherman on the loose. Yeah, I can see that.'

'You got a better theory?' Edris snapped.

'Let's just keep an open mind,' Meadows said. 'While we're here I want to talk to Lloyd Evans to check out his movements on Saturday. Quintin initially lied about going to bed with Kitty after the bonfire and is lying about the time he turned up for the family dinner on Saturday. According to Kitty, Lloyd was also late.'

'We've finished with the others. Sounds like Jac and Arwel had a fair amount to drink and slept it off on Saturday morning. But we only have their word for it,' Blackwell said.

'Celyn left the party before the others and was looking after her children Saturday morning,' Valentine added.

'We know Elsie was with Kitty on Saturday afternoon, but we don't know where she was in the morning,' Meadows said.

'Lottie wasn't around either,' Edris said.

'Did you check their boot sizes?' Meadows asked.

'Yeah,' Blackwell said. 'Jac is a size ten, and Arwel a nine.'

Valentine flipped open her notebook. 'Celyn is a size six, her husband an eleven.'

'One with the right size feet and the other could have put on a thick pair of socks. Celyn's husband could've squashed his feet in a size smaller. I don't think shoe size is of any use,' Blackwell said.

'No but it's still worth checking,' Meadows said. 'OK, we've got a list of everyone who works here.' He gave the sheet of paper to Blackwell. 'Let's find out who saw who, and what time. And mark anyone with size ten feet.'

Blackwell nodded. 'I could do with one of those quad bikes.' He pointed to one parked outside the dairy. 'Lot of ground to cover tracking them all down.'

'The exercise will do you good,' Edris said.

'Sod off,' Blackwell snapped.

'We get plenty of exercise,' Valentine said. 'I don't see you running around the farm. Probably worried you'll get pig shit on your nice shoes.'

Blackwell laughed.

'I've been walking around here all morning,' Edris said.

'OK let's make a start,' Meadows cut in. If this carries on I'll have to speak to them both, he thought.

They walked together to the first field where they found Lloyd and two younger men clearing out the pigsties. All three were dressed in matching green overalls and black wellington boots.

'We'll have a chat to the other two when you talk to Lloyd,' Blackwell said.

Meadows guessed Lloyd to be in his fifties. Solid build with thick, dark grey hair, he had light blue eyes and a friendly smile. He took off his gloves and poured himself a cup of tea from a flask.

'I'd offer you some tea if I had a spare cup,' Lloyd said.

'We're good, thanks,' Meadows said. 'We just need to ask you a couple of questions. It won't take long.'

'No worries. I'm happy to have a break. If I didn't have this lot to sort out I would give Kitty a hand. Bad business with the fish, it's going to give her a knock. She works hard. I expect Quintin is hiding out in the office and letting her get on with it.'

'You don't get on with Quintin?' Meadows asked.

Lloyd shrugged. 'He's family, so we put up with each other. He's not easy to get along with, likes to think he's above the rest of us. Not one to get his hands dirty. I don't know what he does in that office all day.'

'He doesn't get involved in the farm work?' Meadows asked.

'No, he just gives out orders.'

'So he's like the boss,' Edris said.

Lloyd laughed. 'He'd like to think that. Llew made both me and Quintin sort of joint managers. We have different ideas of what that means. I find you only get the best if you put in the work yourself. I wouldn't ask someone to do what I wouldn't do myself. You get more respect and more work done. Quintin has no interest in farming. He hasn't a clue. All he cares about is the bottom line, how much money he can make. Kitty could've done better. I think he married her because it was convenient.'

'What do you mean?' Meadows asked.

'I've worked here since I was fifteen. I grew up with Lottie and Kitty. We went to school together. Kitty was always, well you know, a little bit special.'

'Do you mean she has learning difficulties?' Edris asked.

'I wouldn't say that. She did struggle with school, not the brightest. She also had other problems; she was a tiny little thing and she was bullied relentlessly. I guess that's why she's timid. Don't get me wrong. I love her to bits, she has a big heart, like Madog. Do anything for you. She nursed her mother and took care of Madog. Made sure his clothes were washed and he had a cooked meal every day. She works hard and never complains. All she wanted to do was to stay on the farm, get married, and have a family of her own.'

'And why was that convenient for Quintin?' Edris asked.

'Quintin had nothing to do with Lottie and Kitty when they were young. He went to boarding school and came home for holidays. He never gave them the time of day. Walked past them without saying a word. Then Kitty and Lottie inherit money from their grandmother in Ireland. A considerable amount. Lottie bought our house and Kitty bought the cottage and renovated it as well as putting the money up for the lakes and the fishery. Quintin suddenly became interested in Kitty. Old man Hugo was all for it as he wanted some land. Next thing Quintin marries Kitty and quits his job in London, or so he says. He said he wanted to help build the business, make it a success and improve the farm finances.'

'Did he improve them?' Meadows asked.

'I suppose to start with, yeah. He turned a good profit with the fish and the farm. Then the profit became less, or so I heard from Lottie. I don't get to see the paperwork. Quintin files all the necessary tax forms now. Madog and Connie had their share, well, on paper. They drew down some of it but left the majority for the estate.'

'Do you think that Quintin is mishandling the money?' Meadows asked.

'I didn't say that,' Lloyd said. 'I'm not accusing him of anything. I'm just saying he's always talking about cutting costs. Buying cheaper food for the livestock, that sort of thing. The farm should be doing well. I'm not sure he's putting his best into it.'

'Did Madog talk to you about this?' Meadows asked.

'No, not really. He did mention looking at the accounts once or twice.'

'What about last Thursday when you went fishing? Did he bring up any concerns?'

'No, he was quiet. Then again fishing is not a noisy sport. He talked a bit about Llew and Connie, and that he was the last of the generation. He seemed sad, if anything.'

'What about the day of the funeral? Did you talk to him much?' Meadows asked.

'No, I was at the bonfire with the others. Madog went home early. I dropped Celyn home not long after that, then went home myself.'

'What about early Saturday morning and evening?' Edris asked. 'We're asking everyone for their movements that day.'

'Yeah, that's alright,' Lloyd said. 'Saturday morning was the same as any other morning. I was with the cows by five. I'm always here for the first batch.'

'Did you see or talk to anyone?' Edris asked.

'Luke gave me a hand then he went into the dairy.'

'Did you see Quintin at all that morning?' Meadows asked.

Lloyd laughed. 'Not at that time of the morning. You're lucky if you see him before ten.'

'What about the evening?' Edris asked.

'I was the last in the shed, cleaning. I went home for a couple of hours' kip as we had a family dinner that evening. Lottie and Arwel were out. I overslept so I was a bit late getting there. We left before ten and I came home and went straight to bed as I needed to be up by four.'

'It sounds like a hard job,' Edris said.

'Yeah, it can be and I'm not getting any younger.'

'Has there been any disputes with any of the farm workers recently?' Meadows asked.

'No, everyone gets on well. We have a laugh most of the time.'

'Kitty said there was some problems with the fishing competition this year. Were you involved?' Meadows asked.

'No, I'm too busy. I attended the closing ceremony on the Saturday. It all went smoothly.'

'Is there anything you can think of that was out of the ordinary in the last couple of weeks? Family arguments, livestock being left out, even local gossip. Any reason why Madog or this farm would be a target?'

Lloyd shook his head. 'No, honestly, there's nothing. No reason for what happened to Madog. He gave me my job here. I loved that man. In all the time I've lived and worked here I've never heard one person say a bad word about him. He was a quiet, gentle man.'

'One more thing, what size boots do you wear?' Meadows asked.

'Eleven, I like them a bit bigger than my shoes so I can wear thick socks.'

'We'll let you get back to your work now,' Meadows said. 'Thank you for your time.'

They gave Blackwell and Valentine a wave before heading back to the car.

'How does Lloyd or any of them stand the smell?' Edris asked.

'I suppose after a while you don't even notice it. Besides, all this fresh air every day, working outdoors. I can think of worse things.'

'I'm going to smell like pigs all day,' Edris said.

Meadows laughed. 'I guess farm life isn't for everyone.'

'Lloyd seems happy enough,' Edris said.

'Yes but he's got to be thinking of his future. If Jac was to inherit then he'd probably have to keep working. If Lottie takes a fifty percent share then he could step back and live off the profits. It's enough reason to keep the codicil from being read. That's if he knew what was in it.'

'Yeah, and he was quick enough to point us in Quintin's direction.'

'Both of them claim to be on the farm Saturday morning and evening but were only seen by one person,' Meadows said.

'Yeah, seen by the same person,' Edris said. 'Luke Henry is tight with Kitty. He'd probably lie for the family if asked.'

Meadows nodded. 'A lot of people work here. You'd think they would've run into someone else. Particularly Lloyd as he would've been moving cows around the farm. We'll see what Blackwell and Valentine's impression is of Luke when they talk to him. On the other hand there's a chance that this is nothing to do with money and all about the fishing contest. Let's go and talk to Rhodri Morgan.'

'With a bit of luck we'll get a confession, and the case will all be wrapped up by the weekend,' Edris said.

Meadows laughed. 'Yeah, I can see that happening.'

Chapter Twenty-one

Lloyd returned to the pigpen after Meadows and Edris left. The two men, James and Dan, who had been helping him were still talking to Blackwell and Valentine. He moved along the fence hoping to be able to hear what they were saying, but they were too far away. He didn't know why he felt nervous. He got on well with everyone that worked the farm. They wouldn't say anything bad about him, he was sure of that. It was the fact that one of them could've seen something. He moved away and started shovelling out the muck, letting his worries drift away. He wasn't the type to dwell.

'Are you OK, Lloyd?' James asked as he stepped back into the pigpen.

'Yeah, it's just all these questions about Madog. It still doesn't feel real.' Lloyd picked up the shovel and pushed it down hard into the muck.

'You should go home,' Dan said as he followed James into the pen. 'We can manage here, can't we?'

James nodded. 'Yeah, you shouldn't be working at a time like this.'

'We've all had a shock,' Lloyd said. 'But the farm won't run itself. Besides the work helps. I don't want to be sitting at home. Are you two OK?'

Dan nodded.

'Yeah, it's not going to be the same without him,' James said. 'Then Kitty's fish on top of it. As if she hasn't got enough to deal with. Who would do such a thing?'

'I don't know,' Lloyd said. His first thought had been Quintin. Then he realised that Quintin would lose money and he was too greedy for that. However, he was sure that Quintin was responsible in some way. 'Best thing we can do for Kitty and Lottie now is to keep things running smoothly.'

'That's something you don't see every day,' Dan said.

Lloyd turned to see what Dan was looking at. Quintin was striding towards them.

'The only time he comes out of his office is to have a go at someone,' Dan said.

'I better go and see what he wants,' Lloyd said.

'Rather you than me,' Dan said.

As Lloyd let himself out, Quintin stopped short of the pigpen. 'Can I have a word, Lloyd?'

Lloyd followed Quintin until they were a far enough distance not to be overheard by Dan and James.

'We've got a problem,' Quintin said.

'You think?' Lloyd said. 'Madog is dead and Kitty's fish have been poisoned. I don't think it can get much worse.'

'That's where you're wrong,' Quintin said. 'The police are all over the farm asking questions. On top of that a forensic team are looking at the fishery and summer house.'

'Well, they're not going to find anything there, are they?' Lloyd said.

'It means I won't be able to do it this afternoon. You'll have to.'

'No,' Lloyd said. 'It's your problem, you sort it out.'

'It's our problem,' Quintin hissed. 'It will look odd if I just take off now, and I've got other business to sort out this evening. What if the police are watching me?'

'Why would you think the police are watching you?' Lloyd asked.

'That's what they do. They'll be watching the whole family.'

Lloyd couldn't believe it. He knew Quintin was selfish, but this was taking it to the next level. 'So you expect me to take the risk.'

'No one will notice if you take off for a few hours. I'll cover for you.'

'Forget it,' Lloyd said. 'Do it yourself or get someone else. I kept to my side. I'll be on my own in the morning and up at stupid o'clock as it is.'

'There is no one else,' Quintin said. He ran his hand through his hair. 'Oh wait. I suppose I could get Luke to do it.'

'No, not Luke,' Lloyd said. 'You're not throwing him under the wheels.'

'You're not leaving me much choice,' Quintin said. 'It will be fine. Luke wanted to leave early to meet with Theo this evening. He'll come and ask you if it's OK. Tell him he can go straight home when he's finished. Luke will be happy with that. Problem solved.'

'If anything happens to Luke it will be on your head,' Lloyd said.

'If you want to swap places with him, be my guest,' Quintin said.

'I can't,' Lloyd said.

'Then I'll get him to do it.'

Lloyd felt disgusted with himself. He just hoped that Luke would be OK.

Chapter Twenty-two

It took hours to track down Rhodri Morgan who they finally located in hospital recovering from an operation.

'Is it even worth speaking to him?' Edris asked. 'It's not like he's had much of an opportunity to murder three people, have an operation and pop out to poison fish.'

'We're here now,' Meadows said. 'Let's at least talk to him and see how long he's been in. He may still have been up the Usk Reservoir last Saturday and the fish could be unrelated, or he could've got someone to kill the fish for him. It's also worth finding out if he did try to cheat or if he thinks someone was trying to sabotage the competition.'

'If it is him, it's enough to put anyone off fishing,' Edris said. 'Garrotted by fishing line, thrown in the reservoir, not to mention the flies. All for a competition.'

Meadows smiled. 'You haven't been fishing since you were a boy.'

'Well, I'm not about to start again.'

Meadows' phone pinged and he checked his messages. 'My brother has arrived.'

'Let's ditch this and you can go and spend time with him. I know you're dying to see him,' Edris said.

'This won't take long,' Meadows said. 'Besides it could be the catch of the day.'

Rhodri Morgan was sitting up in bed with a drip attached to one arm. Meadows introduced himself and Edris.

'Sorry to disturb you,' Meadows said, 'if you're feeling up to it we'd like to ask you a few questions.'

Rhodri smiled. 'Don't know what you'd want with me, but I'm bored stiff. Grab a chair.'

'Thank you,' Meadows said. 'We are investigating the murder of Madog Jones.'

'I heard about that on the news. It was a bloody shock, I can tell you.'

'We understand you knew him from the fishing contest held at Bryn Glas Farm,' Meadows said.

'The White Moth, yeah. I've been going to the competition for years. Great week and a hell of a party on the Saturday night.'

'This year was different though,' Meadows said.

'Yeah, some sneaky bastard put paste in my bag,' Rhodri said.

'Has that ever happened to you before?' Meadows asked.

'No, never.'

'You were angry with Madog?'

'Yeah but I did apologise afterwards. He had no choice but to turn me in. I did create a bit of a scene when I was disqualified. Both Kitty and Madog looked uncomfortable, but Quintin looked like he enjoyed himself. I didn't cheat if that's what you're thinking. I've won the cup before, four years ago. What would be the point of winning again with an unfair advantage? No pride in that, is there?'

'Do you have any idea who put it in your bag?'

'No, but a couple of anglers were staying in the pub with me. They have a B&B there. One of them was Scott Whittaker, the winner. I suppose he could've slipped it in my bag when I was having breakfast.'

'How long have you been in hospital?' Edris asked.

'Nearly a week. I came in last Thursday with a ruptured appendix. I had to have emergency surgery.'

Edris closed his notebook and looked at Meadows.

There isn't anything more to ask, Meadows thought. Clearly Rhodri had nothing to do with Madog's murder. 'I think that's it,' he said. 'Thanks for answering our questions. I hope you get well soon so you can go home.'

'Me too,' Rhodri said.

'I don't think you'll get a better alibi than that,' Edris said as they walked down the hospital corridor.

'No, and he's the only one that got disqualified,' Meadows said. 'I think it will be a waste of our time talking to the other anglers. I'll get uniform to talk to the ones that were there that day. Just to cover all bases.'

'Right, enough about work,' Edris said. 'Get home and see your brother.'

* * *

When Meadows arrived home the lights were on in the cottage and he could hear happy chatter from within. He felt a fizzle of excitement as he pushed open the door. Daisy was sitting on the sofa opposite his mum in the armchair, and on the floor, sitting cross-legged, was his brother.

'Winny, love, you're home,' Fern Meadows said.

Rain Meadows jumped to his feet and launched himself at Meadows almost knocking him off his feet as he wrapped his arms around him.

'It's so good to see you,' Rain said and planted a kiss on Meadows' cheek.

'You too,' Meadows said as he released his brother. He could feel himself tearing up. 'You look good.'

Rain had the same green eyes and dark curly hair as his brother except he wore his long and tied back. At six foot he was a couple of inches shorter than Meadows, and years spent working in Asia had given him a deep tan.

'It's so nice to have my boys together,' Fern said.

Meadows walked over to his mother, leaned down to kiss her before joining Daisy on the sofa.

'Sorry I'm late,' Meadows said.

'It's fine,' Rain said. 'The lovely Daisy has been keeping us entertained.' He gave her a wink. 'She did tell us that you're working on a difficult case.'

'Yeah but let's not talk about that now. I want to hear all about your travels,' Meadows said.

'I sent you emails when I could get to a café, and we've talked on the phone. I want to hear about what's going on with you.'

Meadows smiled. It was Rain's special quality. Listening to people, taking an interest in their lives. He had a way of making you feel special and cared for.

'You first,' Meadows said. 'I need the distraction.'

'Yeah, we want to hear all the gossip,' Fern said. 'We haven't heard you mention anyone special since Dave. It'd be nice for you to have someone to share your adventures with.'

'There's been a few guys but no one I want to settle down with. I'm happy as I am. I've met some wonderful people,' Rain said. 'You'd be amazed by the love and generosity of those who have nothing but a one-room tin shack to share with five or six others. We've manged to build a community centre with a school. As well as lessons for the kids, we teach adults basic skills to make a decent living. The project has made a real difference.'

'I'm so proud of the work you do,' Meadows said.

'As I am of you, brother,' Rain said. 'Now let's eat and talk about your case. I bet Daisy knows everything and you know it won't go further than this room.'

They talked until late, and Fern grew tired. Daisy drove Fern home while Meadows and Rain cleared away the dishes.

'I'm sorry you arrived in the middle of a case,' Meadows said as he hung up the tea towel. 'I was hoping to take a couple of days off to spend some time with you.'

'You worry too much,' Rain said. 'I'm going to be around for a while. I thought I'd go home for a few days, take Mum with me.'

Meadows knew that home meant the commune. 'She'll like that.'

'Come and join us when you're free and bring Daisy with you.'

'Maybe.'

'Don't tell me you haven't taken her.'

'No, not yet,' Meadows said.

'Don't be ashamed of where you come from,' Rain said. 'It's what makes you who you are.'

'I'm not ashamed. She knows my background. It's just, well I'm not sure she'll like it there.'

'I think you'll be surprised. Besides, if me and Mum are there as well it will be easier for her. You know we'll look after her and everyone will welcome her.'

'Yeah, I know. I'll ask her.'

Daisy came back and hung up her coat. 'I'm off to bed.'

'Me too,' Rain said. 'I take it I'm in my old room.'

'I kept it just the same for you,' Meadows said. He gave his brother a hug then made his way upstairs with Daisy.

For a few hours he had put the case to the back of his mind. Now as he lay in bed he thought of the killer. If this was about money then he had a feeling it was far from over. Madog had been fond of Kitty, if anyone was to inherit the farm it would be her, he thought. He just hoped she took his advice and locked her door.

Chapter Twenty-three

When Meadows walked into the office the next morning all the team were sat at their desks.

'Sorry I'm late,' he said as he shrugged off his coat.

'You're not late,' Edris said. 'How did the evening go with your brother?'

'Fantastic, thanks.'

'You should have taken the day off,' Blackwell said. 'We could have managed.'

'Not too late,' Valentine said. 'Put your coat back on, we'll pretend we never saw you.'

Meadows laughed. 'It's very tempting but now is not a good time. It's five days since Madog and the Wilsons were murdered and so far we don't have a suspect. We need to put our heads together and solve this case before someone else dies.'

He stepped up to the board and filled the team in on the hospital visit.

'I agree,' Blackwell said. 'It doesn't sound like this has anything to do with the competition. We're getting sidetracked with fishing because of the flies and fishing line.'

'Yeah, but our killer has to be an angler,' Edris said.

'Not necessarily,' Valentine said. 'She or he could've nicked that stuff from the summer house. The flies may not have any meaning at all.'

'They meant something to Kitty,' Edris said.

'This whole thing could've started back in May,' Paskin said. 'If someone is trying to drive Kitty away from the farm it would be a good place to start. Upset enough anglers and it could put a stop to the competition and the income it generates. If anglers thought they were going to be framed for cheating then they wouldn't take part. Word gets around.'

'Good point,' Meadows said. 'Blackwell, Valentine, did you learn anything of interest from the farm workers?'

'Not a lot,' Valentine said. 'No one saw Madog early on the Saturday morning or anyone who shouldn't have been there. One of them' – she checked a notebook – 'James Hopkins, saw Kitty; she'd been sorting out the chickens.'

'We asked about the family,' Blackwell said. 'Madog was well liked, as is Kitty. Quintin is a different matter. The general opinion is that he spends his time twatting around the farm and barking orders. Not my words. Lloyd is one of them. Works hard but rumour is that he's had enough and is looking to get out and retire early.'

'Interesting,' Meadows said. 'Both Lloyd and Quintin only have one witness to corroborate their alibis during the time of the murder, Luke Henry. Did you talk to him?'

'No but it wasn't through lack of trying,' Blackwell said. 'He was all over the farm. By the time we got to one place he had moved to another. Then he went out delivering cheese. We have arranged to speak with him this morning. Lloyd said he would get Luke to meet us at the dairy.'

'Good,' Meadows said. 'He's close to the family, and he may have been asked to cover for one of them.'

'Yeah, don't worry,' Blackwell said. 'I'm sure I can get the size of him.'

Meadows nodded. 'Paskin, how did you get on?'

'I spoke to the family solicitor, Mr Howells. He wasn't prepared to give any details on Llew or Connie's will as we expected. He did say that Madog didn't leave instructions with him. Only that when the time came Kitty would know where to find his will.'

'She didn't tell us that,' Edris said. 'She said they were waiting for the family solicitor.'

'Maybe she doesn't know where it is, or she does and has destroyed it if it isn't in her favour,' Valentine said.

'She may have it and is waiting for the family solicitor to visit so he can read it to the family,' Meadows said. 'Anything else?'

'Madog's phone records,' Paskin said. 'Not a lot of calls. He made one to Theo on Monday, 13th of September. It lasted just over twenty minutes. A few to Kitty's landline. There were quite a few calls received from Pippa's mobile phone. Some lasting a few minutes, others less. She could've been leaving messages. I'm waiting on transcripts of any messages left.'

'We need to look at the family members in detail,' Meadows said. 'Financial records, full background check, social media, even gossip. Anything you can find. This must be about money. It started after Connie Jones' death when Llew Jones' codicil would take effect. The family claim they don't know who the beneficiary is from that codicil; on top of that there is now Madog's share. He owned the land so with Connie and Madog out of the picture someone stands to gain a lot or lose a lot if the codicil is found.'

'That means that someone knew what was in the codicil and Madog's will,' Blackwell said. 'The closest to Madog is Kitty.'

'Yes,' Meadows agreed. 'But it appears that it is Kitty who is being targeted. Why? We know the white moth found with Madog had a special meaning to her, probably more than she is saying. Madog told her when he gave her the white moth that it was a gift, and she shouldn't give it

173

away. Was he preparing her for taking over the farm? If so, is someone trying to drive her away?'

'The flies found with the Wilsons were ones used in the fishing contest,' Edris said. 'Then there's the poisoning of the fish, the only one to suffer is Kitty. It does look like this is all about her.'

'And Quintin,' Blackwell said. 'The loss of the income from the fish and potentially the competition will affect him. I can't see he would be responsible for that – he strikes me as being too selfish.'

'Unless he thought he had more to gain,' Meadows said. 'If Kitty inherits and he gets her to give up the farm then the land could be used for access to the housing estate he wanted to build. He would be the main winner from that.'

'If that's his intention then what about Lottie and Lloyd?' Edris asked. 'They would lose out. The farm isn't supposed to be under the control of one person.'

'No, but if Madog left the land to Kitty, and Connie's fifty percent is split between Lottie and Kitty, Kitty would hold the majority interest,' Meadows said.

'In which case Lottie wouldn't want Kitty to get control of the farm as Quintin controls Kitty, or that's how it seems,' Edris said.

'And if Jac inherits, Quintin loses an opportunity,' Blackwell said.

'If Jac inherits and Lottie gets her share, that would give them the majority interest,' Paskin said.

'They all have motive,' Valentine said.

'Anything back from forensics?' Meadows asked.

'Plenty of prints on the boat,' Paskin said. 'Four of them were out on the boat last Thursday so it doesn't help.'

'Jac wasn't out with them,' Edris said.

'Yes but he's family, he would have reason for his prints being on the boat if they were found,' Valentine said.

'The blood was fish blood. Skin cells found match Madog's, which was expected given the scrapes on his arms,' Paskin said. 'Nothing more of interest from the Wilsons' crime scene. Mike sent details of the footprints found. Nothing remarkable about the make of boot that matches the print. You can buy a pair in any shoe shop or online. The only good thing is we can match the tread to the suspect's boots.'

'If we had a suspect,' Blackwell said.

'Mike's theory is that the Wilsons were rolled part of the way into the trees before being dragged,' Paskin said.

'Which means that the killer didn't have the strength to drag them all the way in. Could be a man or a woman,' Valentine said.

'Probably the former,' Edris said, 'given the size of the footwear, and I can't see a woman dragging two dead bodies and moving a boat.'

'Well that's just sexist,' Valentine said.

'No, I'm just stating a fact.'

'Do you want to test that? I bet I could match you pulling a weight,' Valentine said.

Paskin shook her head and raised her voice. 'Waiting on results from the fishery and they are processing the summer house this morning.'

'Thank you,' Meadows said. 'Another point of interest is Theo's father, or rather the absence of a father. We need to—'

Meadows was cut off by the trilling of a phone. Edris picked it up and they all listened. The look on Edris' face put Meadows on edge.

'On our way.' Edris ended the call. 'A body has been found in the dairy of Bryn Glas Farm.'

* * *

Tension knotted Meadows' stomach as he drove to Bryn Glas Farm. They hadn't been given any more information so all they could do was wait until they got there to see what they were dealing with.

'It must be bad if Hanes couldn't tell us if the body was male or female,' Edris said.

'That's what worries me. It could be any one of the family. There's been enough police presence on the farm; the killer is taking a big risk. Either they are extremely clever, or they don't care if they get caught. It can only escalate from here.'

When Meadows pulled the car up outside the dairy he was relieved to see Kitty. She was standing next to Quintin who was talking to Hanes. Quintin was clearly agitated. They could hear his raised voice before they got out of the car.

'Shall we calm things down?' Meadows said as he approached.

Quintin turned to face Meadows. 'I just want to go back into the office and get my computer.'

'Quintin, someone has died in there. How can you be thinking of work now?' Kitty said.

Meadows saw a flash of anger in Kitty's eyes. He guessed there was only so far you could push a person before they reach their limit.

'Why don't you and Kitty go back home,' Meadows suggested.

Quintin huffed. 'Fine.' He stomped off leaving Kitty.

'Can I stay?' Kitty asked. 'I want to know who it is. I can't bear it.'

'It's better you wait at home. As soon as we know anything I'll come and talk to you.'

Kitty nodded and as she walked away, Blackwell and Valentine arrived.

'OK, what have you got for us?' Meadows asked Hanes.

'The body was discovered by Betsan Rees and Lauren Ellis. They both work in the cheese processing side of the dairy. Betsan said there was a strange smell when they arrived, so they opened the windows. The vat was on, so she opened it to check and that's when she saw the body. Her screams brought Quintin down from the office and he called it in. He was with the two women when I arrived.'

'Do any of them have an idea who it is?'

'No. Lloyd showed up and rang the rest of the family so it's not one of them. He's gone to check on all the workers. He didn't want to phone around in case he started a panic. I thought it was OK to let him get on with it.'

'That's fine,' Meadows said.

'SOCO were already here processing the summer house, so they were quick to make a start. No one else has been in. I had to stop Quintin going back to the office. He wasn't too happy about it, as you saw. That one is a bit of a dick,' Hanes said. 'Makes you wonder what he's hiding in the office.'

'Might be worth looking,' Blackwell said. 'How about me and Valentine go up? Just to check no one's hiding.'

Meadows smiled. 'I think that's reasonable cause to go in there. You should be able to get up there without disturbing the crime scene. Best put on a suit first.' He turned to Edris. 'Let's take a look.'

Once they were dressed in protective clothing with their masks fixed in place, Meadows and Edris stepped inside the dairy. Mike was standing by one of the vats with two other forensic officers.

'I think you better rent me a cottage here,' Mike said. 'We haven't processed the summer house yet. The fishery was a nightmare, plenty of footfall. All I can tell you is that a large amount of chlorine was dumped in the water, if that helps.'

'Not really,' Meadows said. 'This scene is going to have to take priority now, but I think you'll find they are all linked. I take it the body is still in there.' He nodded towards the vat.

'Yeah, come and look,' Mike said.

Meadows stepped along the metal plates that had been laid out and peered inside the vat. The body was squashed inside, face down and bent at the back. One turning blade was against the head, another pressing on the victim's back. The vat was filled with a thick, creamy yellow liquid which was streaked with blood around the victim's head. The smell from the cheese and an overheated dead body, together with the blood, turned Meadows' stomach.

'I don't think I'll be eating cheese for a long time,' Edris said.

'I think I'm with you there,' Meadows said.

Mike laughed. 'I thought you two were tougher than that. Still, I suppose it's like finding a fly in your soup.'

Meadows stepped back from the vat. 'Can't have been easy getting the body in there, and it would've been messy.'

'I think someone has cleaned up by the look of it,' Mike said. 'As for moving the body, I noticed a forklift outside. Probably used to move the pallets.'

'I reckon that would do it,' Meadows said.

'I'll get it tested. We're just waiting for the vat to cool down then we'll get the body out.'

'There's not much to see until that happens,' Meadows said. 'We'll come back.'

They stepped outside and Meadows removed his mask and drew in a lungful of fresh air. The noise of an engine made him turn around. Lloyd pulled up on a quad bike and turned off the engine.

'I've been all over the farm,' Lloyd said. 'Checked who was in. The only one I can't find is Luke. Has anyone seen him?'

'Have you got his phone number?' Meadows asked.

'Yes.'

'OK, can you call it for me please.'

Lloyd took his phone from his pocket and called up Luke's number. When he hit call, a ringtone could be heard coming from the dairy. Meadows stepped over to the door.

'Can you see where that phone is please, Mike?' Meadows asked. He waited as Mike looked around the dairy.

'Ah, it's here. Coming from a coat pocket,' Mike said.

'Can you pass it out and the coat please?' Meadows asked.

'That's Luke's coat,' Lloyd said from behind the cordon.

The phone in Meadows' hand had stopped ringing and the screen displayed three missed calls. One from Lloyd and the other two from Theo.

'Oh, God, you don't think it's Luke in there, do you?' Lloyd asked.

'It looks as though it may be,' Meadows said. 'We are going to need someone to identify the body and I don't want to contact Luke's family until we're sure. Would you be willing to do that?'

The colour had drained from Lloyd's face. He stepped back and rubbed his hand over his chin.

'Don't worry if you can't,' Meadows said. 'It can be quite traumatic.'

'No, it's fine. I'll do it. If it is him, I don't want his parents to have to come and do it.'

'Thank you. If you want to go and get yourself a cup of tea, that's fine. It will be a little while.'

'Yeah, I think I'll do that,' Lloyd said.

'We're going to go and see Kitty, but Sergeant Blackwell will be here when you get back.'

Meadows took off his protective clothing and got into the car.

'If that is Luke Henry then it's quite a coincidence that he was killed before talking to Blackwell,' Edris said as he clipped in his seat belt.

'The thought hadn't escaped me,' Meadows said. 'He was the only one who could confirm that Quintin and Lloyd were on the farm at the times they said they were. Then again there could be a different reason he was killed.'

'Like he saw someone else with Madog on the Saturday morning? He would've said something to the family. He was out looking for Madog. We should just arrest Quintin and Lloyd before anyone else gets hurt.'

'Both of them?' Meadows asked.

'It has to be one of them,' Edris said.

'We have nothing on either of them. No forensics that could tie them to the Wilsons' murder. Both were on the boat with Madog on Thursday so their prints can be explained if they are found. We need to find something on one of them.'

'Maybe Blackwell will turn something up in the search of Quintin's office.'

'We can't use anything he finds. He's just checking no one was hiding up there, remember?' Meadows smiled.

'Well it will be a start.'

As soon as Meadows stopped the car, the door to the farmhouse opened and Kitty came out.

'We still don't know anything for certain,' Meadows said as he approached her. 'Let's go back inside.'

'I've just made a pot of tea,' Kitty said. 'Would you like one?'

'That'll be great, thanks,' Edris said.

They sat around the pine table as Kitty made the tea. Quintin sat with a stony expression.

When Kitty handed Meadows a mug of tea, he took a sip before placing it on the table.

'Lloyd has checked all the farm employees,' he said. 'Everyone has been accounted for except Luke.'

'Not Luke,' Kitty said bringing her hand up to her chest.

'We don't know for certain but Lloyd has agreed to stay at the dairy to assist us with the identification.'

'I could've done that,' Quintin said.

'Why don't you sit down, Kitty?' Meadows said. He could see she was struggling.

'I feel like I should be doing something,' she said.

'There's nothing you can do,' Quintin said. He rubbed his hand over his head. 'Just sit down, you're driving me mad with your flitting around.'

Kitty took a seat at the opposite side of the table to Quintin.

'When was the last time either of you saw Luke?' Meadows asked.

'He helped me yesterday,' Kitty said. 'Once he had disposed of the fish, we cleared out one of the troughs. We scrubbed it down and flushed it with water. Then he had to catch up with some work. He said he had to be at the dairy this morning then he was coming back to help me with the other troughs.'

'Did he talk to you about what happened to the fish or about Madog?'

'He was angry about the fish.'

'Did he say who he thought was responsible?' Meadows asked.

'If he'd said something we would've told you,' Quintin said.

Meadows ignored the comment. 'Kitty?'

'No,' she said. 'He just said that he hoped whoever did it would be caught soon. He offered to camp out at the dairy to keep an eye on things, just in case someone went after the other animals.'

Maybe he disturbed someone, Meadows thought. 'Do you think he slept in the dairy last night?'

'No, I told him we were getting security cameras and locks fitted so he didn't have to worry.'

'When was this decided?' Quintin asked.

'I haven't had a chance to discuss it with you. Lottie and me talked about it yesterday. I was going to speak to you last night but—'

'Fine,' Quintin said. 'But these things cost money.'

'I think extra security would be wise now,' Meadows said.

'Do you think you will be able to give us some protection?' Kitty asked. 'Maybe a policeman could watch over the farm at night.'

'Do you think they're going to post an officer here, at Lottie's, and Celyn's house. What about Jac and Elsie? The rest of the farm workers? Oh and Pippa.'

'It was just a thought,' Kitty said.

'I think it would be difficult to cover everyone,' Meadows said. 'Given the farm seems to be the main target I can look into having an officer keep watch at night.'

'We'll do with the cameras,' Quintin said. 'I don't feel comfortable having our every move watched. I prefer to have privacy in my own home. I tell you what would be more helpful. You catching the person doing this instead of sitting around drinking tea.'

'Quintin, they're trying to help,' Kitty said.

'We do need to ask questions,' Edris said.

Meadows looked at Kitty who appeared uncomfortable. 'Were you near the dairy early this morning?' Meadows asked.

'Yes, I always walk past that way on the way to the coops.'

'Did you see anyone?'

'Lloyd and then James, they were switching the cows.'

'What about you, Quintin? When was the last time you saw Luke?' Edris asked.

'At the dairy yesterday. He went out on a delivery. He had plans to go out in the evening, so I didn't see him after that.'

'What time did you leave the dairy?' Edris asked.

Quintin didn't answer immediately, and Meadows wondered if it was because he was trying to work out a time that would leave him in the clear.

'It was before six. I went up to see my mother and Pippa. We ended up having a few drinks, so I got home late.'

'What time did you get to the dairy this morning?'

'I was late in this morning; it was nearly nine. Bit hungover,' Quintin said.

'Did you notice anything unusual when you arrived at the dairy?' Meadows asked.

'No, other than there was an odd smell. The window had been opened. I went straight up to the office. I was working when I heard the screams from the floor. I looked in the vat then got the women out and called you lot. How long is this going to take? I've a lot of work to do today.'

'You won't be able to go back into the dairy until forensics have finished. We can't risk contaminating the area. It won't be today,' Meadows said.

'The office is above the processing room. The staircase is panelled. It's separate,' Quintin said. 'I've already been there this morning so what difference will it make?'

'I'm afraid it doesn't work that way,' Meadows said.

'This is ridiculous. How am I supposed to work? We've already lost the fish, now the processing floor is out of action. It's going to have to be professionally cleaned. How much more are we going to lose?'

'Quintin! That's Luke up there,' Kitty said. 'What we lose is nothing compared to what his family have lost.'

'We're doing everything we can,' Meadows said. 'The more information you can give us, the better the chance we have of finding the person responsible.'

'We've told you everything,' Kitty said. 'I still can't think of anyone that would be doing this.'

Meadows nodded. 'We have to look at everyone and that includes family and those close to you. We spoke to your family solicitor this morning. While we don't know the terms of your late father's codicil, it's important that we establish the beneficiaries of Madog's will. The solicitor informed us that although he doesn't possess a copy of Madog's will, Madog told him that you, Kitty, would know where it is. We need to examine the document to see if it has any bearing on the case.'

'But I don't know where Uncle Madog's will is,' Kitty said.

Quintin looked at Kitty. 'If he told Howells then he must have told you. Think!'

'He didn't tell me. Maybe he meant to and forgot. He probably thought he had more time. I don't know where it is.'

'You're bloody useless, just like Madog. If he couldn't be bothered to sort it out then he could've asked me to do it for him. You should've made sure it was dealt with. Especially after your mother got sick. You know what is at stake.' Quintin stood up. 'I'm going for a walk. I can't deal with this now.' He left the kitchen slamming the door behind him.

'I'm sorry,' Kitty said. 'He has a short fuse.'

'There's no need for you to apologise. We understand how difficult the situation is. I'm guessing Quintin has quite a temper when things are not going well.'

Kitty nodded.

'Did he ever lose his temper with Madog?' Meadows asked.

'He loses his temper with everyone. He doesn't mean anything by it. He thought Uncle Madog was getting too old to have any say in the running of the farm. That he didn't understand that the farm needed modernizing. Quintin installed the new vats as he wanted to increase the production of cheese and yogurt. He set up a website and wanted more things automated. Uncle Madog didn't care much for technology, so he dug his heels in. He thought the large vat was a waste of money as we weren't supplying that much cheese. Quintin said it would save time and money and Uncle Madog said it would take people's jobs. He didn't want to splash out on newer expensive equipment.'

'Was this a recent thing?' Meadows asked.

'No, they've been disagreeing for years. Quintin was always on at him. Uncle Madog said he switched off.' Kitty smiled. 'Uncle Madog used to tell me that Quintin had been to see him, and he wasn't interested in his blah-blah.'

'I expect that made Quintin angry,' Meadows said.

'Quintin would never hurt Uncle Madog if that's what you're thinking,' Kitty said.

Meadows caught a flick of doubt in her eyes. 'When we talked about the white moth, I got the feeling that there was more to it than you told me.'

'There is nothing more to tell really,' Kitty said. 'It was just Uncle Madog's way of making me feel better. I told him I gave it to Lottie because she was pretty. I think that's what made him cross. I was bullied at school mostly because I didn't grow like the other kids. My spine was crooked, so I was hunched over. I had to have a lot of operations to straighten me out. You know how cruel children can be. Uncle Madog said that the white moth was small and beautiful, and I was his little white moth. He told me that kids had bullied him for being too tall. We laughed because he wanted to be smaller, and I wanted to be taller. I told him that he was a white moth too. Just a longer one. It became a thing between us. That's all, it's just a bit of nonsense.'

'Is that why you named the competition and the fishery, The White Moth?'

'Yes, it was something we shared. The white moth was Uncle Madog's and my thing.' She touched her necklace. 'It makes me think of love and security. I guess that's why I like it here so much. It's away from people and judgement. Now it no longer feels safe.'

'It will again,' Meadows said. 'But for now you need to stay safe and lock your door. Don't trust anyone.'

Kitty nodded.

A thought occurred to Meadows. 'Was there ever anyone special in Madog's life?'

'No. Well, not that I can remember. I'm sure he must've had the odd girlfriend when he was younger. His cottage is out of sight so I guess he could've had a fling and none of us would have noticed.'

'OK, well if anyone comes to mind let us know.' Meadows stood. 'We'll keep you informed of any development.'

As they drove back to the dairy Meadows turned over the events of the past week. There was something that didn't make sense.

'You're quiet,' Edris said. 'What's on your mind?'

'Too much,' Meadows said. 'I think it's likely that Madog would leave his share to Kitty. If that's the case then I'm guessing that he discussed it with Llew before he died. Llew would then have passed his share to Lottie, so it was equal.'

'Right,' Edris said.

'Well both families would be in favour of the codicil being read. They would have no reason to harm Madog. Unless—'

'There is someone else in the running,' Edris said. 'Madog was single so it's not impossible that he has a child somewhere.'

'So we are looking for another stickman, as Quintin called him,' Edris said.

'Not necessarily. Daisy said there's only a fifty percent chance of getting Marfan syndrome. So a child of Madog's wouldn't necessarily have the same physical characteristics as him and Llew.'

'Theo doesn't have a father and, according to Kitty, Madog took an interest in him when he was a child.'

'The thought had crossed my mind. Pippa would want Theo to inherit if that was the case,' Meadows said.

'Yeah, and so would Quintin. He could get his hands on the land. Maybe we should get them all in and interview them formally.'

'We don't have any evidence. It doesn't sound like Theo knew his father. If it is Madog then chances are Pippa didn't tell anyone.'

'Apart from her father who apparently paid off baby daddy.'

'We need to talk to Pippa again but for now let's see what's happening at the dairy.'

* * *

Blackwell and Valentine were waiting for them at the dairy.

'They got him out,' Blackwell said. 'Bit of a mess but Lloyd seemed certain it's Luke Henry. That and the fact his coat and phone were left there, and nobody's seen him since yesterday.'

'I've taken a statement from Lloyd,' Valentine said. 'We told him to go home but he said he would rather keep working. I did ask him not to talk to anyone about Luke or what he had seen as his family needs to be informed first.'

'Anything interesting in the office?' Meadows asked.

'We had a good look around. Some of the drawers were locked. Lots of paperwork. He should really be more careful. There was a small notebook with passwords. Anyone could see it,' Blackwell said.

'I may have accidently bumped into the computer,' Valentine said.

Blackwell grinned. 'Yeah, we had to check that it wasn't damaged.'

'The loan application he was working on just popped up,' Valentine said.

'All the other files – more loans, mortgages – were undamaged,' Blackwell added.

Meadows smiled. 'I'll leave that information with you. See what you can dig up.' He turned to Edris. 'We better go and see Luke's family. In a community like this gossip will spread fast. I don't want them hearing it from someone else.'

Chapter Twenty-four

Paula Henry sat next to her husband, Greg, on the sofa. Both looked at Meadows with uncomprehending expressions. When Meadows and Edris had arrived to break the news Paula was on her own, so they had sent uniform to collect Greg from work. She'd paced around phoning Luke's number and leaving messages convinced that it wasn't true. Once Greg had arrived she had clung to him, and they both sobbed. Only now that they had regained some composure did Meadows feel able to ask questions. It was Paula who spoke first.

'Was it an accident at the farm?'

'We don't know the full circumstances yet, but I have to tell you that we will be treating his death as suspicious,' Meadows said.

'No one would want to hurt Luke,' Greg said. 'Are you sure it's him?'

'A formal identification will need to be made by a family member but Lloyd Evans confirmed it was Luke. I'm very sorry.'

Greg put his arm around his wife and pulled her close.

Edris took out his notebook and pen. 'When was the last time you saw Luke?'

'Yesterday evening. We all had dinner together. Usually he's tired and goes to bed not long after, but he showered and changed. He said Quintin had called and he was going up the dairy to set the machines and lock up, then he was going for a couple of pints with Theo,' Greg said. 'He seemed happy that they were friendly again.'

'Had they had an argument?' Meadows asked.

'Not recently. They grew up together and were good friends until they had a falling out,' Paula said.

'Do you know what about?'

'A girl. Theo was going out with Celyn. I'm guessing that Luke liked her. There was some accusation of Luke seeing Celyn behind Theo's back. They had a fight.'

'A physical fight?' Meadows asked.

'Theo hit Luke and Luke hit him back. There was a black eye and bloody nose but nothing more serious than that. Luke was afraid that he would lose his job at the farm, given that Theo is family. But it was OK, he kept his job.'

'When was this?'

'About six years ago. Wasn't it?' Greg looked at his wife.

'No, it was longer than that because just after that Madog bought Luke a car for his twenty-first birthday.'

'A car? That was very generous of Madog,' Meadows said.

'He was like that,' Greg said. 'Luke would never have been able to afford a new car and the insurance. We thought it was a big gift at the time, but Madog said Luke was a good worker and it was a bonus. We thought maybe Madog was worried that Luke would leave after the fight with Theo. Theo did hit Luke first and he could have made a scene, but he didn't.'

'And then Theo and Luke made up?' Edris asked.

'No, not until recently. They hadn't spoken for years, and Theo moved away. Then he came back for Connie's funeral, and they started to talk again. Luke was happy that Theo had asked him out for a drink.'

'What time did Luke get back last night?' Edris asked.

'I don't know. It must have been late because we were in bed,' Paula said.

'What about this morning?'

'He's up early, before both of us,' Greg said, 'so we wouldn't have seen him.'

'Is it possible that he didn't come home last night?' Edris asked. 'Would you mind if we checked his room? See if his bed was slept in.'

'It would make no difference. He never made his bed.' Paula choked back a sob.

'Have you noticed anything different in Luke's behaviour over the past week?' Meadows asked.

'No,' Paula said. 'He was upset when he found out about Madog. He was very fond of him.'

'I know it's usual for families to discuss local news. Did Luke talk about what happened to Madog? Mention any theories he had about who was responsible?' Meadows asked.

'No.' Paula shook her head. 'He said he couldn't imagine anyone hurting Madog or the family.'

'Did he tell you what happened at the farm yesterday?'

'The fish?' Greg asked. 'He did tell us, and he said he thought it was disgusting that someone would do that to Kitty after what happened to Madog.'

'So, he thought that Kitty was being targeted?' Meadows asked.

'Yes. Well, she runs the trout farm. He was worried about her.'

'Was there anything else he mentioned? Anything he thought was out of the ordinary?'

'No, nothing,' Greg said.

'OK, a family liaison officer will be here shortly. They will be able to answer any questions you have and will talk you through what happens next. I'm so very sorry for your loss,' Meadows said as he stood up. 'We'll see ourselves out.'

* * *

'Odd, don't you think, that Madog bought Luke a car,' Edris said when they were back in their vehicle.

'Yeah, my thoughts exactly.' Meadows started the engine. 'It's the type of gift given by a parent. I'll give Daisy a call and ask her to check if Luke's DNA is a match to Madog. I don't want to have to ask Luke's mother. She would probably deny it anyway. Let's go and see Theo and Pippa. I want to know if he met up with Luke last night and if so why did Luke go back to the dairy?'

'If Luke was Madog's son, why keep it a secret?' Edris asked when Meadows had finished the call to Daisy.

'Because Paula was married. But he would've told someone. I'm thinking his brother, Llew. If Madog was going to leave the land to Luke then Llew would make sure that his share went to one person so they would have equal control.'

'Kitty?' Edris asked.

'Possibly, as the oldest. The family wouldn't want an outsider to inherit, so they silence Madog and kill Luke, so he has no claim,' Meadows said.

'Then why put it in a codicil? Why not just say it in the will?'

'I don't know. Maybe because as long as Connie was alive nothing would change.'

'But the truth would've had to have come out at some time.'

'Yeah, I guess it doesn't make a lot of sense. Maybe we are reading too much into the car and there was another reason Madog gave the gift to Luke. Then there's Theo. Kitty said Madog took an interest in him. No father involved and Pippa pestering Madog with phone calls before he died.'

'Kitty said that Hugo paid off the father. Madog would've been a lot older than Pippa and she would likely have been embarrassed, so she gets her father to pay him off. He has to just be a sort of uncle to Theo.'

'It's a good theory but I can't see Madog taking money,' Meadows said. 'Besides, Pippa would want Theo to inherit so she would've been shouting about it by now. There is only one thing for it, we'll have to ask her outright and see what reaction we get.'

It was Theo that answered the door. Dressed in grey joggers and a black sweatshirt.

'Mum's not in,' Theo said. 'She's gone out to do some shopping. She mentioned something about Cardiff.'

'With Quintin?'

Theo looked puzzled. 'No, I don't think Uncle Quintin is into shopping.'

'Her car is parked outside,' Meadows said.

'Oh, yeah. No, a friend picked her up. Uncle Quintin called around earlier, but she had already left.'

That confirmed Meadows' suspicions that Quintin would run straight to Pippa for an alibi.

'Actually, we wanted to have a chat to you as well,' Meadows said.

'OK, come in.'

As Meadows followed he noticed that Theo was having trouble walking.

'Your back is bad today?'

'Yeah,' Theo said. 'I'm trying to cut back on painkillers. Exercise more, but I'm struggling.'

'How did you hurt your back?' Edris asked.

'On a building site. We were putting in a metal girder and it slipped on the pulley. I put up my hands to stop it coming down on me. Not the brightest idea. Still, it could've been worse. I spent a couple of weeks in hospital in traction. Now it's just a matter of time to heal.'

'Do you mind if Sergeant Edris has a chat with your grandmother while we have a talk?' Meadows asked.

'No, I'll take you in.'

Theo led them to the sitting room where a woman with grey hair twisted into a bun was sitting in an armchair. She wore a navy dress with a flowered scarf draped over her shoulder.

'Grandma, the police want to have a talk to you,' Theo said.

Eleanor looked them up and down. 'Well take a seat.'

'We'll go into the kitchen,' Theo said.

Meadows followed Theo into the spacious room and waited for him to lower himself into a chair.

'I expect you've heard by now about Luke Henry,' Meadows said as he took a seat.

'Luke, no, what's happened?'

'Did Quintin not say anything?'

'No.'

'Luke Henry was found dead this morning in the dairy.'

'Luke, dead? I only saw him yesterday.' Theo shook his head. 'I can't believe this. He's the same age as me. What happened?'

Meadows thought that Theo looked genuinely shocked. 'All I can tell you is that we are treating his death as suspicious. It would help if you can tell me about when you saw him yesterday.'

'I went up to the dairy. We had a chat and I asked him if he wanted to go for a couple of pints after work in the Trout. He didn't show up.'

'What time were you supposed to meet him?' Meadows asked.

'We agreed between half seven and eight. He didn't want a late night as he had to be up early for work.'

'Did you go up to the dairy when he didn't show?'

'No, I assumed he had gone home and had a nap before coming out and hadn't woken up. I called him a couple of times. I stayed for a few pints then came home.'

'I heard you used to be good friends with Luke,' Meadows said.

'Yes, we've known each other since we were children.'

'But you had a falling out.'

'Yes, I didn't want to bring it up. It's not fair when he's not here to tell his side of things. Anyway it was years ago.'

'I'd like you to tell me about it if you wouldn't mind,' Meadows said.

'I was seeing Celyn for a while. I suppose you'd call it first love. You know, when you think you know everything, and you are planning a future together.'

'It sounds like it was serious.'

'It was at the time. Then Celyn went with Luke behind my back.'

'How did you find out?'

'My mother saw them together. She was out riding and caught them at it in one of the barns. Celyn denied it. I confronted Luke and he admitted it. He said I would thank him one day. So I hit him. We had a fight and that was it. I moved to Cardiff not long after.'

'Celyn didn't stay with Luke though,' Meadows said.

'No, they never got together. That's what I heard at the time. Maybe they were ashamed. It seems such a waste now.'

'What do you mean?'

Theo shrugged. 'Celyn isn't happy with Kai, maybe she would've been happier with Luke. Instead, you had three unhappy people at the same time.'

'What do you think Luke meant by you'd thank him one day?'

'I've no idea. Maybe he thought we wouldn't last. I don't know.'

'Did you and Celyn talk about it when you went for your walk after the funeral?'

'Yes, we did. The strange thing is, she still denies it happened. She said Luke and my mother lied.'

'Do you believe her?'

'What would they have gained by lying? I think Celyn denied it so much that she convinced herself it wasn't true.'

'But you forgave Luke.'

'Yes, that's why I asked him out for a drink. I thought it was time to put the past behind us. Especially as I'm going to be living here for a while. After what happened with Uncle Madog it didn't seem important anymore.'

'How was Luke when you spoke to him yesterday? Did he seem distracted or upset?'

'He was angry about Auntie Kitty's fish, and he was behind on his work because he'd been helping her dispose of them. He was busy but other than that there was nothing unusual.'

'Who else was at the dairy when you spoke to Luke?'

'Uncle Quintin. He said Luke had to do a delivery for him. Luke said he would talk to Uncle Lloyd to see if he could leave a bit earlier so he could eat and get changed. That was it.'

Edris came into the kitchen. 'All done,' he said.

'I'd like to ask you, if I may, about your father,' Meadows said.

'My father?' Theo laughed. 'I couldn't tell you anything about the man. I've never met him. Mum never talked about him when I was young. When I was a teenager I got it in my head that I wanted to meet him. I imagined this perfect scenario of him welcoming me into his life and making up for lost time. After a lot of arguing Mum gave me his phone number. I called him. He was married with a family and wanted nothing to do with me. Is there a reason that you wanted to know about him?'

'We just have to cover all angles. We'll leave you to get some rest,' Meadows said. 'Can you let your mother know we need to speak to her as soon as she gets back?'

'Will do,' Theo said. 'I'll see you out.'

'How did you get on with Granny?' Meadows asked as they walked back to the car.

'I had to listen to her whole life story. I don't think we can rely on anything she says. I'm not sure she knows what postcode she's in, let alone the time and the day of the week. Did you get anything out of Theo?'

'He knew Luke's plans but so did Quintin and Lloyd. He gave me the same story as Luke's parents. They had a fight over Celyn and didn't speak for years. He seemed shocked by the news of Luke's death.'

'So what now?' Edris asked.

'We keep looking and hope we turn something up before someone else dies.'

Chapter Twenty-five

Pippa looked down into the pit she'd dug. The items were still smouldering, but she was satisfied they were burnt enough. She was in the furthest field from the house in an area that dipped down. She hoped that it was far enough away from Bryn Glas Farm that the smoke wouldn't be noticed. As she passed the highest point of the property that looked over the farm she saw police cars parked at the dairy. She hadn't lingered for fear of being seen. She had no doubt they'd be back to see her so the longer she stayed out the better.

She shovelled the earth back into the hole, stamping it down as it filled. Then she placed the clods of turf she had carefully cut before stepping back to look. It was obvious that the ground had been disturbed but rain was forecast for the next few days so she was confident it would settle. Besides, there was no reason for anyone to be on her land. She felt very weary now and tears of self-pity tracked down her cheeks. She took a tissue from her pocket and wiped her face before blowing her nose. She needed to pull herself together. She didn't want anyone to see her like this. She couldn't afford to let the cracks in her life widen.

She walked slowly back to the house and when she reached the courtyard Quintin came hurrying towards her.

'I've been looking for you everywhere. You didn't tell Theo where you were going. The police are all over the dairy. They'll want to talk to you. Luke–'

'I know, Theo told me,' Pippa said.

'What? How did he find out? I didn't say anything when I came around earlier. The police weren't sure.'

'I think Elsie called him.'

'Kitty must have rung her,' Quintin said. 'What have you been doing?' He looked at the shovel in her hand.

'Just clearing some of the ditches before winter sets in. They'll flood otherwise.'

'Ditches?' Quintin shook his head. 'Are you alright?'

Pippa wanted to say that she wasn't alright. 'I'm fine. I just needed to get out of the house and clear my head.'

'OK, well I need to talk to you. We better go inside.'

'I'll put this away.' Pippa put the shovel into the shed and pulled off her boots before carrying them inside and setting them down on a mat.

'Right, what do you want? Make it quick because I want to have a shower.'

'When the police come to see you, I need you to tell them that I was with you last night.'

'Why?' Pippa asked.

'Because I had to see to our problem. That meant–'

'I don't want to know,' Pippa said. 'I've got other things to worry about.'

'Like what?'

'Never mind. Fine, I'll tell the police you were with me and Theo last night, but I expect you to return the favour when I need it.'

'Of course,' Quintin said. 'We stick together as always. It'll be over soon. Kitty knows where Madog's will is.'

'She has it and hasn't told anyone?' Pippa said.

'No, the solicitor said that Madog told him that Kitty would know where the will is. She claims she doesn't know. I think she's lying, and if she knows where the will is then she must know where the codicil is.'

'Why would she lie? I thought you had Kitty under control. Sounds like she has other ideas. Maybe she plans on keeping the money and getting rid of you.'

'Why would she do that?' Quintin asked.

Pippa was astounded by the look on Quintin's face. 'You're my brother and I love you, but you can be a dick sometimes. I'm surprised she has stayed with you all these years. Then again she's always been a mousy little thing. You never know, this may be her way out.'

'No,' Quintin said. 'Where would she go?'

'More like, where would *you* go? Think about it, if she inherits the land and Madog's money she can do what she wants. You better find that will and the codicil before she does because I'm betting you won't be included.'

'Yeah, well, if it's not in Kitty's favour she's going to need me to fight for her. She won't do it by herself. We better keep an eye on her, see what she does.'

'We?' Pippa said. 'I'm not following her around.'

'You've got as much to lose as I do,' Quintin said. 'You just have to keep an eye on her when I'm not around. I can't see her going out after dark. She'll be too afraid. I have to go out for a couple of hours tomorrow morning. Just watch her then. I'll do the rest.'

'Fine,' Pippa said. 'If there's nothing else, I want to get out of these clothes.'

'I'll see you later. Let me know when you've talked to the police. I want to know what they say.'

Quintin left without bothering to see his mother. Typical, Pippa thought. He only thinks of himself. She was about to go upstairs when Theo appeared.

'You're going to lie for Uncle Quintin now, are you?'

'Everyone tells a little lie now and again,' Pippa said.

'Yes, but this isn't a little lie, is it? You're both sneaking around and now the two of you are going to spy on Auntie Kitty. Is there something you want to tell me?'

Pippa felt like her heart had stopped for a moment. Theo was looking at her with a strange expression on his face.

'There's nothing to tell. Quintin has some business to deal with and he doesn't want the police knowing. That's all.'

'Maybe he deserves the police knowing,' Theo said.

'Quintin has nothing to do with it.'

'To do with what, Mother?'

Pippa couldn't stand much more of this. If Theo knew then she wished he would just come out and say it. Put an end to it.

'I think I'll go out for a while,' Theo said.

'Where?'

'I don't know. Maybe I'll go and see Celyn. You haven't got a problem with that, have you?'

Pippa had a problem with anyone he planned to visit but she didn't say. 'Fine, do what you want.'

'See you later.' Theo smiled. 'Try to stay out of trouble when I'm out.'

He left the house and Pippa picked up a vase from the table and hurled it at the door.

Chapter Twenty-six

Kitty was sitting in the old wooden armchair in the farmhouse kitchen. Darkness had crept in without her noticing. The only sound came from the crackling of the fire in the Aga. She felt numb and cold. Even the heat from the hotplate she'd left open didn't seem to penetrate her skin.

Quintin hadn't been back since he left in a mood that morning. The police had returned showing her another photo of a fly. According to Quintin, Luke had been found in the vat covered in gloop. So where had they found the fly? She didn't want her mind to travel down that dark path, but she couldn't help it. Had someone stuck it in him? If so then they had stuck one in Madog and that other poor couple. It made her feel sick. It was another one of her White Moth Cup flies, a message left for her. She rubbed her hands over her face and tried to chase away the thoughts.

She was afraid now. Was she going to be next? It was alright for the police to tell her to lock the doors at night but what if she was locked in with a killer?

The back door opening made her jump. The light was switched on and she blinked in the brightness.

'Why are you sitting here in the dark?' Quintin asked.

'I don't know,' Kitty said. 'I just don't have the energy to move.'

'Are you sick?'

'No,'

'What about dinner?' Quintin asked. 'Are we going to eat tonight?'

'I'm not hungry. You can make something for yourself.'

She wished he would go away. Leave her alone to her thoughts. She didn't feel like watching him brooding all night as he drank glass after glass of wine. It was wearing. She had to watch everything she said as one wrong word could set him off on a tirade. Part of her wished Elsie was still there instead of in her own home. But the greater part was glad. At least away from the farm she would be safe. Quintin was staring at her, and she guessed he was waiting for her to talk. Maybe if she pissed him off enough, he'd go back out, she thought.

'Where have you been?' she asked.

'Out for a walk, then I went to see my mother.' Quintin opened the fridge and took out a bottle of wine.

'Where were you last night?'

'What is this?' Quintin pushed the corkscrew into the top of the bottle. 'I was with Pippa. You heard me tell the police this morning.'

'Yes, but you didn't come home.'

'You were asleep.'

'I'm not a heavy sleeper. I'd have heard you come in.'

'Oh, so you think I was out killing Luke, do you?' There was a dangerous look in Quintin's eyes.

Kitty turned her head away without answering.

'I tell you what,' he said, 'why don't we talk about what you're hiding?'

Kitty stood up. 'I'm not hiding anything.'

'Madog's will and the codicil.'

'I told you I don't know where the will is, and if I knew where the codicil was I would have given it to Mr Howells,' Kitty said as she slid her feet into her boots.

'Where are you going?' Quintin asked.

'Out for a walk.'

'After what happened to Luke? No, you're staying here.'

'You can't tell me what to do.'

She put her hand on the door handle but Quintin grabbed her arm. Kitty yelped.

'I said no.' He yanked her away from the door and forced her into a chair.

'I know you and Lottie are up to something. Do you think you can find the will and hide it from me?'

Kitty rubbed her arm. 'Why would I do that?'

'Maybe because you think Madog left the farm for me to run.'

'He wouldn't do that. The farm stays in the family.'

Quintin slammed his hand down on the table. 'I am bloody family. I haven't worked my balls off on this farm for years to be cut out. Is that what you are planning? You think if you get the land you'll be boss. Well think again because you haven't a clue how to run this place. You can't manage without me. If I were you I would put your efforts into finding that will and the codicil before Lottie does. Don't think for a minute that she and Lloyd are going to play fair. If they're destroyed there will have to be a legal battle. Best scenario is you get fifty percent of the shares. Worst case is Jac gets the lot. Is that what you want? You will lose the farm without me.'

He is right, Kitty thought. She wouldn't be able to go through the courts. She wouldn't know where to start. She was stuck with him. She should have taken more interest in learning how the finances work.

Quintin sighed and sat down. 'You don't want to lose the farm, do you?'

'You know I don't.'

'Madog would want you to have the land and the money,' Quintin said. 'That's why he left the will somewhere you'd know where to look.'

The kitchen door opened, and Lottie walked in. She looked from Quintin to Kitty. 'Everything alright?'

'What are you doing here?' Quintin asked.

'I've come to see my sister. You got a problem with that? Come on, Kitty, get your coat, we'll go for a walk. It'll do you good.'

Kitty stood up and brushed past Quintin. She put on her coat without looking at him. She knew he'd be angry.

'I thought you wouldn't come tonight,' Kitty said once they were outside.

'We'll be safe enough. There's still police hanging around at the dairy. No one will know we're out. Where do you want to start?'

'We should finish Uncle Madog's garden.'

'OK. What's up with Quintin? He looks really pissed off,' Lottie said as they picked up the path that led to the bridge.

'He knows I'm looking for the codicil.'

'What?' Lottie stopped. 'You told him?'

'No, Mr Howells told the police that Uncle Madog said that I'd know where his will is. The police asked me about it this morning and Quintin was there. I told them I don't know anything. Now Quintin thinks I know where the codicil and Uncle Madog's will are hidden.'

Lottie started walking again. 'I think we're right, he's put it in a jar and buried it, he's probably done the same with his will. We just have to think logically. They're going to be in a place with a special meaning. So it's either somewhere special to you or special to Dad and Uncle Madog.'

'He expected to read the codicil himself so I don't think they will be together,' Kitty said. 'Maybe we should tell the police. The jars could be anywhere on the farm.'

'No, they'll dig up the whole farm. Besides, what if...'

'We're still going to have to deal with that. I hope you're not thinking of destroying the codicil.'

'We'll think about that when we find it. We'll do the garden tonight then we should make a list of all the places they could be and split up. It'll be quicker,' Lottie said.

Kitty didn't like the idea. She wanted Madog and her father's wishes to be honoured, no matter what it cost her. Was Quintin right? Would Lottie and Lloyd fight to make sure they had their share? Would they destroy the codicil and will if they weren't in Lottie's favour?'

'I just want this over with,' Kitty said.

'It will be soon. We find the will and codicil then we'll know. No one can do anything about it once we have it. No one else gets hurt.'

'Unless one of us is next.'

'Kitty! You know I'm not going to let anything happen to you. You know Lloyd and I will look after you no matter what. As for Quintin...'

'You think he's the one doing this?' Kitty asked.

'I don't know,' Lottie said. 'If I'm honest, no, but then I can't imagine anyone in the family hurting Uncle Madog. I do worry about you. You've been unhappy for a while and now you just seem to have given up. It's like all the life left you when Uncle Madog died.'

'It's just so much harder without him. I miss him. When he was around, I didn't notice things so much.'

'Now it's just you and him,' Lottie said.

'Yeah, he hardly talks to me. When he does it's some criticism. I never seem to do anything right. He drinks every night so I have to stay quiet, or I could say the wrong thing and start him off. Not once has he said he's sorry about Uncle Madog.'

Lottie put her arm around Kitty. 'He's always been like this. The rest of us see how he treats you.'

'It's more than that.' Kitty sighed. 'He didn't come home last night.'

'It wouldn't be the first time if you're honest.'

'No, I mean…'

'Oh shit,' Lottie said. 'Did the police say when Luke died?'

'No, but it wouldn't matter if it was last night or early this morning, would it?'

'What about Saturday morning, when Uncle Madog went missing or the evening?'

Kitty didn't say anything. She wished she hadn't started this.

'Did you see him Saturday?' Lottie asked.

'No, not until dinner.'

'And he was late.'

'He wouldn't do something like that. I've been married to him long enough. He isn't a lunatic.'

'Just a dick,' Lottie said.

'Yeah.' Kitty laughed but doubts had crept in.

'Why don't you leave him?' Lottie asked.

'I don't want to leave the farm and where would I go?'

'You don't have to go anywhere. It's your cottage and your fishery.'

'Yes, but he works on the farm and controls the money.'

'Then it's time you took back control. If we get the land and money we can sack him.' Lottie laughed. 'Can you imagine his face?'

'I couldn't do that. He's still Elsie's father.'

'Elsie is a grown woman. She'll understand.'

'I don't know if I want to be alone,' Kitty said.

'You're alone in that marriage now. Anyway you have me, and Lloyd. You'll never be alone.'

'He'd never agree to leave. He'll fight for his share of the cottage.'

'I don't think he'll be entitled to any money. Come on. Let's find this codicil and will, then at least you'll know where you stand.'

They moved around the garden pushing their forks into the earth testing for resistance. Kitty tried not to look at the empty cottage. Think nice thoughts, she told herself. Her fork hit something, and she called out to Lottie. Together they carefully dug around the jar and lifted it out.

'You open it,' Lottie said and trained the beam on the jar for Kitty to see.

Kitty twisted the lid and pulled out a roll of money. Inside was a piece of paper saying, "Warmer".

'We're on the right track,' Lottie said. 'Do you remember Uncle Madog used to follow us around shouting "warmer", "colder"?'

Kitty smiled. 'Yeah, and we used to get so excited when he said "hot". This jar could have been here for years though.'

'No, look at the notes. They're polymer, they haven't been in circulation for that long.'

'I guess he wanted us to have one more treasure hunt,' Kitty said. 'Here.' She handed the money to Lottie.

'No, you keep it; it is meant for you.'

'For both of us,' Kitty said.

'Then we'll split it and you can buy something nice. Nothing to do with fishing.'

'OK.'

A noise from the side of the cottage made them both jump. Lottie moved quickly and Kitty followed. As they rounded the front of the cottage a figure could be seen moving swiftly towards the gate. Lottie shouted and gave chase.

'Don't!' Kitty yelled but Lottie didn't stop.

Kitty ran after her sister. As small as she was she could move at speed. She caught up with Lottie at the fishery, her sister was gaining on the figure heading towards the lake.

'Lottie, stop!' Kitty yelled.

'I know it's you, Quintin,' Lottie shouted as she slowed.

Kitty came to a halt next to her sister. 'Let him go. It's too dark and dangerous.'

'We're going back to the farmhouse,' Lottie panted. 'I'm calling the police and telling them that someone is out lurking around. Let them catch him.' She set off.

'We can't do that, the police will think he's responsible for killing Uncle Madog. He's probably only watching to see if we are looking for the will and codicil,' Kitty said.

'I don't care,' Lottie said.

They arrived at the farmhouse and Lottie opened the door and stopped.

'What is it?' Kitty asked.

Lottie moved in and Kitty saw Quintin sat in the armchair by the Aga, a glass of wine in one hand and a book in the other. Kitty knew that it was impossible for Quintin to have been heading towards the lakes and to get back to the farmhouse before them. The only way was to go around the lakes and up the steep bank onto the track, or to come back and pass them. She could see Lottie was thinking the same. Kitty felt a coldness creep over her. If it wasn't Quintin out there, then it was the killer watching them.

Chapter Twenty-seven

The next morning, as they gathered for their morning briefing, Meadows pointed at the four photographs pinned to the incident board.

'David and Anna Wilson, Madog Jones, and now Luke Henry. All suffered a brutal death, were defiled post-mortem, and discarded. All have grieving families waiting for answers. Luke Henry we now know died sometime between seven and ten in the evening. Hit over the head and garrotted with a fishing line or something similar. Then he was put into the vat. He also had a fly hooked into his tongue.'

'Kitty identified it as a *diawl bach*, a little devil,' Edris said.

'We're dealing with someone who has no compassion or is vengeful beyond reason,' Meadows said. 'Someone who managed to lure Madog onto a boat, convince the Wilsons to meet up on the Saturday evening, and was known to Luke Henry. They are clever and probably manipulative. They are likely to have convinced someone to give them an alibi. So far we have concentrated on the family. We know for a fact that a great deal of money and land is due to be inherited. It's enough motive for any one of them to murder. That includes Pippa Eccleston who also benefits indirectly.'

'The land?' Paskin asked.

'Yes, and her son Theo would also gain,' Edris said.

'We also need to look at the possibility of the existence of another family member. Maybe someone who feels they are intitled to that inheritance. We are awaiting test results from Luke Henry to see if he is a match to Madog. That may be the reason he was killed. To stop him making a claim. The other reason being that he was the only one able to provide an alibi for these two.' Meadows pointed to Lloyd and Quintin. 'We will speak to Pippa Eccleston this morning, not only about her calls to Madog but also Theo's parentage. Theo tells us he has spoken once to his father; he wanted nothing to do with him. Could Pippa have lied about the identity of Theo's father? She could have got anyone to take the call from Theo. Theo could be Madog's son.'

'Wouldn't Luke or Theo have Marfan syndrome and have the same characteristics as Madog?' Valentine asked.

'It's only a fifty percent chance of being passed down,' Edris said.

'I found something that may be of interest,' Paskin said. 'Theo lost a child. I'm still working on the details, but I saw some memory posts on his ex-wife Ffion's Facebook page. Grace Eccleston was just two years old when she died. Just over three years ago. I'm waiting on the death certificate. It may not be connected.'

That accounts for the sadness I saw in Theo's eyes, Meadows thought. 'Good work, Paskin. Follow it up. Even if Theo is not Madog's son he spent a lot of time on the farm as a child. It could be that he took his daughter there. We could be looking at an accident. Both Madog and Luke could be involved. That would certainly be motive. We need to tread carefully. These are grieving parents.'

'Why didn't any of them mention it?' Edris asked.

'I'm guessing it's too painful to talk about. The family wouldn't tell us for fear of us asking Theo about it. They would want to protect him,' Meadows said.

'I can see that but three years is a long time to wait to take revenge,' Blackwell said.

'Three years is also a long time to have grief eating away at you,' Meadows said. 'We still need to rule it out. Paskin, I'd like you to arrange for Theo and Pippa to come in to give a voluntary DNA and fingerprint sample. See what reaction you get. OK, who are we left with?'

'We checked out the whereabouts of Jac, Arwel, and Celyn the night before last,' Valentine said. 'All alibis check out. So they're not in the frame for Luke's murder.'

'That leaves us with these four as prime suspects.' Meadows tapped the photographs. 'Bridget or Kitty as she is known, Charlotte known as Lottie, Quintin, and Lloyd. Kitty would easily have persuaded Madog to go on the boat but given her size I very much doubt she would have the strength to overpower him. She certainly wouldn't have been able to kill the Wilsons alone. It may be that she had help from Quintin, but I can't see that she would play any part in her uncle's death. She was very close to him. While I feel she isn't telling us everything, I don't think she is involved.' Meadows looked at the team.

'I agree,' Edris said. 'I think we can rule her out. I can't see that she would poison her own fish either.'

'She could be afraid of Quintin,' Blackwell said. 'I get the impression that he controls her. If she suspected anything she'd be unlikely to tell us for risk of retribution. We also did a bit of digging into his finances.'

'Go on,' Meadows said.

'Quintin and Kitty are in a lot of debt. Quintin more so. We checked with the Land Registry. Bryn Glas Manor is now owned by Pippa and Quintin. Title was transferred from Eleanor Eccleston eight months ago. It also has a charge over the property and land. The mortgage is in joint names, Pippa and Quintin.'

'We also found that Kitty's cottage is held in both her and Quintin's names, again with a charge. The trout farm has been used as collateral for a sizable loan,' Valentine added.

'I was under the impression that the cottage and the trout farm could only be owned by Kitty and not passed out of the family,' Meadows said.

'Like I said, he's controlling. He's managed to get her to sign over half the title,' Blackwell said. 'It looks like he's a gambler among other things. I spoke to a couple of investors that were involved in the proposed property development on Bryn Glas Manor years ago. They, with others, put in a substantial amount of money. Work was started on the land, but it never went ahead because of the access. When the investors tried to get their money from Hugo Eccleston and Quintin they found themselves tied up in a legal battle. Hugo and Quintin hid behind the company they'd set up. Eventually the court ruled in the investors' favour. It took a long time for them to get all their money back and the manor house couldn't be touched. It looks like Quintin has started up the proposed housing estate again. Planning application was approved with the proviso that the access would be granted by Bryn Glas Farm. I think if we dig deeper we'll find more.'

'I think you're right. If Bryn Glas Manor is mortgaged, where has the money gone?' Meadows asked.

'Exactly,' Blackwell said. 'Add the mortgage on the cottage and loan on the fishery. You're talking a lot of money. If Kitty doesn't inherit, they are in a lot of trouble.'

'I think it's time we brought him in for formal questioning,' Meadows said. 'That leaves Lottie and Lloyd. Anything on them?'

'Lottie owns a hairdressing shop in Llandeilo,' Paskin said. 'She tried to sell the property a couple of years ago, but it has subsidence and rising damp. It would require a lot of money to complete the remedial work. She is renting another property to carry out her business. The family home is in joint names and mortgaged.'

'I thought she bought the house with her inheritance,' Edris said.

'More than likely they mortgaged the property to start the hairdressing business,' Meadows said. 'I think we should bring Lloyd in as well. I have to see Pippa Eccleston this morning. I have a feeling she will cover for her brother, but I still want to find out about Theo's father and why she made so many phone calls to Madog before he died. Blackwell, can you organise bringing in Quintin and Lloyd? See if they will provide a voluntary DNA and fingerprints. You and I can interview them when I get back from speaking with Pippa. Edris and Valentine, I think it would be worthwhile you talking to Lottie and Kitty while Quintin and Lloyd are here. It may be that Kitty will be more forthcoming with Quintin away. It's worth a try.'

He saw the look of horror on both Edris and Valentine's faces. The time together can give them some time to work out their problems, he thought.

* * *

Pippa answered the door this time. As on the previous occasion she was dressed well with flawless make-up and sleek hair.

'Theo told me you wanted to talk to me yesterday. It was late when I got back from shopping, and I didn't think it was appropriate to phone you at that hour.'

'No matter,' Meadows said. 'We were able to get most of the information we needed from Theo.'

Meadows expected some reaction to this statement, but none came.

'You'd better come in,' Pippa said. She led them to the same room as the last time she had spoken to them.

Meadows took a seat without waiting to be asked. Edris did the same and took out his notebook.

'What can I do for you this time?' Pippa asked as she seated herself and crossed her legs at the ankles.

'We'd like you to go over your movements on Wednesday evening.'

'Which Wednesday?' Pippa asked.

'The 22nd of September,' Meadows said. 'Two nights ago.'

'We had dinner early, about five. Mummy gets an upset stomach if she eats too late. Quintin came around not long after we finished eating and we had a few drinks.'

'Just you and Quintin?' Edris asked.

'Yes, Theo went out to the pub. He came back and went to his room. He didn't want to join us.'

'What time did Quintin leave?' Edris asked.

'Late, maybe after one in the morning. He's been stressed with everything that's been going on. He's worried about Kitty and the family.'

Edris jotted a few notes down then flipped through his notebook. 'We've been looking at Madog's phone records. You made calls to him on the 10th, 12th, 14th, and 15th of September and a few before those dates. Can you tell me the nature of those calls?'

'You can't expect me to remember every conversation I had with Madog,' Pippa said.

'Just a general idea,' Meadows said. 'There were no calls going back the previous weeks.'

'I was just calling to make sure he was OK after Connie died.'

'But you called before she died,' Meadows said.

'Yes but I knew she was very ill.'

'It's only a short walk to Madog's cottage from here if you use the bridle path. Why not visit him if you were worried?'

'It's not always convenient to leave my mother.'

'Other than Connie, did you talk about anything else?' Edris asked.

'Not that I recall.'

Meadows was convinced she was lying although she showed no outward signs. 'That's fine,' he said. 'We know you left a number of messages, and we will be looking at the transcripts so we should be able to refresh your memory.'

Pippa clasped her hands together. The first time she had shown any discomfort since they arrived. 'I may have mentioned the codicil,' she said.

'Why?' Meadows asked.

'Because Connie had died, and I knew there would be a change in ownership. I wanted Madog to sell me some land. I thought it would be a good time to try and persuade him.'

'Land for the proposed housing development?' Meadows asked.

'Yes, it would've made sense for Madog and the new partner to sell. They don't need all that land. Everyone would benefit, including the village.'

'We understand that Madog didn't want to sell,' Edris said.

'I think he was coming around to the idea.'

'Did he tell you who was going to inherit?'

'No, I didn't ask him. I assumed it would be Kitty. That would've made things neater. Kitty would've sold the land as, being married to Quintin, she benefits twice. The money from the land and the income from the housing estate.'

'What if Kitty doesn't inherit?'

'Then it would been down to who holds the remaining interest. I thought it best to get Madog on side. Of course now things are different.'

'Yes,' Meadows agreed. 'Although it's probable that Kitty will inherit. She would be easier to persuade to sell, especially if she was frightened of staying on at the farm.'

'You're forgetting that Kitty can't sell unless the other party agrees.'

'Lottie? Or someone else?' Meadows asked.

'I wouldn't know,' Pippa said.

'What about Theo?'

'Theo? Why would Theo inherit?'

'We understand that Madog was very fond of him.'

'Yes but not fond enough to leave him an inheritance. Besides, it has to remain in the family or that's what I understand.'

'There has been a suggestion that Madog is Theo's father,' Meadows said.

Pippa's eyes widened. 'I would laugh if it wasn't so insulting. He was about twenty-five years older than me, and you must've seen what he looked like. I can assure you I have better taste.'

'Nevertheless, we still have to look into the rumours. Would you mind telling us who Theo's father is?'

'Yes I would mind. It's none of your business.'

'I'm afraid under the circumstances it is. We think it's possible that Madog may have fathered a child. Now if that is Theo then he could be in danger. I'm sure you don't want that. Our only other option is to ask Theo for a DNA test.'

Pippa's eyes narrowed. 'That's not going to achieve anything. Look, Theo's father has played no part in his life. I don't want that man dragged into this to satisfy your curiosity.'

'We understand there was a payoff. You didn't want Theo's father around,' Edris said.

'Quintin had no right,' Pippa said.

'It wasn't Quintin but I'm guessing from your reaction it's true,' Meadows said.

'I made a mistake, a few too many drinks at the time. I didn't love him. It was just a one-night stand. I thought Theo would be better off without a father rather than have one who was forced into a relationship. He guessed when he found out I was expecting Theo. Daddy did offer him some money. I'm guessing he took it as I never heard from him again.'

'We still need a name,' Meadows said.

'Last I heard he had a wife and family of his own.'

'We will be discreet.'

Pippa sighed. 'Simon Taylor.'

'Do you have contact details for him?'

'Last I heard he was living in Kent but that was years ago. You're detectives, you should manage to track him down.'

'What about Theo's birth certificate? Can you provide us with a copy?'

'I could but Simon is not named. Now, is there anything else?'

'Yes,' Meadows said. 'And I'm sorry to have to ask. I understand that you lost a granddaughter three years ago. That must've been very hard for you and Theo. Was it an accident?'

Meadows saw a wave of sadness wash over Pippa. 'No, it was an aneurysm. It was very sudden, and Theo was with her at the time. I'd appreciate it if you don't mention Grace to Theo. As you can imagine it hit him hard and he is still grieving.'

'Of course,' Meadows said. 'There's no reason why we would need to ask him about it.'

'Good.' Pippa stood up. 'I'll see you out.'

She moved at a pace to the front door and Meadows got the feeling that she couldn't get them out fast enough.

'Do you believe her?' Edris asked when they were far enough away from the door.

'No. The mention of a transcript of Madog's phone messages got her rattled. I don't think her phone calls had anything to do with the land. At least we got a name for Theo's father.'

'Yeah, but that's all. She didn't show us proof.'

'I'll ask Paskin to try and track him down. What's more worrying is Pippa's willingness to cover for Quintin. I suppose some families will lie for each other even if it's to cover up a murder.'

Chapter Twenty-eight

When Meadows and Edris arrived back at the station Blackwell was sitting at his desk cradling a mug of tea and talking to Valentine.

'I've put Lloyd and Quintin into the interview rooms with a cup of tea,' Blackwell said. 'Lloyd seems OK, but Quintin hasn't stopped complaining and is now waiting for his solicitor.'

'Interesting why he thinks he needs one,' Meadows said.

'Both gave DNA and fingerprint samples,' Blackwell said. 'Doesn't mean they're innocent. Both can explain prints on the boat. We just have to let them think we have something from the other crime scenes.'

'If only,' Meadows said. 'The killer is bound to have left some physical evidence behind but time is not on our side. Mike and his team are working as fast as they can. OK, let's start with Lloyd.' He turned to Edris. 'I'll see you later.'

'Ready?' Edris asked.

Valentine grabbed her coat and walked out of the office without answering him.

'Nice move putting them two together,' Blackwell said. 'I'm fed up with the bickering.'

Meadows smiled. It was usually Blackwell and Edris that sniped at each other. He guessed they did it so often that neither one noticed anymore.

They walked together to the interview room where Lloyd appeared to be dozing in the chair. Meadows guessed it had been another early morning for him.

'Sorry to have kept you,' Meadows said as he took a seat opposite.

'It's OK,' Lloyd said then yawned and stretched. 'I'm not used to sitting down this time of day. The minute you stop it catches up with you.'

'We will be recording the interview,' Blackwell said as he settled himself next to Meadows.

'Alright,' Lloyd said.

Meadows thought that Lloyd was remarkably calm given the situation. Even those who were innocent tended to show some nerves. Lloyd could easily be sat in a pub having a chat over a pint. He wondered if it was a trait of character and if that extended to a lack of compassion and any feelings of guilt.

Blackwell switched on the recording device and announced the time, date, and those present.

'Firstly we'd like you to go over your movements on Wednesday the 22nd of September,' Meadows said.

'I was in at the usual time, before five, to bring in the first batch of cows with Luke. Once they were done milking, we cleaned for the second batch. Then the family got together to make the announcement about Madog. We went back to the house for a cuppa then I went back to the dairy. It wasn't long after that I heard about Kitty's fish. I asked Luke to go and help. I got some of the other lads together to dig a pit. We filled it in after we burned the fish. You saw me with the pigs. Luke came by not long after, asked if he could get off early to meet up with Theo.'

'How did he seem to you?' Meadows asked.

'OK, well, he was a bit upset about Madog and angry about Kitty's fish. He said he felt sorry for her.'

'Did you see Luke after that?'

'No, Quintin asked him to go out on a delivery.'

'What time did you leave the farm?' Meadows asked.

'I was home by five and asleep by seven.'

'What about yesterday morning?' Blackwell asked.

'Same thing. I got the first batch of cows in. James helped me with the milking. He and Luke take the first batch in turns.'

'Did you go into the dairy?' Blackwell asked.

'No, just the milking shed. Quintin called me when he found Luke; well, we didn't know it was Luke then. I checked around to see who was in.'

'Luke was with you on the morning of Saturday, the 18th of September?' Blackwell said. 'The morning Madog was murdered.'

'Yeah.'

'So he was the only one who could confirm your whereabouts that morning.'

'I suppose so. I didn't see anyone else until James came in later.'

'And that afternoon?'

'Like I told you before. I went home early for a sleep.'

'Is that usual?' Blackwell asked.

'No, but with the funeral and the family dinner in the evening I was tired.'

'We talked to all the employees on the farm. They hold you in high regard,' Blackwell said. 'Call you a hard worker. As well as managing the farm they tell me you've been working in the dairy, cheesemaking. Why all the extra work?'

Lloyd shuffled in his seat, and it was the first time during the interview that Meadows noticed any discomfort.

'Just helping out,' Lloyd said. 'It's in my family's best interests that the farm does well. We've had large orders recently and we haven't had the time to employ new workers and train them. I'm picking up the slack until that happens.'

'And you need the money?' Blackwell asked.

'I don't get any extra in my wages,' Lloyd said.

'We know about the hairdressing shop,' Meadows said. 'You can't sell the property. You must've lost a lot on what should've been a good investment. Now you have a mortgage and rent to pay.'

'Yeah, OK,' Lloyd said. 'We're not as well off as I'd like to be. University fees for Jac and Arwel; Celyn's wedding. It all added up, but we're doing OK.'

'You'd be doing even better if Lottie inherits fifty percent shares in the farm. There's a fair amount of money in the estate,' Blackwell said.

Lloyd shrugged. 'We have to wait for probate.'

'Yes but you're in a better position now that Madog has gone,' Blackwell said. 'If the codicil revealed that Kitty inherited her father's share then it would've been a long wait before Lottie saw any money. Madog could've lived for years.'

'What are you saying?' Lloyd asked. 'Yeah we need the money, but we are managing. If you think I had anything to do with what happened to Madog then you're nuts. If we were that desperate Lottie would've asked Madog for help. He helped us before. You can check. He paid for half of Celyn's wedding. He didn't want it back. Just gave it to Lottie. That's what he was like. Generous and kind. I could never hurt him.' Lloyd's voice cracked and he cleared his throat.

'Somebody hurt him,' Blackwell said. 'The only people who will gain from Madog's death are Kitty and Lottie and possibly your son Jac. So if you didn't kill Madog...' Blackwell left the statement hang in the air.

'We're a family,' Lloyd said. 'We have arguments now and again, but we don't go around killing each other. And what about Luke? He wasn't family, no one gains from his death.'

'But he was the only one who could confirm the time you were at the farm,' Meadows said. 'You see our problem.'

'We're going to be looking into your finances, your phone records, even your fishing tackle,' Blackwell said. 'So if you have anything to tell us, now would be a good time.'

'There's nothing. I've told you everything I know,' Lloyd said.

'OK, Lloyd. As you've provided us with a DNA and fingerprint sample voluntarily, we'll leave you to go back to work. I would advise you to stay local as we may need to interview you again.'

'I can go now?' Lloyd asked.

'Yes,' Meadows said.

Meadows asked the custody sergeant to see Lloyd out.

'What do you think?' Blackwell asked.

'I'm not sure,' Meadows said. 'He seems genuine enough, but he was twitchy when we asked him about working late in the dairy.'

'Yeah, I picked up on that too.'

'Ask SOCO to go over every inch of the dairy. I want to know what Lloyd is hiding. Then we'll interview Quintin.'

'My money is on him,' Blackwell said. 'Be interesting to see him try and explain his way out of his debt.'

Chapter Twenty-nine

Quintin glared at Meadows and Blackwell when they entered the interview room.

'About time,' he said. 'Do you know how long I've been waiting?'

'I apologise,' Meadows said as he took a seat.

Blackwell took a seat next to him and put a file on the desk. Meadows saw a look of worry flit across Quintin's face before he sat up a little straighter and looked at his solicitor.

The solicitor introduced himself as Alan Williams and asked a few questions before Blackwell switched on the recorder and listed those present along with the time and date.

Blackwell pulled out a sheet of paper from the file. 'You gave us an account of your movements on Saturday, the 18th of September. Is there anything you would like to add or change?'

'No,' Quintin said. 'I was at the farm working in the dairy as I told you.'

'You've been working long hours. Is there a reason for that?' Meadows asked.

'We've had a number of large orders for the cheese, so I've been helping to fill the orders.'

Same answer as Lloyd, Meadows thought. 'So you've been working with Lloyd processing and packing cheese? We understood that you worked in the office managing the finances.'

'I oversee the processing. I do give a hand when it's needed. We're looking at employing more staff. It didn't make sense financially to take anyone on until we increased orders. It just happened that the increase in orders came faster than we anticipated.'

'Luke also worked with the cheese processing,' Meadows said.

'Yes, in between his other work.'

'You called him Wednesday evening to ask him to set the vats,' Meadows said.

'Yes,' Quintin said.

'But Luke had left early and was planning an evening out. Wasn't there anyone else who could've set up the vats? You, for example.'

'Does it matter?' Quintin snapped. 'I don't see what cheesemaking has to do with any of this.' He turned to his solicitor. 'Are you going to say anything?'

'Is there a point to this?' Williams asked.

'Yes,' Meadows said. 'We need to establish why Luke went back to the dairy after he'd already showered and changed. The killer would've had to know Luke would be there. Luke is also the only one who can confirm your client's whereabouts on the day the Wilsons and Madog Jones were murdered. Unfortunately Luke was murdered before we had an opportunity to interview him.'

'Well I'd be stupid to call him to ask him to come to the dairy if I was going to kill him,' Quintin said.

'Where were you on Wednesday evening?' Blackwell asked.

'I already told you, I was with Pippa.'

'Yes, your sister.' Blackwell gave Quintin a tight smile. 'If you were only going to see your sister then why ask Luke to make a special trip in to set the vats? Why not do it yourself before you left?'

'Luke is paid, was paid, to do a job. Why would I work late when I can delegate?'

'Yet you've been happy enough to work late filling cheese orders,' Blackwell said.

'I think my client has adequately answered your questions with regards to the times he was asked to account for,' Williams said. 'It's also perfectly reasonable for him to ask an employee to return to work. I don't see what more can be gained from looking into the work practices of the farm. I trust that you've already asked Pippa Eccleston to confirm the times that my client was with her on Wednesday evening.'

'Yes,' Meadows said. 'Although she couldn't give a firm time that your client left her property. There is also the question of Saturday, the 18th of September. We have no witnesses that can place your client in the dairy.' He turned to Quintin. 'How well did you get on with Madog?'

Meadows noticed that Quintin visibly relaxed now that they had moved on from the dairy and Luke Henry.

'We got on very well,' Quintin said with a smile. 'I'm going to miss him.'

'No arguments?' Meadows asked.

'Not really. We had the odd disagreement about the running of the farm but nothing major.'

'Kitty could stand to inherit a substantial amount of money from Madog, and possibly the land,' Meadows said.

'We don't know anything for certain,' Quintin said.

'Would you agree that there's more of a chance of her inheriting now both her mother and Madog are dead?'

A smile played on Quintin's lips. 'Are you suggesting that Kitty killed Madog?'

'No,' Meadows said. 'If Kitty inherits it will put you in a favourable position, particularly if she inherits the land. If some of that land is sold to Bryn Glas Manor then access to the housing estate could go ahead. I imagine that would be very profitable for both you and your sister.'

Quintin's eyes narrowed. 'It would benefit both families. That's only if it goes ahead. I've made no secret of my plans for Bryn Glas Manor.'

Meadows gave Blackwell a nod.

Blackwell opened the file, took out a sheet of paper and pushed it towards Quintin. 'Bryn Glas Manor has a charge over the property. You took out a mortgage eight months ago. Why?'

'Do I have to answer that?' Quintin looked at Williams.

'Is this relevant?' Williams asked.

'Yes,' Blackwell said. 'It demonstrates that your client is in financial difficulty.'

'Fine,' Quintin said. 'The manor needed a lot of repair work.'

'What about the cottage on Bryn Glas Farm? That's also mortgaged.'

'Yes, we took out a mortgage a number of years ago to finance the fishery, and before you ask, the loan against the fishery was to set up the cheese processing business.'

'You can see how it looks,' Blackwell said. 'You and Kitty are in a lot of debt.'

'Not really. If we liquidised the assets it would more than enough cover the debts. It's how businesses work. You take out loans to expand. It doesn't mean that we had anything to do with what happened to Madog. A lot of people have debts.'

'But they're not your assets, are they?' Meadows said.

'The fishery is.'

'Rumour is that you lost a lot of money you invested in a crypto scam,' Blackwell said.

'Yes but I've also made a lot of money in other investments,' Quintin said.

'You're in charge of the farm finances,' Meadows said. 'Anyone else have control?'

'I share all information with the stakeholders.'

'That's not what I asked,' Meadows said.

'Yes, I take care of the financial side of the business.'

'Madog had been asking to see the accounts.'

'I provided him with a copy.'

'We didn't find any documents in his cottage,' Blackwell said.

Quintin shrugged. 'I don't know what he did with them.'

'If we take a look at the books would we find them in order?' Blackwell asked.

Quintin looked at Williams. 'Can they do that?'

Williams nodded.

'We have enough cause to request a warrant for both your financial records and the farm's,' Meadows said. 'We can hold you until we've had a chance to examine them.'

'This is ridiculous. You can't do this,' Quintin said.

Meadows saw the panic on Quintin's face. It confirmed that they were onto something. 'Perhaps it would be better for you to disclose any information on the farm's finances now.'

'If we find discrepancies then it doesn't look good for you if you fail to inform us,' Blackwell added.

Quintin looked at Williams.

'If you have any information that would assist with the inquiry then I'd advise that you disclose it now,' Williams said.

'I don't know what I'm paying you for,' Quintin said. 'I would've been better off on my own.' He looked at Meadows. 'You'll find everything in order with the farm finances.'

'Really?' Blackwell said. 'The finance on the fishery and the cottage. How did you manage that? Madog owned the land. You would need his permission.'

'Who says I didn't have his permission?'

'We know that Madog was unwilling to sell the land. I doubt we will find any documents supporting the application for loans. We will be looking,' Meadows said.

'The fishery and cottage are Kitty's,' Quintin said.

'Which are both mortgaged. What did you do with the money?'

'I told you. It was used to set up the fishery and the cheesemaking.'

'We know the money from the fishery came from Kitty's inheritance from her grandmother. You're just digging yourself a bigger hole. I think maybe some time to reflect will be helpful. We'll be holding you while we have an expert look over the farm's finances,' Meadows said.

The colour drained from Quintin's face

The solicitor started to object but Blackwell held up his hand. 'As you will be fully aware we can hold your client up to twenty-four hours. Given the serious nature of the crime, we can apply for thirty-six to ninety-six hours without charge.'

'Are you formally arresting my client?' Williams asked.

'That's easily arranged,' Blackwell said. 'Quintin Eccleston, I'm arresting you on—'

'Wait,' Quintin cut in. 'OK, I used some money from the farm for investments and some didn't go so well.'

'I'm guessing you mortgaged the manor to cover the deficit when Connie became ill,' Meadows said.

'Yes, so you will find that all the money is in the accounts.'

'You stole money from the farm,' Blackwell said.

'No, borrowed. Connie and Madog knew about it.'

'It's not like we can ask them though, is it?' Blackwell said.

'You're just going to have to take my word for it,' Quintin said.

'Anything else you would like to tell us about?' Meadows asked.

'No.'

'I think my client has provided enough information,' Williams said. 'He also gave fingerprints and a DNA sample voluntarily. Do you intend to arrest him? If not I think we are done here.'

Good question, Meadows thought. 'Your client will be released under investigation.'

'What's that supposed to mean?' Quintin asked.

'I'll explain everything to you,' Williams said. 'But for now you are free to go.'

Quintin stood up and left the room without saying a word. His solicitor followed.

'I'm not sure we should've let him go,' Blackwell said.

'We don't have enough to charge him. We do have him worried though,' Meadows said. 'Did you see his face when we talked about holding him?'

'Yeah but that goes for most. No one wants to spend a night in a cell.'

'It was more than that, he looked afraid. It was as though he needed to be out. He basically confessed to stealing money from the farm.'

'Which means he's done something worse that he doesn't want us to know.'

'Or maybe he's protecting someone.'

'Nah, he seems like a selfish bastard,' Blackwell said.

'I think we need to keep a presence at the farm.'

'He won't like that.'

'No, but we can have uniform check the place over periodically. Just let him know we are watching.'

* * *

Meadows was sitting at his desk when he had a call to go to the front desk. Downstairs he saw a woman he recognised talking to the custody sergeant.

'Betsan Rees,' the custody sergeant said. 'Works in the dairy on Bryn Glas Farm. She has some information for you.'

Meadows smiled. 'We met briefly at the dairy. Come on through.'

'Were you at the dairy when we found Luke?' Betsan asked as they walked towards the interview room. 'Everything is a bit of a blur. I remember speaking to a uniformed officer. I don't suppose I made much sense at the time.'

'It must have been a shock for you,' Meadows said.

'Yeah, I still can't believe it. Luke was lovely.'

Meadows stepped back and let Betsan enter the room first. 'Please, take a seat.'

Betsan sat down with her handbag clutched to her chest.

'What can I do for you?' Meadows asked.

'I… well…' Betsan stood up. 'I'm sorry, I don't think I should've come.'

'It's OK,' Meadows said. 'You've done the hardest part. Why don't you sit back down and tell me what's on your mind? Would you like a cup of tea?'

Betsan shook her head as she lowered herself into the seat. 'I'm afraid they will know it's me that said something. I'll lose my job, or worse, end up like Luke.'

Her eyes were wide, and Meadows noticed the tremor in her hands.

'I understand your concerns,' Meadows said. 'Anything you tell me will be in confidence. Why don't you start from the beginning, and we'll take it from there?'

Betsan nodded. 'We don't get paid a lot for the work in the dairy, but it does come with perks. Free eggs, cheese, and yogurt, meat at Christmas. There's always cheese left over from the orders, so we just help ourselves. I was working on Wednesday when Luke came in to pick up the order for delivery. We have different-coloured crates. Red for local delivery and green for the new orders which go all over. Luke usually takes the local deliveries, so I gave him the red crates. Luke was great but he could be a bit *twp* – forget things. He said something about taking the green crates, but I told him Quintin would be mad if he mixed up the order. The red ones were ready to go, with the green ones stacked behind. It was my fault.'

Meadows wondered where all this was going. 'You're saying that Luke delivered the wrong order and Quintin was angry?'

'Yes, well no, it's more than that. Quintin did come into the dairy later, it was just before I went home. He was furious, he stormed off calling Luke all sorts of names. He also said something about wasted cheese, so I took a few from the crate home. I was cutting it up this morning for sandwiches and... it's better I show you.' She opened her handbag, took out a clear plastic bag and handed it to Meadows.

Meadows held the bag up for inspection. Inside a cheese round had been cut in two. Each half was hollow and contained a bag of white substance.

'It's drugs, isn't it?' Betsan asked.

'Yes,' Meadows said. Now Quintin and Lloyd's unease regarding questions about the dairy made sense. 'Betsan. I'm going to ask you to keep this to yourself for now.'

'I won't tell anyone. Not after what happened to Luke.'

'Do you think that Luke knew about the drugs?'

'I don't know but he wouldn't have taken the wrong ones by mistake if he did.'

Meadows smiled. 'I think you may be right. How many of you work in the dairy?'

'It's just me and Lauren. Luke came in during the afternoons for a couple of hours when he had finished the rest of his work. When we got the big orders Quintin and Lloyd came in during the evening to do the waxing.'

'Are the batches that were left by mistake still at the dairy?' Meadows asked.

'No, Quintin took them. There's still some cheese drying out ready for waxing but we haven't been able to get back in. Quintin said we'd have to start from scratch after the cleaning, as all the cheese in stock has to be thrown away.'

'OK, thank you. You've been very helpful,' Meadows said. 'I'm going to ask someone to take a formal statement from you, if you have time right now?'

'Yes, no work until the clean-up is done, but I don't know what I'm going to do after that.'

'Maybe take a couple of days off. Under the circumstances I doubt anyone will question it.'

'No, I don't want to leave Lauren there alone, but do you think it's safe?'

'Yes, we will be keeping an eye on the place. If you have any worries give us a call.'

Meadows asked a PC to take Betsan's statement then he filled the team in on what he had learned.

'Drugs,' Edris said. 'So that's what all this is about.'

'I'm not sure,' Meadows said. 'It accounts for Quintin and Lloyd's behaviour but why murder Madog, Luke, and the Wilsons?'

'Madog must have found out,' Blackwell said. 'One of them kills Madog. The Wilsons are killed because they were witnesses and Luke, well, he might have wanted a share, or he was going to blow the whistle.'

'Why take Madog to the reservoir? If Madog knew about the drugs he wouldn't have gone with one of them,' Meadows said.

'I doubt he expected his own family to kill him,' Paskin said.

'They could've told Madog they wanted to speak to him away from the farm. Pretend they were going to give him an explanation,' Valentine said.

'I still think the will and codicil have something to do with it. Even if it's to cover the money for their enterprise,' Meadows said. 'We need to find them. Did you get anything from the sisters?' He looked at Valentine and Edris.

'Kitty denied there was a mortgage on the cottage and a loan on the fishery,' Edris said. 'She must have known about it.'

'I didn't get that impression,' Valentine said. 'She looked shocked.'

'She could be a good actress,' Edris said.

'Or maybe you're not a good judge of character,' Valentine snapped.

Putting them to work together obviously hasn't helped, Meadows thought. 'What about Lottie?'

'She hates Quintin,' Valentine said. 'She thinks he has something to do with Madog's murder.'

'But she didn't have any evidence to back it up,' Edris said.

'Anything else?' Meadows asked the team.

'Theo and Pippa came in to give fingerprint and DNA samples together,' Paskin said. 'She wasn't happy but if they had something to hide I think they would've refused or at least tried to delay. Also, SOCO found nothing in the dairy. Are we going to send them back in now we know what we are looking for?'

'No,' Meadows said. 'The drugs will be long gone but I have a feeling they're going to make up another batch. If we question them now they will blame it on Luke. I want surveillance set up day and night. There are only two ways out of the village. We watch until they make or receive a delivery. My feeling is they will move fast to shift what they've got. Uniform can make their presence known around the dairy. Once the two women workers have left for the evening we'll leave the way clear for Lloyd and Quintin to go in. Let them feel that they are safe. I just hope no one else is involved. We don't want another death.'

Chapter Thirty

Fury bubbled in Kitty's veins. It was a feeling she wasn't used to. It twisted her stomach and clenched every muscle in her body. She wanted to scream and kick. This rage had surfaced after the officers had asked her about the mortgage on the cottage and loan on the fishery. Up to that point the shock of Madog's death had subdued her feelings. Now it all came raining down on her – the injustice of his murder, the loss of her mother, Luke Henry, and now Quintin's betrayal. He'd made her look stupid or worse, the police would think she was lying. She was glad Quintin was still at the police station. She wanted to claw at his face. Hurt him.

She marched up the old bridleway and across the fields to the dairy. The walk had left her breathless, but the anger spurred her on. The police had left the dairy and the cordon had been removed from the entrance. She took the stairs to Quintin's office trying not to think about how close she was to where Luke had been found. She tried the door, but it was locked. Letting out a scream of frustration she kicked the door before running back down the stairs and into the cowshed where she jumped on a quad bike. It didn't take her long to find James in one of the fields.

'You OK, Kitty?' James asked.

'Not really,' Kitty said. 'I need some help getting into the dairy office. Can you break the lock on the door for me and open any locked cupboards or drawers inside?'

James didn't ask any questions. 'Yeah, no problem. I'll grab some tools and meet you there.'

While Kitty waited for James to open the door she called Lottie. She told her what had happened as she struggled to hold back the tears. Lottie said she was on her way. Kitty was grateful, her sister was the only person she trusted now.

Once the door was opened and James was sure nothing was left locked, he left the office. Kitty opened every drawer and cupboard, took out the paperwork, and piled it on the floor where she sat and started to read.

'Bastard,' Lottie said as she came through the door and joined Kitty on the floor.

'He took a mortgage out on the cottage years ago,' Kitty said. 'It's my signature on the document as well as his. There's another document.' Kitty handed some papers to Lottie. 'It's a transfer for joint ownership. I don't remember signing any of this.'

'Has he ever asked you to sign anything?' Lottie asked.

'Just insurance documents, stuff for the fishery, that sort of thing.'

'Did you read them?'

'Well no,' Kitty said.

Lottie shook her head.

'If Lloyd gave you something to sign would you question it?' Kitty asked.

'I guess not. Knowing Quintin, he probably put these among other documents. He tricked you. Don't worry, we'll find a way out of this. I'm sure there's paperwork with the solicitor that states ownership can't be transferred to someone outside the family. It was to stop him making a claim if you got a divorce.'

'All this debt is still in my name,' Kitty said. 'I can't get out of that.'

'We'll fight it,' Lottie said.

They looked through the rest of the paperwork, getting one shock after another. They found Quintin had his own bank account, was the sole director of a company Kitty had never heard of, and had a power of attorney he'd drawn up for their mother. It wasn't signed but dated the week before she died.'

'I bet he was going to try and take the farmhouse and get his hands on her money,' Lottie said.

'If we hadn't been looking after her twenty-four hours a day then I guess he would've succeeded. I wondered why he asked so often to take a turn to give me a rest. I didn't let him because I thought Mum would be more comfortable with one of us or Uncle Madog. Right, enough.' Kitty picked up the papers she had piled to one side and stood up. 'I'm going to have it out with him.'

'I'm coming with you,' Lottie said, scrambling to her feet.

'No, I can do this. I need to stand up to him on my own. Go and look for the will and codicil. I want an end to this. If one of us gets control of the farm we can use it to get rid of him.'

Lottie nodded. 'I'd love to see the look on his face when we sack him. I'm going to try up where Dad and Uncle Madog had a tree house as boys. It was a special place to them both. I'll ask Theo to come down and check on you. I don't trust Quintin.'

'He wouldn't hurt me. It's not his style.'

'Even so, I'd feel better if Theo is there. He can just wait outside the house. That way if you have a problem you can just scream.'

'What about you? I don't like the idea of you wandering around the farm in the dark.'

'No one will know where I am. You can join me when you've finished dealing with Quintin.'

It was dark outside, and all the farmworkers had long gone home. Kitty was glad to get a lift with Lottie. She wouldn't have liked walking back through the fields. Lottie dropped her off outside the farmhouse and Kitty watched her sister drive past the cottage and park up. Quintin's car was sitting outside and there was a light on in the kitchen, so she knew he was home. Anger fizzled in her stomach as she pushed open the door. Quintin was sitting at the kitchen table with a glass of whiskey in his hand. The dogs came around her legs and she stroked the top of their heads while staring at Quintin.

'What's the matter with you?' Quintin asked and took a gulp of whiskey.

'How could you?' Kitty said.

'What?'

'I know what you've done.' Kitty threw the papers on to the table.

Quintin snatched the top one and looked at it. 'What is this? You've been in my office. How dare you? It's private.'

'You've lied, you've stolen from me,' Kitty shrieked. 'The cottage is my home, the fishery belongs to me. I paid for it with my own money. You've taken everything. I want you out!'

The dogs barked and jumped up at her.

Quintin laughed. 'Your signature is all over these. It's all above board.'

'You tricked me.' Kitty moved to the door, opened it, and ushered the dogs outside. She turned around to find Quintin had stepped up behind her.

'It wasn't that difficult to do.' He inched closer so he was towering over her. 'You and the rest of the family are a bunch of imbeciles. You couldn't run this place without me.'

'You were going to take money from my mother, a dying woman.'

'Yeah, well it's not as if she needed it.'

Kitty drew back her hand and swiped at Quintin's face, but she was so much shorter than him that she only caught him on the chin. He reacted instantly. Kitty heard the crack of his hand as it collided with the side of her face. The force knocked her sideways, she put out her hand to break her fall and let out a yelp as she felt the impact dislocate her wrist.

The kitchen door flew open, and Theo appeared. He looked from Kitty on the floor to Quintin then charged, pinning Quintin against the wall.

'Stop!' Kitty yelled as Theo drew back his fist.

Quintin held up his hands. 'I didn't mean to do it,' he said. 'It was an accident.'

'You hit her,' Theo said.

'She hit me first.'

'That's no excuse,' Theo seethed.

'It was a reflex.'

'You're nothing but a bully,' Theo said.

'Let's just calm things down,' Quintin said. 'It's been a difficult day.'

'Are you OK, Auntie Kitty?' Theo asked.

'I'm fine.' Kitty got to her feet. Pain shot from her wrist to her elbow, her face stung, and she could taste blood.

'You don't look OK,' Theo said.

'I'll be OK,' Kitty said. 'She grabbed a torch from the counter. 'I'm going out for a walk. I want you to get him out of here. I don't want to see him when I get back.'

'You can't throw me out,' Quintin said.

'Yeah I can. I'm going to see the solicitor first thing in the morning.'

'Well good luck with that. You're in a lot of debt. You need me to run this farm. Your only choice now is to sell the land to the manor, build the houses and get the money back.'

'That's the last thing I'm going to do,' Kitty said. 'I don't care if I have to pay back the debt for the rest of my life. I want nothing to do with you.'

She didn't stay around to hear Quintin's reply. She stepped out of the door and slammed it behind her.

She could feel her body trembling as she walked to the fishery and sat down on one of the empty troughs. She didn't want to find Lottie just yet. She knew her sister would be furious and would call Lloyd. Kitty couldn't bear the idea of any more fighting. She suddenly felt exhausted, it was as though her legs couldn't carry her any further.

It was quiet at the fishery, the usual movement of fish in water was gone. She turned off her flashlight and sat in the dark. Her thoughts turned to Madog and all the time they had spent setting up the fishery and the competition. She let her mind wander, letting the memories play out like a film. Time drifted by as she sat as if in a trance. The cold seeped through her jumper as she chased her memories through the years. Something from the last time she had seen Madog jolted her back to the present. It had been the evening of her mother's funeral and they had been standing on the bridge. Did he have an idea of what was going to happen? Kitty thought. He talked about the white moth. It became clear now what Madog had been trying to tell her. She had to find Lottie.

The dogs that had been sat at her feet followed her now as she crossed the bridge. The stiffness in her legs was easing but her face and wrist still throbbed. She had no idea how long she had been sat by the fishery and hoped that Lottie was still in the same place digging. She passed Madog's cottage and took the path that led into a small, wooded area. She trained the beam of the torch on the ground, careful not to take another fall. As she came through the trees she saw a dark figure bending over and the light from a torch lying on the ground.

'Lottie,' she called.

The figure moved so fast it took Kitty a moment to realize what was happening. It wasn't Lottie, and as the figure moved through the trees and disappeared she saw another figure lying on the floor. Fear paralyzed her for a moment then she ran forward. Lottie was lying face down on the ground with blood coming from the back of her head. Kitty screamed.

Chapter Thirty-one

An aroma of spices filled the cottage and Meadows heard his stomach growl in anticipation of the meal.

'Smells wonderful,' Meadows said.

'Vegetable curry,' Rain said as he took the plates from the cupboard. 'Is Daisy joining us?'

'No, she has to work late.'

'That's a shame. Well, bring her up the commune for a few days when you've finished the case. We'll hang out there then come back and do some hiking or whatever you fancy.'

'Sounds great.'

Meadows phone trilled in his pocket. It was Matt Hanes calling to tell him that Lottie had been attacked.

'I'm sorry, I have to go,' Meadows said.

'No worries,' Rain said. 'I'll go and pick up Mum. We'll leave you a plate in the oven.'

'Thanks,' Meadows said and hurried out of the house.

'What do you think? Some drug deal that's gone wrong?' Edris asked as Meadows drove the car along the twisting road of the mountain.

'No, I checked with surveillance. No one has been in or out of the village other than residents. They ran all the plates.'

'Then it has to be one of the family,' Edris said.

'Or one of the farm workers that lives local.'

They arrived at the farm and were met by Hanes.

'Any news from the hospital?' Meadows asked.

'No, all we know is that she was still alive when they took her in. Kitty went with her,' Hanes said.

He led them over the bridge, along the path and into the trees where they found Mike from forensics laying out the pathway.

'What was she doing out here in the dark?' Edris asked.

'There are a number of holes, along with a spade and a trowel. Looks like she was digging for something,' Mike said. 'There was an empty glass jar near to where she was found. I've bagged it. Nothing more I can tell you. We've only just started.'

Meadows turned to Hanes. 'Did Kitty say anything to you?'

'No, I arrived just after the ambulance. Kitty had given directions when she called it in, but Quintin was waiting for us. He showed us where to find them then went back into the farmhouse with Theo. Kitty was kneeling next to Lottie, sobbing. I thought it best to let her go with her sister.'

'That's fine. We'll catch up with her at the hospital,' Meadows said. He looked at Edris. 'Come on, let's go and have a chat with Quintin, I want to know where he was this evening. Hanes, after we've finished I'd like you to stay at the farmhouse and make sure he doesn't go anywhere.'

Meadows could tell from Quintin's eyes that he'd had a fair amount to drink. He was sitting at the kitchen table with half a glass of whisky. Theo was standing with his back to the Aga.

'You again,' Quintin said. 'I'm not in the mood to talk to you. In case you haven't heard, we've had a family emergency.'

Meadows ignored him and sat down. Edris did the same and took out his notebook.

'What happened this evening?' Meadows asked.

'I don't bloody know,' Quintin said. 'I wasn't here. I got a call from Pippa.'

'Kitty called Lloyd and Lloyd called me,' Theo said. 'Because I'm closer and could get to them quicker than he could. He turned up after and followed the ambulance.'

Meadows looked at Quintin. 'If you weren't at home, where were you?'

'Oh just bugger off, will you?' Quintin said.

'He had an argument with Auntie Kitty,' Theo said.

'You can piss off, too,' Quintin said.

Meadows looked at Theo. 'Go on.'

'I walked in on them. Kitty went off for a walk. She wanted Uncle Quintin to leave the house. We went up to the dairy. I thought it best until things had calmed down.'

'What did you do up there?'

'I was sorting out the equipment,' Theo said.

'I had to tidy up my office. Little bitch broke in,' Quintin said.

'You mean Kitty?' Meadows asked.

'How long did you stay at the dairy?' Edris asked.

Quintin ignored the question and picked up his glass taking a large gulp.

'I don't know,' Theo said. 'A while. I had only just got home when Lloyd called me and asked me to go to Kitty and Lottie. I told Mum to call Uncle Quintin and I went to look for them. It took a while to find them. I left Kitty with Lottie and met Uncle Quintin back here. We showed the paramedics the way.'

'Shouldn't have bothered,' Quintin said.

'She was upset and not thinking straight,' Theo said. He looked at Meadows. 'She was screaming at Uncle Quintin, so I thought it best to come back here and wait for news.'

'Did you see anyone else when you went to find Lottie and Kitty?' Meadows asked.

'No, no one,' Theo said.

'OK. I suggest you make your uncle some coffee. We're going to go to the hospital to see Kitty. An officer will stay here with you.' He looked at Quintin. 'Don't go anywhere.'

Meadows got in the car and started the engine. 'As soon as you have a good signal, call Blackwell. Ask him to organise warrants. I want footwear, coats, laptops, and all their fishing equipment.'

'All of them?' Edris asked.

'Yeah, Pippa and Theo included. Make sure it covers the dairy, the hairdresser shop, and any outbuildings. They're all suspects. It's like some sick game of last man standing.'

* * *

At the hospital they met with the doctor who was treating Lottie. He led them into the staff room and closed the door.

'Lottie has swelling on the brain and has not regained consciousness,' the doctor said. 'She's on a respirator and we are monitoring her to see if we'll need to operate to relieve the pressure.'

'Will she be OK?' Meadows asked.

'I'm afraid it's a case of waiting,' the doctor said. 'She's in the ICU. Her husband and sister are with her.'

'We're going to need to speak with them both,' Meadows said.

'I'll take you, but I can only allow one of you in and only for a few moments.'

Meadows left Edris to sit outside the ICU and followed the doctor through the doors. There were only four patients, and the room was filled with the whir of machines, monitors beeping, and the whooshing of oxygen through ventilators. Lottie was lying with a drip in her arm, monitors on her chest, and a tube protruding from her mouth. On one side of the bed Lloyd was sitting holding her hand, his head bowed. On the other side Kitty stroked her other hand. Meadows saw Kitty's arm was held in a sling and when she turned her head to look at him he saw a bruise on her cheek.

'He's done this,' Kitty said.

Meadows stepped closer to the bed. 'Who?'

'Quintin. Lottie knew about what he had done with the money, and the cottage. He must have found her. She was so angry with him.'

'I'll kill him,' Lloyd said.

'Did you see Quintin attack Lottie?' Meadows asked.

'Yes, well no, not exactly,' Kitty said.

'We don't think it was Quintin,' Meadows said. 'He was with Theo and wouldn't have had time. Maybe we should talk outside.'

'No,' Kitty said. 'I'm not leaving her.'

'OK,' Meadows said. 'Can you talk me through what happened? I know it's difficult but the more you can tell me now the better chance we have of catching the person responsible.'

'I saw someone. I thought it was Lottie at first because they were bending over her, Lottie's torch was on the floor. I called out and they ran off.'

'Did they run at you?' Meadows pointed to Kitty's arm.

'No, the other direction. I fell earlier.'

Meadows didn't believe her explanation for her injuries but let it go.

'Did you recognise anything about the attacker? Was it a man or woman?'

'I don't know. It was dark and it happened so quickly.'

'What were you and Lottie doing in the dark in the woods?'

'We were looking for Uncle Madog's will and the codicil. Uncle Madog used to play games with us when we were young. He would bury jars with money and things for us to look for. We thought perhaps that Madog had put the codicil where he and Dad used to have a tree house.'

'We found an empty jar where Lottie was found.'

'She must have found something before…'

'Why didn't you tell us about this?' Meadows asked.

'Because we didn't know for sure, and we didn't think you'd take it seriously.'

'Were you digging somewhere else?'

'No, I was sitting by the fishery. I just wanted to be alone for a while. I remembered something Madog said about the white moth. I thought he may have put his will by the summer house. There's a large wooden moth on the side. I was going to tell Lottie.'

'Did you know all about this, Lloyd?' Meadows asked.

'Yeah, Lottie said they were looking.'

'I have to ask where you were this evening?'

'Seriously, you think I'd do this to my own wife?'

'I'm sorry but we need to know where everyone was at the time.'

'I was home sleeping, and before you ask, I was alone.'

'OK, I'll leave it there for now. First thing in the morning I want you to show me where you think Madog hid his will. As for the codicil it may be the case that Lottie found it and the attacker now has it. It may already be destroyed. I'm going to arrange for an officer to be posted outside the room at all times.'

Meadows met up with Edris outside the ICU and filled him in on the conversation with Kitty and Lloyd.

'Why would he bury his will and the codicil?' Edris asked. 'He must have known there would be a chance they would never be found.'

Meadows nodded. 'It is an odd thing to do but I'm guessing Madog didn't trust anyone, not even the solicitor. Look at the way he led his life. He only left the farm once in his life. There was no television in his cottage, and he didn't use a computer. He barely used a bank account. He cut himself off from the outside world. His life was the farm and Kitty. I suppose the only person he did trust was Kitty and he was probably confident she would know where to look.'

'Hell of a gamble,' Edris said.

'Not really. Kitty did figure it out. If Madog's will and the codicil were not with the solicitor then the only logical conclusion was that they were hidden on the farm.'

'So how many of them knew about Madog burying the jars?' Edris asked.

'I don't know but I'm betting Quintin knew about it. I think we can be sure of one thing. This has nothing to do with drugs. The killer is after the will and codicil. Once we know who inherits we'll have a better idea of who would want the will and codicil kept hidden.'

* * *

Meadows and Edris dug carefully around the area below the white moth carving. Kitty was standing watching them. Meadows thought she looked worse this morning than she had last night. She was pale with dark circles beneath her eyes, a livid bruise on her cheek, and she nursed her arm which clearly gave her a lot of pain. She was quiet as they dug and all that could be heard was the scraping of earth.

There were several holes now and just as Meadows began to feel like their efforts were in vain, he felt the spade hit something. He knelt and used a trowel to free the jar. He pulled it out, brushed off the earth and stood up.

'Do you want to open it?' he asked Kitty.

Kitty nodded.

Meadows loosened the lid and handed the jar to Kitty.

Kitty took the lid off, dipped her hand in and pulled out the paper. Meadows watched as her eyes pooled with tears as she skimmed the words.

'He left everything to me,' Kitty said. 'But I thought…'

'What did you think?' Meadows asked.

'It doesn't matter now.' She held out the paper to Meadows.

Meadows read Madog's final wishes and gave Kitty a nod before handing it over to Edris.

'I thought the farm had to be split in such a way that not one person got control,' Meadows said. 'Still, it's signed and witnessed.'

'Yeah, Dad must have left his share to Lottie, so Uncle Madog left the other half to me.'

'No, read it again. Madog talks about giving you his share and refers to your father's division of shares. That means that you're the majority holder.'

'I don't understand,' Kitty said.

'I guess Madog assumed you would've seen the codicil before reading his will.'

'What do they want?' Kitty said.

Meadows turned to see who Kitty was looking at. Quintin, Theo, and Pippa were walking towards them.

'If Quintin was the one to cause your injuries I can have him arrested,' Meadows said.

'It was an accident,' Kitty said. 'I hit him first and he reacted. He didn't mean for me to fall.'

Meadows felt anger fizzle in his stomach. Domestic violence riled him. There were no excuses in his mind.

'He could have just walked away,' Meadows said. 'You shouldn't have to feel afraid in your own home.'

'I don't want to leave my home,' Kitty said.

'If you press charges we can have him taken from here and help you get a restraining order,' Edris said. 'You wouldn't have to be the one to leave.'

'It doesn't matter,' Kitty said, 'even with Quintin gone I'm still not safe until you catch whoever is doing this.'

'Well what did it say?' Quintin asked as he got nearer to them.

'None of your business now, but he left everything to me. So you can pack your bags and go.'

Colour rose in Quintin's face, and he took a step towards Kitty. 'I'm not going anywhere. This is my home.'

Edris stepped next to Kitty and addressed Quintin. 'Maybe it would be a good idea if you went away for a few days.'

'You're not thinking straight, darling,' Pippa said. 'You've had a shock and you're exhausted. We're all stressed. The police have been all over my house this morning. They've taken away my boots, coat, and my bloody laptop.'

'Yeah and they're in our house now,' Quintin said.

Pippa moved towards Kitty. 'See, it's hard for us all. Quintin can stay with Mum tonight and I'll stay with you. Once you've had some sleep things will look better.'

Even if Kitty agreed Quintin wouldn't be far enough away for Meadows' liking. He imagined that Pippa was used to getting her own way. Kitty didn't look like she could stand up to the two of them at the moment.

'Kitty, I think it would be a good idea if you pack a bag and come with us,' Meadows said. 'We can take you to a place of safety until this is over.'

'No, I want to stay here,' Kitty said.

At that moment Lloyd came around the side of the summer house.

'Is Lottie OK?' Kitty asked.

'No difference since you saw her, but the doctor says the swelling is going down. Celyn is there now, then Jac and Arwel are going to sit with her this afternoon. Only two allowed in the ICU. I'll go this evening. You can come with me.'

Kitty nodded. 'Go home and get some rest, you've been up all night.'

'Nah, I won't be able to sleep. I thought it best to do some work and take my mind off things.'

'Kitty, if you won't let us take you somewhere safe then I'm going to have an officer stay with you,' Meadows said.

'We can look after her,' Quintin said.

'Yeah, looks like you've done a good job of that,' Lloyd said.

'You can shut up,' Quintin said. 'It's not my wife that's lying in the hospital.'

Lloyd lunged forward and Meadows grabbed his arms.

'This is not the time or place,' Meadows said. 'I think you should all be concerned for Kitty's safety. Given the revelation in Madog's will it is likely that she's a target.'

'Kitty, you should go with the officers,' Lloyd said.

'I just want to be left alone,' Kitty said. 'I don't want to be sitting around in some strange place. I'll go mad.'

'OK,' Lloyd said. 'If two of us stay with you at all times, you can potter around the farm to take your mind off things. We'll go and see Lottie this evening and when you come back you can have an officer stay at the house.'

'I don't know.' Kitty cast a look at Quintin and Pippa.

'Either Theo or me will be with you,' Lloyd said.

'Are you saying you don't trust me?' Quintin said.

'Or me?' Pippa added.

'How many of you knew that Lottie and Kitty were looking around the farm for the will?' Meadows asked.

Theo shook his head as did Pippa. Meadows guessed that Quintin would know.

'I'll stay with Theo and Lloyd,' Kitty said.

Meadows didn't like the idea of leaving Kitty with the family, especially given that there was a high chance that one of them was the killer.

'There are plenty of people working around the farm,' Lloyd said. 'She'll be safe.'

'I'll be talking to some of the farm workers as well as checking in on the searches so I won't be far away,' Meadows said. 'I'll make the arrangements to have an officer meet you at the hospital and go home with you.'

'OK,' Kitty said.

Quintin and Pippa were the first to leave, followed by Kitty, Theo, and Lloyd.

'I don't understand why Kitty wants to stay here after what happened to Lottie,' Edris said.

'I guess it's her home and it's not easy to accept that a member of your family would wish you harm.'

'Unless she is involved. She is the one who's benefited from Madog's death.'

'There is that, and Lottie is the only one to stop her getting the entire estate. I just can't see Kitty being involved,' Meadows said. 'We've got the hospital covered. For now, as long as Kitty stays with two members of the family at all times, she should be safe enough.'

'If she picks the right ones.'

'That's what worries me,' Meadows said.

The farm that had a peaceful quality when he first saw it now had an ominous feel. It felt as though the killer was playing with them. What was he missing?

Chapter Thirty-two

Kitty felt so tired she was having difficulty concentrating on any task. She had moved about the farm, always in sight of Theo and Lloyd, or James when one of the others had to do something. Pippa had stormed off home after the will had been found and Quintin was in the office. Now and again she had glimpsed the detectives talking to one of the labourers.

'You look like you could do with a strong cup of tea,' Theo said. 'Come on I'll make you one in Quintin's office.'

Quintin was the last person Kitty wanted to talk to. 'I think I'll give it a miss.'

'Don't worry about Uncle Quintin, I'll chuck him out.' Theo laughed.

Betsan and Lauren were in the dairy so Kitty passed the time talking to them when Theo went up to the office. They asked about Lottie and Kitty felt tears sting her eyes.

'I see you got the vats going,' Kitty said.

'Yeah, Quintin wanted everything up and running again to fill the orders,' Lauren said.

Betsan excused herself and went back to work and Kitty guessed she was still shocked by Luke's death and didn't want to talk.

Quintin came into the dairy. 'Office is all yours,' he said. 'Maybe you should have a lie-down on the sofa. I'll make sure no one disturbs you. I'm sorry, Kitty. Maybe we can talk when you feel a little better.'

If Kitty thought he meant it she may have been tempted to talk to him. But she knew him too well. He would be nice to her now that money was involved.

'It's a little too late to talk,' she said.

Upstairs in the office Theo handed her a cup of tea. 'I'll be down in the dairy if you need me. I'm sure I can make myself useful.'

Kitty took a sip of the tea. 'Thank you.'

'No problem. See you in a bit,' Theo said.

Kitty closed the door behind him and put a chair behind it. She drank some more tea then set the cup down before lying on the sofa. She closed her eyes, but she couldn't sleep. Her mind was too busy whirring over the week's events. So much had happened she found it difficult to believe it was only a short time ago that she only had the grief from her mother's death to contend with. If anything happened to Lottie she would have lost most of her family in a week. She tried to chase that thought away and instead think of the words in Madog's will. She couldn't believe he had left everything to her. The other thing that bothered her was why her father would split his share between her and Lottie. It didn't make sense if he knew Madog would leave his share to her.

She sat up abruptly, causing her head to spin. No, that can't be right, she thought. But it made sense now. How could she have got it so wrong? Meadows had asked who knew about the jars. She didn't think anyone besides herself, Lottie, Quintin, and Lloyd knew. She didn't think anything of it at the time, but she was sure now there was one other person that would know. She felt afraid now. She had to get away from the farm. She should call Meadows, but she needed to speak to Lottie first. She'd have to hide away until she woke up.

Kitty stood up and paced the office. Where would she go? A hotel? She couldn't use her bank card because Quintin would see the payment on their joint bank account. She didn't trust him. He would tell. She couldn't let anyone know where she'd gone. She couldn't go to Elsie as she would put her in danger. She stopped pacing as an idea came to her. Celyn would lend her the money.

She hurried downstairs where she found Theo in the dairy talking to Quintin and Lloyd.

'I'm going to see Celyn,' she said.

'Not on your own,' Quintin said.

'I'll take you,' Theo said.

'OK,' Kitty said.

'You're supposed to stay with two of us,' Quintin said.

'That's when I'm here. I'll be OK with Celyn. I won't be long.'

They took Theo's car as it was already parked at the dairy.

'How are you feeling now?' Theo asked as he drove.

'I'm OK. It's just so much to take in. I expect poor Celyn is worried sick. It will do me good to think of someone else instead of feeling sorry for myself.'

'No one could ever accuse you of being selfish,' Theo said. 'You nursed your mother, took care of Madog as well as working on the farm. I'm glad he left the farm to you. You deserve it.'

'I haven't done any more than most would do,' Kitty said. She was tempted to tell Theo what she suspected but thought he had enough to deal with. He would find out soon enough.

Theo parked outside Celyn's house. 'Give me a call when you are ready to go home, and I'll pick you up.'

'Thank you.' Kitty leaned over and gave Theo a hug. 'Be careful,' she said before getting out of the car.

* * *

Celyn looked as tired as Kitty felt. She was sitting on the floor stacking plastic shapes with her toddler.

'How is she?' Kitty asked.

'The swelling has reduced so the doctor is hopeful that she'll wake up soon. At least it doesn't look like they'll have to operate. She's still on oxygen but I thought she looked a bit better when I left. Maybe it's just wishful thinking. You don't look much better yourself.' Celyn smiled. 'You should get some rest. She'll be pissed if you make yourself ill worrying.'

Kitty nodded. She didn't know how to ask Celyn for help without explaining why. In the end she just blurted out the request for money and gave an explanation that even sounded garbled to her own ears.

'You're worrying me,' Celyn said. 'You're not making any sense.'

'I'll be OK,' Kitty said. 'I just really need your help to get away.'

'I don't have that amount of cash on me,' Celyn said. 'I can go to the bank.'

'If it's not too much trouble,' Kitty said. 'Then if you can, drop me back at the farm so I can get my car. I promise I'll pay you back and explain everything.'

'OK.' Celyn picked up the child. 'Come on let's go.'

* * *

When they arrived at the farmhouse all was quiet and Kitty guessed they must all be still at the dairy.

'Do you want me to come in with you and wait until you are ready to go?' Celyn asked.

'No, it's fine.' Kitty glanced at the little boy sleeping in the back. 'Go home. With a bit of luck he'll stay asleep, and you can get a rest before you go back to see your mum.'

Celyn nodded. 'Call me to let me know you're OK.'

Once inside the farmhouse Kitty locked the door and hurried upstairs. She grabbed a holdall and threw in a change of clothes and some nightwear before collecting toiletries from the bathroom. She was zipping up the bag when she heard a noise downstairs. She stood still listening.

'Quintin?' she called.

There was no answer, so she grabbed her bag, tucking the strap over her shoulder and hurried down the stairs. Another noise stopped her. It was coming from the kitchen. A sort of scraping sound. Part of her wanted to run out of the house but her car keys were on the kitchen table.

I locked the door, she thought. There can't be anyone in the house. She took a deep breath and pushed open the door. There was no movement. She could see her keys on the table, she pitched forward and grabbed at the keys. As she straightened up she heard a whooshing sound, felt something collide with the back of her head, then blackness came.

Chapter Thirty-three

The team gathered around the incident board where Lottie's photo had been added alongside that of Madog, Luke, and the Wilsons.

'I can't see Lloyd attacking his wife,' Valentine said.

'No,' Meadows agreed, 'but you never know how far some will go when they are desperate. He was home at the time. Sleeping, he claims, and Theo and Quintin were together.'

'Or so they say,' Blackwell said. 'Quintin is neck-deep in drugs, so he'll agree with anything that's said as long as it gives him an alibi.'

'Kitty was also alone,' Edris said. 'She's just inherited Madog's share. With Lottie out of the picture she'll get the lot.'

'She could've surprised her sister,' Blackwell said. 'Possibly killed Madog but I don't see her being able to overpower Luke or the Wilsons. Besides, she would've made sure Lottie was dead before calling for help.'

'That leaves Pippa,' Paskin said. 'She was at home when Theo got the call from Lloyd about Lottie's attack. She could've attacked Lottie and got home before Theo. She looks strong enough to have killed the others. Especially as the Wilsons were taken by surprise. Shoe size is wrong but all she would need is a couple of pairs of socks and to put on Theo's boots.'

Meadows rubbed his hand over his chin. 'What's the motive?'

'The land. She's in a lot of debt. If the mortgage payments aren't met she could lose the house. She could also be involved with the drugs. They must be getting them in somehow. Easy access from the manor to the farm.'

'Why attack Lottie?' Meadows asked.

'Lottie and Kitty were in Quintin's office. They could've found out about the drugs,' Edris said. 'Or maybe they are in on it.'

'I don't think this is about the drugs,' Meadows said. 'The killer was after the codicil and will. The waters have just got muddied with drugs, poisoned fish, and the fishing competition. It's down to the family and the inheritance. They all knew about Madog hiding jars, even though Pippa and Theo deny it. So our prime suspects are, Quintin, Lloyd, Pippa, and Theo.'

'Maybe Kitty is in on it as well,' Edris said.

'OK,' Meadows said. 'I guess anything is possible and we can't discard her because of her size.'

'Quintin, Theo, and Lloyd's fingerprints were matched to ones found on Madog's boat,' Paskin said. 'They all have a good reason for them being there. No match from any of the footwear seized this morning to the footprints concentrated around the Wilsons crime scene. Fishing line was found near where Lottie was attacked.'

'They're all anglers so it doesn't help,' Valentine said.

'So, we arrest them all,' Blackwell said. 'Put the pressure on. We haven't had Pippa or Theo in yet.'

'We still have to wait for the results of the testing on the coats and maybe tech will get some information from the laptops. Paskin, have you tracked down Simon Taylor?'

'Not yet, there are a few of them. I'm working through the list and waiting for a couple to call me back. Death certificate for Grace Eccleston shows cause of death as an aneurysm. Nothing to do with the farm or the family. Oh, and Daisy called in the results of Luke Henry's DNA. He was not a match to Madog.'

'So he wasn't killed because of the inheritance,' Blackwell said. 'It has to be Quintin and Lloyd because they used him as an alibi.'

'We've still got surveillance watching the exits to the farm. With a bit of luck Quintin and possibly Lloyd will try and move the drugs. At least we can get them away from Kitty. I'll go back to the farm and keep an eye on things until Kitty goes to the hospital. Lottie is improving and the doctor thinks she'll wake up soon. With a bit of luck she saw her attacker; at the very least she may know what's in the codicil. Two officers will stay at the farmhouse this evening and overnight. Another two are going to watch the manor house so they can keep an eye on Pippa and Theo.'

Meadows' phone vibrated in his pocket. He saw Hanes' name flash across the screen before he answered it.

'What's up?' Meadows asked.

'Kitty is missing,' Hanes said. 'I don't think she left voluntarily.'

'On our way,' Meadows said and ended the call. 'Blackwell and Valentine, you'd better come with us. Paskin, can you check with surveillance and see what vehicles have been seen going in the direction of the farm? They also need to stop every vehicle trying to leave the village to check for Kitty. Can you also get as many uniform as can be spared? If she is still on the land it's a lot of ground to cover. Thanks.' He grabbed his coat.

They drove in convoy over the mountain. Paskin called as they reached the top.

'Only two vehicles of interest. Theo, who left the village with Kitty earlier then came back alone, and Celyn, who was heading towards the farm with Kitty and came back out alone.'

'Thanks,' Meadows said and ended the call.

When they arrived at the farm Hanes was waiting outside the house.

'Quintin, Lloyd, Theo, and Pippa are out looking for Kitty with some of the farm employees,' Hanes said. 'You'd better come inside.'

'Best you stay here,' Meadows said to the others. 'We don't want to contaminate a possible crime scene.' He followed Hanes into the kitchen.

Hanes pointed. 'There's blood on the floor.'

Meadows knelt to look and saw Kitty's white moth necklace lying under a kitchen chair. A holdall and handbag were near the blood splatter.

'It looks like she was trying to leave,' Meadows said. 'Who called it in?'

'Theo. He came to check on Kitty. He said Celyn had sent Lloyd a text message to say she was dropping Kitty off. He was going to take her up to the dairy until it was time for her to visit Lottie at the hospital. The door was closed. When he didn't get an answer, he came inside.'

Meadows stepped outside and filled the others in on what he had seen.

'Looks like we're too late,' Blackwell said.

Meadows felt a churning in his stomach. He wished now that he had insisted that an officer stay with Kitty at all times. 'I really hope not,' he said. 'Why did the killer move her? If they were going to kill her then they would've left her on the kitchen floor. It's more risk to take her out of the house.'

'Maybe they moved her to buy some more time,' Valentine said.

The sound of footfall made them all turn. Theo and Lloyd were running towards them.

'We can't find her,' Theo panted. 'We've been all around the lakes, checked the boathouses and outbuildings. Nothing.'

'I thought Kitty was going to stay with the two of you. What happened?' Meadows asked.

'She wanted to go and see Celyn, so I took her. She was supposed to call me to be picked up, but Celyn dropped her home,' Theo said. 'I came straight here. I opened the door and shouted then went down to the lakes. When I couldn't find her I checked the house again. That's when I saw the blood.' His voice cracked.

'Someone must've been waiting at the house for her,' Lloyd said.

'Where is Quintin?' Meadows asked.

'Taken a quad bike around the fields with Pippa to look.'

'OK, I want you to stay with DS Blackwell and Valentine. We have more officers on the way to help with the search. I will need to speak to Celyn.'

'She's gone to the hospital,' Lloyd said. 'She'll have her phone switched off.'

'Right, we better go and see her. We'll meet you back here,' Meadows said to Blackwell.

'Are you thinking Celyn saw something or that she's the attacker?' Edris asked as they drove towards the hospital.

'She could have noticed a car, or someone near the farmhouse and not thought anything of it. What I really want to know is what made Kitty decide to leave. I'm hoping she said something to Celyn.'

There was activity around Lottie's bed when they were let into the ICU. A nurse was taking Lottie's blood pressure and a doctor was shining a pencil torch in her eyes.

Celyn turned to them as they approached the bed. 'She hasn't long woken up,' she said. 'I popped outside to call Dad and he told me about Kitty.'

'That's why we're here,' Meadows said. 'We need to talk to you and your mum. It could help Kitty.'

Celyn nodded and moved up the bed when the doctor moved away. She quickly explained the situation to Lottie. Meadows could see Lottie was having trouble taking in the information.

'Lottie, do you know who did this to you?' Meadows asked.

'No,' Lottie croaked.

'Did you find the codicil?'

Lottie struggled to sit up and Celyn helped her and gave her a glass of water. Lottie took a sip. 'I was going to take it out of the jar. I felt something hit the back of my head, then nothing. You have to find Kitty.'

'We're doing everything we can,' Meadows said.

'Celyn, what did Kitty say to you when you saw her this afternoon?' Edris asked.

'She wasn't making much sense,' Celyn said. 'She was afraid, and she wanted money so she could get away.'

'Did she tell you who she was afraid of?' Edris asked.

'No, but she didn't want Quintin to know where she was going.'

'Did she say anything else?' Meadows asked.

'She said something about Madog's will and that she still didn't believe it... no, she said she didn't want to believe it.'

'What?' Edris asked.

'I don't know. Like I said, she wasn't making any sense.'

'Celyn, you need to think carefully,' Meadows said. 'Did she say any more. Mention names?'

'No, just something about there being another white moth.'

'Lottie, Madog left everything to Kitty. He said it was because of your father's share being split. Kitty thought it would go to someone else. Who did she think Madog would leave his share to?' Meadows asked.

'It was just a stupid idea,' Lottie said, 'we'd had a few to drink. It was years ago.'

'Who, Lottie?'

'Theo.'

'Why did you and Kitty think Madog would leave Theo an inheritance?'

'Theo didn't have a father growing up. Pippa made this big thing about it being a secret. She said it was someone up in London once, but we didn't believe her. Then Quintin told Kitty that the father had been paid off to stay out of Theo's life. We thought the only reason Pippa would keep it to herself was either because the guy was married, or she was embarrassed. Pippa is a snob and if it was someone local then she wouldn't want anyone to know. When Grace died of an aneurysm we suspected that Madog was Theo's father.'

'I don't understand,' Meadows said

'Madog had Marfan syndrome. It can cause weakness and stretching in the artery walls; cause an aneurysm. That's what Kitty must have meant by another white moth. When Kitty was pregnant she was unwell. That's when she found out she had Marfan syndrome. Now we know that's what caused her scoliosis. Dad and Uncle Madog got tested. Not a lot was known about it when they were young, so they didn't know. Once they both came back positive I had the test, but I don't have it. It can't skip a generation, so it was safe for me to have children.

'Kitty was so upset. She thought she would pass it to the child. Uncle Madog tried to calm her. He said it wouldn't matter. The child would be another white moth. It was his nickname for Kitty. His little white moth. Of course Elsie was tested, and she was clear, but Kitty wouldn't risk having another baby. Theo doesn't have the same appearance as Dad and Uncle Madog, but he has problems with his back, that's common. Sometimes the symptoms are mild. It was just an idea. We had no proof so we couldn't say anything. I guess if Madog left everything to Kitty then we were wrong.'

'I'm not so sure,' Meadows said. 'Celyn, what happened between you, Theo, and Luke?'

'Nothing, only Pippa said she'd seen me with Luke,' Celyn said. 'I told Theo it was because his mother didn't think I was good enough for him. I swear I didn't cheat on him.'

'Did you talk to Luke about it?'

'Yeah, I asked him why he lied. He said he had to do it, but he wouldn't explain. I never spoke to him again.'

'Thank you both,' Meadows said.

'Please don't let anything happen to Kitty,' Lottie said.

'I'll do everything in my power to find her.' He hurried out of the room with Edris following.

'We're none the wiser,' Edris said. 'We know who Theo's father is. Maybe there's another child around.'

'What if Pippa lied?' Meadows asked.

'But Theo spoke to this Simon Taylor.'

'Did he though? Pippa can be very persuasive. Anyone could've taken that call from Theo. Pippa admitted to paying off Theo's father. What if Simon Taylor took the money in exchange for saying he was the boy's father? People do all sorts of things for money,' Meadows said.

'That's one hell of a deception,' Edris said.

'Yeah, and Pippa wouldn't want Theo finding out.'

'So you're thinking Madog is Theo's father after all,' Edris said.

'No, Celyn told us that Kitty said, "she didn't want to believe it." She wouldn't be shocked that Theo was Madog's son, she already suspected. I think Llew was Theo's father. That's why he left the codicil to be read after his wife died. He didn't want her to know. Madog knew and that's why he left his share to Kitty. I think Kitty must have guessed after reading Madog's will,' Meadows said.

'They were all there this morning when Kitty read the will,' Edris said. 'They all agreed to stay together and keep an eye on Kitty, apart from Pippa.'

'She could have been waiting at the farmhouse for Kitty,' Edris said.

'We need to find Pippa. She must've known about the possibility of Theo having Marfan syndrome and could have possibly prevented Grace's death. She'd never want Theo to find out. I just hope it's not too late for Kitty.'

Chapter Thirty-four

Darkness was falling and as Meadows drove towards Pippa's house fat raindrops splattered the windscreen.

'Keep trying Blackwell,' Meadows said.

Edris pressed redial on his phone. 'It's still going straight to voicemail. The same for Valentine. They must be in a dead spot.'

Meadows drove at speed to the manor house. Adrenaline was tensing his muscles and Edris had become quiet in the passenger seat. Lottie had been the only one to survive after becoming a target and that was because Kitty interrupted just in time. There was no one to save Kitty, he thought.

He screeched to a halt in the driveway and jumped out of the car and grabbed his coat. The first thing he noticed was there were no lights on in the manor. He hammered on the door.

'Her car is still here,' Edris said. 'Surveillance is stopping anyone trying to leave the village so she can't be far away.'

'She could be anywhere on the farm and the chances of finding her in the dark are slim. Our only hope is that she threatened Kitty, made her come up to the house.'

'Then move her later when it's clear. Easier if she can walk her out of here and kill her somewhere else,' Edris said.

The thought made Meadows feel sick. He tried the door handle, but it was locked. 'Let's try around the back.'

They hurried down the side of the house and as they rounded the corner they saw a flicker of light. They moved along until they came to a set of French doors. Meadows peered inside. The light was coming from a television, but it was difficult to tell if someone was in the room. He tapped at the door and turned the handle. It opened. He stepped inside and heard a gasp. Eleanor was sitting in an armchair.

'It's OK,' Meadows said. 'We've come to see Pippa.'

'It's detectives Edris and Meadows. Remember we talked the other day,' Edris said as he stepped forward.

Eleanor looked at Edris. 'You came about Madog.'

'Yes, that's right,' he said. 'We really need to speak to Pippa. Do you know where she is?'

'Probably in the kitchen, drinking. She drinks too much.'

'Thank you,' Meadows said. 'We're sorry we startled you.'

Meadows made his way to the kitchen in the dark. Edris following silently behind him. He didn't expect to find Pippa but when he pushed open the door he saw the outline of a figure sitting in the darkness.

'Pippa?' Meadows asked.

'Mmph.'

Meadows felt around the wall until he found the switch and flicked on the lights. Pippa was gagged and bound to a kitchen chair. Underneath dishevelled hair her eyes were wide and fearful.

Meadows moved quickly to remove the gag while Edris searched in the drawers for scissors.

'What happened?' Meadows asked.

'I don't know. Someone grabbed me from behind. The scissors are in the drawer on the left. Hurry, I've been here for hours, my legs and hands have gone numb.'

Edris grabbed the scissors from the drawer and started to work on Pippa's bonds.

'Don't you think enough people have died?' Meadows said. 'We know that Llew was Theo's father. Theo is responsible for this, isn't he?'

Pippa choked back a sob.

'Where is he?' Meadows asked.

'I don't know,' Pippa said. She rubbed at her wrists that Edris had freed.

'He has Kitty. You need to tell us.'

'He didn't tell me where he was going.'

'Did he have Kitty with him?'

'No. I was helping to look for her. I came back to see to my mother. Then Theo came back. I asked him what he'd done with Kitty; that's when he got angry. He's not himself.'

'Edris, take the car and find Blackwell. We need to get everyone to search for Theo. I'll take the bridle path and meet you at the farmhouse.'

'OK,' Edris said and left the house.

Meadows poured a glass of water and handed it to Pippa. 'How did Theo find out he was Llew's son?'

Pippa took a sip of water and put the glass on the table. 'I don't know.'

'You paid Simon Taylor to say he was Theo's father.'

'He was happy to take the money. He wanted to start up a business. Daddy gave some of the money, but he didn't know. I told him I wanted Simon out of our lives. Llew didn't want Connie to find out, so he paid the rest. I told Simon there would be no comeback on him and besides he could deny it later, say I tricked him. He was happy, I had my son, and Connie never found out. I didn't love Llew, I just wanted a baby.'

'But Madog knew,' Meadows said.

'Yes, Llew left the codicil so Theo would have an inheritance once Connie died. It wouldn't have mattered but…'

'Kitty found out she had Marfan syndrome which was passed down to her from her father.'

Pippa nodded. 'I lied to Llew, I told him that I had Theo tested and he was clear. I didn't see the point, it wouldn't have made a difference to me. I didn't understand enough about it and Theo seemed well.'

'You split up Celyn and Theo.'

'Theo is her uncle. I couldn't let it carry on. Madog paid off Luke.'

'Then Theo's daughter, Grace, died,' Meadows said.

'If I'd thought there was a chance of that happening I would've told Theo. He didn't look like Llew or Madog. I had no reason to believe that he had it. Even after Grace died I thought it was just a chance in a million. Madog questioned me. I told him the same thing I had told Llew. Then Theo started having problems with his back; apparently symptoms can show up later in life. Madog knew then, he told me I should tell Theo. Especially if there was a chance he could father another child.'

'Then Connie died,' Meadows said.

'I begged Madog not to read the codicil. He could've found another way to honour Llew's final wishes. He could've given the land for the housing estate and Theo would've benefited from that. He insisted that Theo deserved to know the truth. Stupid man. He must have told him.'

'Why go after Lottie and now Kitty?' Meadows asked.

'He blames them all for Grace's death.'

'Kitty and Lottie didn't know.'

'He's so angry. I couldn't reason with him.'

'Where would he take Kitty?'

'I don't know, honestly.'

'You could have stopped this.'

'No, I had my suspicions after Luke was killed but I didn't know for sure. He's been acting strange, but I couldn't ask him if he knew, could I? I would have given myself away. He said I was going to see all of them die and I would be the last.'

'Stay here and lock the doors,' Meadows said. He heard Pippa sobbing as he left the house.

The rain was driving into his face as he ran down the bridle path and by the time he reached the farmhouse he was soaked. Blackwell and Valentine were talking to a group of uniformed officers. All holding torches.

Meadows bent forward to catch his breath. 'Where is Edris?' he asked, straightening up.

'Haven't seen him,' Blackwell said.

Valentine shook her head.

'I sent him to find you. We found Pippa tied up. It's Theo,' Meadows said, and quickly filled them in.

'I haven't seen Theo since we arrived. I thought he was out looking for Kitty,' Blackwell said.

'I'll give Rolly a shout,' Hanes said. 'See if Edris is up at the dairy.'

'He was supposed to meet me here,' Meadows said.

They all listened as Hanes spoke into his radio. Meadows felt like a fist had gripped his stomach as he heard the reply. No one had seen him.

'He would've driven up the track,' Meadows said. 'The car is not here. He has to be somewhere between here and the manor.'

'What if he met up with Theo on the way?' Valentine said.

Meadows didn't like to think about that possibility. He could see the concern on everyone's faces.

'I'll go with Hanes,' Meadows said. 'We'll drive down the track and up to the manor. See if we can see the car.'

'I'm coming with you,' Valentine said.

'And me,' Blackwell said. 'I want to give him a bollocking for wasting our time.'

Meadows knew that was Blackwell's way. He wouldn't voice his concern. They all piled into Blackwell's car with Meadows taking the passenger seat. They had only driven part way down the track when they saw the abandoned car. The driver's door was open with the interior lit up. The headlights illuminating the rain.

'Bloody idiot must have gone after him alone,' Blackwell said.

'But where?' Valentine asked.

'Theo and Lloyd said they had checked the lakes and boathouses. What if Theo checked the boathouses because he knew Kitty was inside? Once he said it was clear no one would look there. Come on.'

Meadows took off with Blackwell, Valentine, and Hanes following.

'Call for backup,' Meadows said. 'I want everyone down here looking.'

Hanes called into his radio as they all trained their torches ahead sweeping the area. As they ran down the bank Meadows caught movement on the lake. He stopped and moved the beam until it picked out a boat.

'Theo!' Meadows yelled.

Theo turned his head to look, then started to row. With all the torches pointing towards the boat they could see Kitty at the back, her hands tied in front of her and a gag over her mouth. Meadows could just make out Edris slumped in the bottom of the boat. He wasn't moving. By the time they'd all reached the edge of the lake Theo was almost in the centre.

'Theo, you've got nowhere to go,' Meadows shouted.

Theo stopped rowing. 'I don't need to go anywhere,' he shouted. He stood up and the boat swayed.

'What's he doing?' Blackwell said. 'Is he going to jump over?'

The rain was lashing down and the beams from the torches weren't strong enough to give them a clear view. Meadows could see that Theo was bending over. Then he stood up straight with what looked like a metal pole. He lifted it up in the air and brought it crashing down. They heard the thud from the shore.

'He's going to sink the boat,' Valentine said.

'Theo, wait!' Meadows shouted. 'I know you don't want to hurt Kitty. You couldn't kill her at the house. Let her go.'

Theo lowered the pole. 'She killed Grace, they all did,' Theo said.

'Kitty didn't know, neither did Lottie. Llew and Madog were told you were tested for Marfan syndrome, and you were clear.'

'You're lying,' Theo said.

'No,' Meadows said. 'Your mother told me. She thought you were OK. Bring Kitty and Sergeant Edris back. We can talk.'

'No, it's too late for that.'

'Theo!'

Meadows turned and saw Lloyd, Quintin, and a group of uniformed officers running towards them.

'Stop them,' Meadows said. 'It's OK, Theo. No one is coming near you.'

Blackwell had stopped Quintin and Lloyd. Meadows moved towards them.

'There're two boats on the bank of the second lake,' Lloyd said.

'He'll see you coming,' Meadows said. 'You won't get there before he sinks the boat. Even if you can, he'll likely tip the boat first. Once Kitty and Edris go under we'll never find them in the dark.'

'We can't just stand here,' Quintin said.

'No,' Meadows agreed. He pulled off his jacket. 'I'm going to swim out. Blackwell, keep him talking. Hanes, organise moving the boats. You'll have to keep your torches off. If we can keep him distracted then you'll have a chance to get the boats into the water before he sees you. Once I get to the boat, start rowing out. If I can hold him off damaging the boat or tipping it, you may have enough time to get to Kitty and Edris.'

'You can't,' Blackwell said. 'It's too dangerous.'

'Just keep him talking,' Meadows said as he pulled off his shoes.

'I'm coming with you,' Valentine said.

'No, stay with Blackwell,' Meadows said.

'If he sees you and tips the boat you can't save both Edris and Kitty. I'm a good swimmer.'

She's right, he thought. He didn't want to have to decide who to save if both Edris and Kitty went under.

'OK,' Meadows said. 'But hang back. He's got that pole and the oars. I don't want you too close. Just close enough to get Kitty if she goes in the water.'

Meadows moved further up the lake with Valentine until they were positioned behind Theo. He stripped down to his underwear and Valentine did the same. The water was freezing, and he heard Valentine's sharp intake of breath as they waded in. They moved slowly as Blackwell talked to Theo.

'It must have been a hell of a shock to find out Llew was your father,' Blackwell said. 'All that grief you've been carrying. I understand. It was a moment of madness.'

'Madog thought he was doing me a favour by telling me Llew was my father,' Theo said. 'He took me out in the boat at the Usk. He said he was sorry about Grace. I couldn't take it in at first. He kept on talking, telling me how he thought I'd been given the all-clear. That he and Llew didn't know that I'd inherited the disorder. I just kept seeing Grace that day at the hospital, like a little wax doll. The doctors telling us how sorry they were. Madog turned around and was threading a fly. I just lost it. I threw the line around his neck and pulled. He struggled then he stopped moving. I sat for a while, then realised what I had done. I had to throw him in the water. No one knew we had gone fishing. He'd asked me the night before and told me not to tell anyone. I think he didn't want Mum to try and stop him telling me.'

Meadows was up to his chest in water. He wanted to hurry but couldn't risk Theo catching sight of them. He nodded to Valentine and they started to swim.

'The Wilsons saw you,' Blackwell shouted.

'They were looking at me through binoculars. I didn't know how much they had seen. I started rowing towards them. They didn't run away so I figured they hadn't seen me kill Madog.'

'But they could identify you and the boat.'

'Yeah, I talked to them. He liked to bird watch. I offered to take them out in the evening, told them they would get a good view of the birds. I came back later. Tied line across the trees and waited. It wasn't hard. I hit him first then her. She tried to help her husband, so I had to hit her again. I didn't want to kill them. I'm not a monster.'

Meadows was getting near the boat now. Theo stopped talking and looked around. He ducked down under the water, staying down until he could hold his breath no longer. He rose slowly and Valentine came up beside him. Blackwell's voice carried over the lake.

'What was the point of the flies?'

'Madog always wore a white moth on his jacket, Kitty too. Now I know why. It was to show they were the same.' Theo laughed. 'I guess he should have given me one. I ripped it off his jacket and put it in his tongue. It seemed right. He'd stayed silent all these years, so I silenced him in death. I used the flies I'd taken from the summer house for the Wilsons and Luke. I wanted Kitty to suffer. See the things she loved get destroyed. I took Madog from her, I poisoned the fish.'

'Why Luke?'

'He was supposed to be my friend. He took money to keep quiet. I could've been happy with Celyn.'

'She's your niece. You couldn't be together,' Blackwell said.

Meadows indicated to Valentine that she should go around and come up at the back of the boat. As soon as she was in position he would make a move. He knew the others would have the boat and be waiting for his signal, but they moved too soon. There was a splash from the shore as a boat went in.

'No,' Theo yelled. He raised the pole and started driving it into the bottom of the boat.

Valentine dived under the water and Meadows started swimming.

'Theo, stop!' Blackwell yelled.

Meadows lifted his head and saw the boat tilting. Theo had hold of Edris and was pulling him over the side of the boat. There was a splash as Theo went over, taking Edris with him. The boat capsized taking Kitty with it. Then there was silence.

Chapter Thirty-five

Shouts came from the edge of the lake and Meadows could hear oars hitting the water. Valentine surfaced near the boat, looked wildly around, and disappeared again. Meadows dived under the water and headed in the direction of the boat. It was impossible to see anything in the dark murky water. He went further down groping around, for a limb, a head, or anything. Just when it felt like his lungs would burst his hand met with a tangle of hair. He gripped tight and dragged Kitty to the surface. He heard her gulp in the air as he held her head above water. Two boats were heading towards them with torches lighting up patches of water. Valentine surfaced at the side of the upturned boat and looked at Meadows holding up Kitty.

'Edris?' she shouted

Meadows shook his head. Valentine drew in a lungful of air and went under as one of the boats came alongside Meadows and hands reached out for Kitty. He handed Kitty over and dived down. The torch beams were shining through the water highlighting sediment that had been stirred up with the movement. He swam deeper skirting the bottom and sending up thick clouds until it obscured his view. His lungs screamed and the lack of oxygen made him dizzy. He searched on until he was forced to surface for air. He was about to go under again when Valentine reappeared, holding Edris under the chin. The boat moved towards them and Hanes reached over and grabbed Edris. With the help of two officers they hauled him aboard the boat.

'Go,' Meadows shouted.

Meadows swam after the boat with Valentine alongside him. He didn't have the breath to speak. By the time they reached the lake's edge, Edris had been pulled out of the boat and Blackwell was leaning over him pumping his chest.

'He's not breathing,' Blackwell said.

Valentine fell on her knees next to Edris. 'Don't you dare,' she said. She pinched his nose and put her mouth over his and blew hard.

Blackwell put his head to Edris' chest and shook his head. Valentine blew in his mouth again and Meadows started compressions on his chest.

'Come on,' Meadows said.

Blackwell was feeling for a pulse when a gurgle escaped Edris' mouth. Meadows rolled him on his side as he coughed and spluttered.

'You're OK,' Valentine said. 'We've got you.'

'You bloody idiots,' Blackwell said. 'You could have all died out there.'

Meadows sat back on the grass. His body shaking. 'Kitty?' he asked.

'She's OK,' Blackwell said.

'Theo?'

'Uniform got him as he came out of the water. He didn't put up a fight.'

'Ambulance is on the way,' Hanes said. He looked at Edris. 'Is he going to be OK?'

'I hope so,' Meadows said.

'He was under a long time,' Hanes said. 'For a minute I thought we'd lost him.'

'For a minute, so did I,' Meadows said.

Chapter Thirty-six

Two weeks later

Meadows drove up the track to Bryn Glas Farm. The sun was shining and once again it looked peaceful and idyllic. The scars left by recent events would take a long time to heal, he thought. The physical ones were already starting to fade but the ones left by the lies and secrets within the family would take a lot longer. He parked next to the farmhouse and got out of the car. Edris walked around the back of the car and took a few steps forward and looked towards the lakes.

'Are you OK?' Meadows asked.

'Yeah, I don't remember a thing after getting to the boathouse. I saw Theo, stopped the car, and ran after him. He must have been hiding inside.'

'You were bloody lucky,' Meadows said. 'You shouldn't have gone after him alone.'

'I know but I had no signal to call for backup. I thought he would lead me to Kitty. You would've done the same.'

'Yeah, I guess I would. At least one good thing came out of it.'

'What's that?' Edris asked.

'You and Valentine are back to normal.'

Edris smiled. 'I nearly died, everything else is insignificant.'

Meadows laughed. 'Don't be so dramatic. Still, you owe her. She saved your life.'

'And don't I know it.'

'Come on, let's go and find Kitty.'

They walked past the farmhouse to the fishery where they found Kitty and Lottie sitting on one of the troughs watching the new fish. When Kitty saw Meadows she jumped up and threw her arms around him.

'Thank you,' she said. She moved to Edris. 'And you too, I heard what you did.'

'Just doing our job,' Edris said.

'It was more than that,' Lottie said.

'How are you both?' Meadows asked.

'Just headaches now,' Lottie said. 'At least the line on my throat has faded and I don't look like a horror show. If Kitty hadn't–'

'Don't,' Kitty said. 'Let's not talk about it.'

'That's probably the best way forward,' Meadows said. 'I wanted to come and see you in person to let you know that we have charged Quintin with receiving and supplying drugs. Given the amount he was caught with, he'll be looking at a lengthy sentence.'

'Good,' Kitty said. 'My solicitor thinks that I have a good chance of proving he obtained my signature by deception for the mortgage and loans.'

'What about Lloyd?' Lottie asked.

'I'm sorry, Lottie,' Meadows said. 'I'm hoping he'll get a reduced sentence.'

'From what he told us, he was coerced,' Edris added. 'He got suspicious when Quintin changed the animal feed suppliers and started taking delivery and emptying the feed into the storage barrels. Something he had never bothered with. Madog had questioned this and asked for a copy of the accounts. Lloyd managed to get to a delivery one morning before Quintin, he found the drugs. He confronted Quintin who told him that he would say that Lloyd was involved, and as his fingerprints were over the drugs he would get done. Quintin made a deal with Lloyd that he would stop the supply in two weeks. In return, Lloyd had to help him get the drugs hidden in the cheese so they could be delivered and distributed.'

'Lloyd is not a bad man,' Meadows said. 'He just got caught up in it and didn't know how to get out.'

'I wish he would've talked to me,' Lottie said.

'He was afraid. Madog had been murdered, then Luke. He couldn't say anything as he would incriminate himself. By keeping silent he thought he was protecting you and the family,' Meadows said.

'I heard Pippa was arrested,' Kitty said.

'Yes,' Meadows said. 'She admitted to covering for Theo and destroying evidence. She burnt his clothes and buried them. We also suspect that she knew about the drugs and covered for Quintin.'

'Well, I hope she goes to prison,' Lottie said.

'She was just protecting her son,' Kitty said. 'You've read the codicil.'

'Yeah, I'm surprised Theo didn't destroy it,' Lottie said.

'It was the only communication he had from his father. It must've meant something to him,' Kitty said.

'How did you know about Theo?' Meadows asked.

'Uncle Madog's will. He said Dad's share would be split. If it was split between me and Lottie then Uncle Madog would've done the same. Control of the farm isn't supposed to go to one person. That could only mean that the share couldn't be split equally.'

'More than two of us to inherit,' Lottie said.

'I didn't think that Theo killed anyone,' Kitty said. 'Quintin always told Pippa everything so I guessed she would know about Lottie and me digging for the will and codicil. I thought it was her, but I couldn't prove it. I didn't want to believe that Dad and Uncle Madog had kept a secret like that from us. I just wanted to go somewhere safe and wait for Lottie to wake up. Celyn had texted Lloyd to say she had dropped me home and Lloyd told Theo. He must have been waiting in the house for me. I was in the kitchen and the next thing I remember I'm tied up in a boat in the boatshed. He came back with the chisel bar and lump hammer. I knew then that he was going to sink the boat with me in it.'

'I'm not sure he would have gone through with it,' Meadows said. 'He could've killed you in the house. I think he was conflicted between his misguided need for revenge and his love for you.'

'It's so sad,' Kitty said. 'If Dad would've come clean we would've loved him as a brother.'

Lottie nodded.

'I don't think I can ever forgive him for what he did to Uncle Madog and Luke, but I understand what made him do it. It's not easy to stop loving someone because they've done something terrible. I stopped loving Quintin a long time ago, it was just convenient to stay together, but Theo is family. He's my brother.'

'Give yourself time,' Meadows said. 'Theo was overwhelmed with grief. Sometimes grief can manifest in ways you can't control, either harm to yourself or in Theo's case, harm to others. Maybe one day you'll want to see him. Even if it's just for closure.'

Kitty nodded and looked at Lottie.

'In the meantime we have a farm to run,' Kitty said. 'If ever you want to take a break you're welcome to stay in one of the cottages and fish on the lakes. That goes for both of you.'

'Thank you,' Meadows said.

They walked to the car and Meadows took a last look around.

'Are you going to take her up on her offer?' Edris asked. 'You're taking some time out with your brother. It might be nice to relax with a rod.'

'Relax!' Meadows laughed. 'After this case I don't want to see a lake or hear the word fishing for a long time.'

List of characters

Eleanor Eccleston – Quintin's mother
Phillipa Eccleston (Pippa) – Quintin's sister
Theodore Eccleston (Theo) – Pippa's son
Bridget Eccleston (Kitty) – Quintin's wife
Elsie Eccleston – Kitty's daughter
Grace Eccleston – Theo's daughter
Llew Jones – Kitty's father
Connie Jones – Kitty's mother
Madog Jones – Kitty's uncle
Charlotte Evans (Lottie) – Kitty's sister
Lloyd Evans – Lottie's husband
Jac Evans – Lottie's son
Arwel Evans – Lottie's son
Celyn Evans – Lottie's daughter
Luke Henry

If you enjoyed this book, please let others know by leaving a quick review on Amazon. Also, if you spot anything untoward in the paperback, get in touch. We strive for the best quality and appreciate reader feedback.

editor@thebookfolks.com

www.thebookfolks.com

Also available:

Following a fall and a bang to the head, a woman's memories come flooding back about an incident that occurred twenty years ago in which her friend was murdered. As she pieces together the events and tells the police, she begins to fear repercussions. DI Winter Meadows must work out the identity of the killer before they strike again.

When the boss of a care home for mentally challenged adults is murdered, the residents are not the most reliable of witnesses. DI Winter Meadows draws on his soft nature to gain the trust of an individual he believes saw the crime. But without unravelling the mystery and finding the evidence, the case will freeze over.

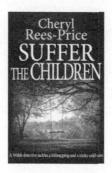

When a toddler goes missing from the family home, the police and community come out in force to find her. However, with few traces found after an extensive search, DI Winter Meadows fears the child has been abducted. But someone knows something, and when a man is found dead, the race is on to solve the puzzle.

When local teenage troublemaker and ne'er-do-well Stacey Evans is found dead, locals in a small Welsh village couldn't give a monkey's. That gives nice guy cop DI Winter Meadows a headache. Can he win over their trust and catch a killer in their midst?

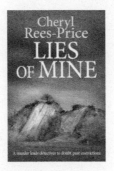

A body is found in an old mine in a secluded spot in the Welsh hills. There are no signs of struggle so DI Winter Meadows suspects that the victim, youth worker David Harris, knew his killer. But when the detective discovers it is not the first murder in the area, he must dig deep to join up the dots.

When a family friend is murdered, a journalist begins to probe into his past. What she finds there makes her question everything about her life. Should she bury his secrets with him, or become the next victim of Blue Hollow?

All available FREE with Kindle Unlimited and in paperback.

Made in the USA
Las Vegas, NV
02 April 2022

46773895R00173